"*Burying Daisy Doe* is a gripping story that exposes the secrets of a small Southern town caught up in three generations of evil. It took the courage of Star Cavanaugh, searching for her grandmother's and father's murderers, to uncover the truth in a tale that will keep you in suspense to the end."

—**Patricia Bradley**, author of the Logan Point, Memphis Cold Case Novels, and Natchez Trace Park Rangers series

"I'm reminded yet again why Ramona Richards is one of my favorite suspense writers. And this may be her best book yet! Riveting from the beginning and filled with suspense . . . I bet you can't just read one chapter!"

—**Kathy Harris**, author of The Deadly Secrets series

"*Burying Daisy Doe* is Ramona Richards's most chilling, most captivating work yet. When Star Cavanaugh moves into Pineville to investigate the cold case murders of her grandmother and her father, she has no idea of the Pandora's Box she is about to open . . . and I had no idea how late I was about to stay up reading to find out what happened next. The intricate storyline goes beyond a simple 'hero versus villain' suspense tale to the dueling capacities for good and evil that reside in us all. *Burying Daisy Doe* is the kind of book that makes you want to sleep with the light on yet compels you to read into the night, as answers reveal more questions. It kept me guessing and kept me up late . . . and I can't recommend it highly enough."

—**Jodie Bailey**, award-winning author of romantic military suspense

"I absolutely loved *Burying Daisy Doe* and cannot wait for the next Star Cavanaugh Cold Case. Richards seamlessly combined all the things I love into one fabulous story: a heroine to root for—and a hunky police chief she'd be a fool to resist—a tightly-plotted mystery, a small town peppered with lovable, quirky characters, and ultimately, justice for those who'd waited much too long to receive it. This series will definitely go on my 'auto-buy' list. Highly recommended!"

—**Connie Mann**, author of the Safe Harbor and Florida Wildlife Warriors series

BURYING DAISY DOE

A STAR CAVANAUGH COLD CASE

BURYING DAISY DOE

RAMONA RICHARDS

Burying Daisy Doe: A Star Cavanaugh Cold Case

Published by Kregel Publications, a division of Kregel Inc., 2450 Oak Industrial Dr. NE, Grand Rapids, MI 49505.

Library of Congress Cataloging-in-Publication Data
Names: Richards, Ramona, 1957– author.
Title: Burying Daisy Doe : a Star Cavanaugh cold case / Ramona Richards.
Description: Grand Rapids, MI : Kregel Publications, [2020]
Identifiers: LCCN 2020031495 (print) | LCCN 2020031496 (ebook)
Subjects: GSAFD: Suspense fiction. | Mystery fiction.
Classification: LCC PS3618.I3438 B87 2020 (print) | LCC PS3618.I3438 (ebook) | DDC 813/.6—dc23
LC record available at https://lccn.loc.gov/2020031495
LC ebook record available at https://lccn.loc.gov/2020031496

ISBN 978-0-8254-4652-8, print
ISBN 978-0-8254-7682-2, epub

Printed in the United States of America
20 21 22 23 24 25 26 27 28 29 / 5 4 3 2 1

CHAPTER ONE

Pineville, Alabama, 1954

WHEN THE WOMAN with the daisy in her hair sauntered into the Pineville Drugstore and Soda Fountain that hazy Saturday morning in May 1954, every man in the room turned and looked. Her lavender dress fit loosely, and the lightweight fabric, cinched at the waist with a matching belt, flowed easily around her as she walked. Thick curls undulated around her face with each step toward the counter, the strands so black that a bluish highlight caressed each one. Her lips formed a tight red bow in the middle of a face pale with carefully applied powder. More than one of the old farmers sitting at the cluster of tables near the soda fountain found himself staring unwaveringly at the stranger.

Roscoe Carver stared too, from his chair in the colored section of the fountain's tables. His fourteen-year-old body responded to the woman's long legs and curvy hips in a way that would have made his mother pray for his soul and his father for his life. Noticing Roscoe's gaze, his father squeezed his arm in the same grip that could pull a mule out of the mud. Roscoe flinched, his eyes darting to his father's tense face.

Ebenezer Carver shook his head, his voice a taut whisper. "Don't you be gawking at no white woman. Doc barely lets us sit inside as it is."

Confusion shot through Roscoe. "White? But she's—" The grip tightened. "White!" The word was a harsh whisper. "Don't let them catch you looking!"

Almost in reflex, Roscoe looked down at the table. It wasn't the first time he'd heard the warning. It would not be the last. He squelched the rage it produced in his gut and found a safer outlet for his anger and curiosity: He watched the woman in the broad mirrors behind the soda fountain in furtive glances that danced between her and his plate. Unlike his father, who focused only on his food, the white men in the fountain area stared openly at the woman, occasionally nudging each other and motioning at her with quick points or nods of their heads.

Her curls glistened as they bounced out of control around her shoulders and down her back, as if she'd forgotten to brush her hair that morning. Low-heeled pumps, a light lavender that almost matched the dress, thwacked on the yellow tile floor, as if they, too, were a size too big. She ordered a root beer float instead of breakfast, and Doc Taylor started drawing it up, being that his fountain girl Ruthie had the day off. The woman clopped over to the magazine rack and picked up one with the latest movie gossip. After studying the display a moment, she plucked up a comic book as well. She paid for all three, then leaned against the fountain, sipping the float.

Roscoe tried to finish his breakfast, but his attention kept turning back to the woman's reflection in the mirror. Maybe his father was right; she was white. But Roscoe knew that she didn't look like any white woman around Pineville. And there was that thick makeup. She faced the fountain again, and Roscoe studied her profile. The wide dark eyes, prominent cheekbones, and sloping jawline. The smooth curls of her hair weren't straightened like his mama's, but Roscoe had never seen a white girl with hair that rich and black. Maybe his daddy had. His father had traveled, been overseas with the army during the war. He'd seen lots of things no one around here had.

The woman set the soda glass down and stirred the ice cream into the mixture. Doc tried to talk to her, but she met his questions with soft shakes of her head, and after a bit, he gave up and went to the high counter at the back where he made up prescriptions. The girl ate the ice cream slowly and dabbed her lips.

The clop of her shoes echoed against the high ceiling as she strolled toward the door, the magazine and comic book tucked neatly under one arm, her hips swaying beneath the pale purple dress.

Roscoe finally looked back at his biscuit, now cold on his plate. *Beautiful, so beautiful that she should never be forgotten.*

A thought he remembered with pain the next morning. This time he stared openly at her—her face, her nude body, the waxen look of her bloodless skin. Beautiful, even dead, with those scarlet lips now a bluish gray, marred by a dark protruding tongue. She lay at the edge of his daddy's newly planted cornfield, a leather strap around her neck, a bright daisy crushed beside her.

He stared, then ran to get his father, knowing that he would never forget that face.

CHAPTER TWO

Pineville, Alabama, Present Day

Roscoe Carver stared at me, the look in his rheumy eyes steadily moving from bored to puzzled, then to intrigued. I had been working at the Pineville drugstore only a month, doing a short-order dance during the morning shift with the cook behind the soda fountain and grill. We served up breakfast, mostly, with the occasional ice cream treats. This was Roscoe's first appearance in the sunrise crowd, having just returned from a long stay at the hospital in Gadsden after his last stroke. His daughter, Imajean, had told me Roscoe had eaten breakfast at the drugstore most of his life. He'd once had a store on the square and knew the breakfast hour was prime for new gossip and potential clients. Even retired, he still came, and he always made the drugstore his first stop after getting out of the hospital.

"Still stuck in the past, that man is," his grandson Charles had muttered, causing his mama to make a shushing noise at him. Charles, who gave a whole new definition to tall, dark, and handsome, had no clue how encouraging his words were to me.

A guy stuck in the past was exactly what I needed. Especially if his name was Roscoe Carver. I had searched the morning rush every day, dodging between the tables as I delivered plates of hot biscuits, gravy, grits, and an assortment of eggs, looking just for him.

Now he was looking at me. Roscoe had emerged from Charles's beloved red 1992 Thunderbird like a king descending to his court. Charles sped off to work as Roscoe moved slowly into the drugstore, using a four-point cane for balance, weaving among the scattering of tables, and acknowledging the dozens of greetings that sailed his way, the handshakes, and the welcome-backs. Miss Doris Rankin even rose from her table with "the girls" and gave him a gentle hug. Everyone wanted to know where Imajean was ("Working too hard") and how Charles was doing ("Spending too much money and time on that Spencer girl").

He moved his girth almost gracefully toward a table in the middle, and he eased down in the chair slowly, settling with a huff of air, as if getting off his feet brought serious relief. He rearranged the napkin holder, the cream and sugar, and the salt and pepper shakers, then leaned back. He clutched his hands over his stomach and looked around, ready to rule.

He spotted me quickly, the new blonde behind the familiar counter. His glance skirted over me head to toe at first, then he sniffed, as if testing the air, and settled in for a long examination.

I set a thick white mug down in front of him, extending the silver-and-glass pot that had become the morning extension of my right hand. "Coffee OK, sir?"

He cleared his throat. "Please." The word had a whispery *h* at the end, and the left side of his face didn't quite cooperate with the right. Leftovers from the stroke.

I poured the coffee, careful not to splash any, ignoring the heads that turned my way, like NASCAR spectators waiting for a crash. Pouring too fast or too hard caused the coffee to hit the bottom and bounce back out, usually all over the customer. The way I found this out was now legendary among the drugstore patrons, alienating a few but endearing me to a number of folks who disliked a certain Alabama legislator who had seen the drugstore as the perfect campaign stop. They loved that part of the story, but they rarely hoped I'd repeat the event.

I picked up the tiny pitcher from the middle of the table to check the cream level. Almost full. Most of the morning folks liked their coffee black—the stronger the better.

"You're a drive-in, aren't you?" His lispy voice sounded like new tires on gravel.

I paused. The question still caught me off guard, even after I figured out what it meant. Once upon a time, Pineville had been a small, isolated town, with the folks here reveling in their own self-sufficiency and survival. But it was now an easy driving distance from Gadsden and Birmingham, less than an hour for each up and down I-59. As in so many other small towns in America, developers had snatched up abandoned or unwanted farmland, constructing a series of fast-built, vinyl-siding-encased subdivisions. The ones that had popped up around the Pineville exit were mostly populated by commuters whose lives centered on the work and culture of the two cities, allowing them to arrive home only to sleep and attend the occasional school function or football game.

Vic Beason, editor of the local Pineville paper, had dubbed them "drive-ins." It was not a compliment.

"Actually, I'm a move-in." I pulled my order pad out of the apron pocket. "Can't stand being cooped up in a car." I pulled my pencil from behind my ear and pointed it at the ceiling. "For now, I live upstairs in Doc's rental room. What can I get ya?"

"Didn't realize Doc had hired a new girl. You're a tall one. Surely you ain't gonna stay upstairs in that dump for long. You have people here? Must. I see it in your face."

He wasn't supposed to see it *that* soon. "No sir, not here. I do have a grandma down in Birmingham. She's got an Airstream I'm going to bring up soon. Doc said I can park it in his back yard for now. Eggs? Toast?"

"Three eggs, over easy, yellows runny. Toast, extra brown, dry. Grits, extra butter. Bacon, larger order. Large OJ, if there's any left. Is it one of the classic Airstreams or one of those new fancy RVs? You sure I don't know your people?" Every *s* ended with the whoosh.

A dozen answers flitted through my head as I scribbled. Finally, out came one that wasn't a lie. "I'm afraid my people aren't from around here. And it's a classic. A 1969 Overlander."

"Humph." This sound came from deep within his gut and rode out on a thick exhale, not so much a word as a noise I would have associated with Jabba the Hutt, had I been less polite.

"I'll get this in." I scooted to the counter and the short-order grill. Rafe, the cook who worked wonders with eggs and gravy but kept a stash of pot taped to the underside of the dumpster out back, plucked the order slip from my hand and stuck it on the metal rack over the steaming kettle of grits. The marijuana, which he rarely used on the job, was, in part, retaliation against the pharmacist for some unknown slight. Rafe was a man of action, and he seldom spoke more than three words during the morning shift.

He motioned toward two plates near the edge of the grill, and I switched out the coffeepot for a fuller one, balanced the plates, and headed back to the floor.

After only a month, a new respect for servers had been born, and I prayed I'd never have to do this for real. To make a living at it. Some people have a calling for it. I did not. But there was no better way to find out what was going on in Pineville, or any other small town in the South, for that matter. Like a bartender, my job gave me instant access and a built-in trust.

Take Miss Doris, for instance. She and her girls—all of them retired businesswomen—clustered in the drugstore every morning to talk God, guns, and guys. Bible study with a twist, and they knew every iota of gossip floating around town. Miss Doris never met a stranger and had spotted me for a kindred soul right away, a woman who was as interested in the town's goings-on as she was. She had invited me to the Pine Grove Baptist Church, a white clapboard structure that was the spiritual heart of the town. According to her, Sunday school was the best place for news as well as soul saving.

She started on that last part pretty soon as well. God and I hadn't been on speaking terms in a while now, despite my grandmother's best efforts. I'd attended Pine Grove Baptist last Sunday, although not for the preaching and singing. By Monday at lunch, Miss Doris had filled this new kindred soul in on more local gossip than I could keep straight without a scorecard, as well as working on my heathen soul. I was far more interested in the former.

Local gossip is an essential tool in my real job.

I grabbed another plate from Rafe, delivered it along with another shot of coffee, then caught my breath as I stopped to combine the contents of the two pots and start a fresh one. The smell of the burnt coffee made my nose twitch as I dumped out the old grounds.

"Got anything left for me, sugar?" Even with my back to the counter, I knew the owner of the thick, and quite fake, Southern accent.

I dropped my own a few notches into Hollywood hick. "Sure, honey-babe. I've got lots for you right here." I turned, empty mug and coffee-pot at ready.

Mike Luinetti's grin broadened, and his accent returned to normal, settling somewhere between Pittsburgh and Erie. "You're getting to be a girl I can count on." He slid onto a stool, his uniform shirt ominously tight.

A quick glance over his shoulder showed Miss Doris's slightly mischievous smile. Not surprisingly, she'd been the first to notice that since I took over the morning shift, Mike had started eating breakfast every day at the drugstore, with a few extra pounds as a result.

I certainly didn't mind the playful chatting. While he had focused on the fact that we were both transplants, I considered it a stroke of luck that the first man in Pineville to show an interest just happened to be the local police chief. Besides, with the dark looks of his Sicilian father, flirting with the man wasn't exactly a chore. His dark-blue eyes, a gift from his German mother, provided a mesmerizing contrast, and I pitied any miscreant who tried to stare him down.

I set the mug in front of Mike and filled it. "You can always count on me, kind sir. So what can I get ya?" I pulled the pencil and pad to ready.

He paused, his blue eyes still bright, but a more serious expression on his face. "How about a real date?"

I blinked. Twice. "Are you asking me out?" Finally. We'd been flirting for a month. Apparently we both could give *reticent* a new definition.

He cleared his throat and shot a quick glance over his shoulder. The grin on Miss Doris's face had moved from mischievous to wicked.

He focused back on me. "Yes."

"When?"

He was Boy Scout prepared. "Saturday night. I'll pick you up at six, and we can drive into Gadsden for dinner. We could do a movie or go to one of the clubs . . ." He stopped. "What's wrong?"

I stood a bit straighter, annoyed at myself. Having a good poker face was a fundamental part of a being a private investigator, and even more so for a cop. I could do it, but it wasn't one of my natural skills. I had to struggle to maintain it, or my eyebrows twitched, my lips puckered, and my eyes went through more gyrations than an actor in a melodrama.

I cleared my throat. "Miss Doris has her great-granddaughter this weekend. Carly. I told her I'd babysit so she and the girls could go to a retirement dinner." There would be a new "girl" at the drugstore table come next Monday.

Stoicism apparently wasn't one of his gifts either. The disappointment shone on his face.

I made a peace offering. "How about Friday?"

He grimaced. "Work." As chief, Mike should have been able to keep regular hours, but he filled in when needed. It was a small force.

I shifted my weight to one foot and held up a finger at two guys motioning for more coffee. "Well, since I suspect Miss Doris is at least a little bit behind this, my guess is that she'd be OK if you helped me take care of Carly. She's only seven. Her bedtime's at eight. We could do takeout from Baker's, maybe watch a DVD."

Mike's eyes narrowed, and his examination of me almost turned official. "Are you serious?"

I nodded. "And honestly, I prefer talking on a first date to being entertained."

He remained silent a moment, still watching for any sign I was joking. Finally he nodded. "What do you want from Baker's?"

He took my order, then I took his. I handed the slip to Rafe, then hit the floor again with the fresh pot of coffee. I filled cups and checked on everyone's progress, then delivered a plate of brown toast and runny eggs to Roscoe, who nodded his thanks and pointed at his mug for more coffee.

Most people watch the cup when I pour, in case they need to dodge a bit. Roscoe, however, watched me. As I tilted the pot back upright, he clicked his tongue against the back of his upper teeth. "I know your face. I must know your people. What's your name?"

"Star O'Connell."

His eyebrows narrowed. "I don't know any O'Connells around here."

"No sir. Most of the ones I know are up in Tennessee." Plus, it was my married name, no longer in use officially. No need to bring that up. A touch on my arm told me the adjacent table needed coffee. "You let me know if you need anything else."

I poured the coffee into the waiting cups and returned to the counter. Rafe had finished Mike's breakfast and slid the plate to the young chief. Mike grabbed it on the fly and pulled a napkin from the holder near the cash register. I changed out the pots again and filled Mike's cup. His stare got my attention. "What?"

"You want to tell me what's making you jumpy?"

"I'm not jumpy."

"You forgot my silverware."

I stopped, looking all around his plate. His hands waited on either side of it, empty. "Sorry," I muttered, then I dug a rolled napkin from a gray side-work tub under the counter.

As I placed it in front of him, he closed his fingers around my wrist. "What's wrong?"

My breath caught. In all our flirting and banter, Mike had never touched me. The warmth of his hand and the concern in his eyes stopped me in my tracks, even though I knew the answer to his question all too well.

Roscoe. I'd been waiting and hoping he'd show up for a month. Now I found myself wanting to hold him at bay, not answering the very questions that could open a door and get to the real reason I was here—an investigation. My mouth was as dry as Roscoe's extra-brown toast, and I kept flashing on two of the crime scene photos waiting up in my room, in a file I'd reviewed yet one more time just last night.

One, with a faded "1954" penciled on the back, showed a waxen female corpse, posed in the exact same position as the Black Dahlia. Murdered in 1947, the body of the Black Dahlia, Elizabeth Short, had been dumped at the edge of a deserted lot in LA, her arms arched over her head. The body in my photo, with the same hair and frame, had been found at the edge of a cornfield near Pineville. Unlike the Black Dahlia, this one, while still intact, had no real name as far as the public knew, just the nickname. The handwriting on the back of the photo identified her only as "Daisy Doe."

According to the records I'd found, "Daisy" was buried in the Pine Grove Baptist Church cemetery, still considered an "unknown" individual. Only she wasn't truly unknown—not to me, nor to her son, Bobby, who'd returned to Pineville in 1984, looking for her killer. He'd been murdered just as she was, and dumped in the same location. Which explained the second photo in my file.

A photo of my father's murder.

Roscoe was my greatest living source of information about both crimes. Somewhere deep in that mind curious about the local connections of a stranger lay answers that might be dangerous to both of us. Maybe . . . maybe it was time to step out a bit, get a look at the local files, and not just the ones I had been able to put together from resources on the other side of the country.

"Star?"

Mike's voice pulled me from the past. My cheeks grew warm as I swallowed and turned my hand, squeezing his fingers. His eyes widened at the gesture, and he tightened his grip. Firm and reassuring, and my throat constricted.

Maybe—just maybe—another door had been opened.

My voice rasped a bit as I whispered. "Saturday. If you can wait, I'll tell you everything Saturday."

A crease appeared between his brows, his expression now more cop than friend. "So this is more than you being a little nervous this morning."

I nodded, then pulled away from him. Folks needed coffee.

I felt his eyes follow me, the way a street officer would watch a suspect walk away from his cruiser. My stomach tensed, and I took a deep breath. I had to trust someone.

I just hoped Mike was the wisest choice. And that it didn't get both of us killed.

CHAPTER THREE

Pineville, Alabama, 1954

ROSCOE RAN, THE broad leaves of the corn plants slashing at him like airborne needles. He tripped over a clod of dirt, landing hard on his elbows, but he bit back the cry of pain and rolled over onto his back, gulping in air and trying to listen for the pursuit.

The shouts of the two men chasing him sounded flat, deadened by the tall stalks of corn, but they were no more than thirty yards off to his left. Over them, he could hear the bass of his father's voice, still confronting the other men crowding the front yard, white-sheeted figures illuminated by the cross they'd lit an hour earlier. Looking up, Roscoe could see the pale light of the flames against the night sky.

Fear oozed from Roscoe's skin, an acrid odor that made him glad the men had not brought dogs. His muscles tensed, cramping as his feet dug into the clods, pushing him backward, the seat of his jeans scraping hard in the dirt. Roscoe knew he'd never felt anything this intense, this consuming. The black community in Pineville had always kept to themselves for the most part, and the local KKK had been reluctant to turn on them—too many of the white men under the white sheets had been raised by black housekeepers and maids who could easily recognize voices, shoes, even the expressions in their eyes. Anonymity was a vital element to the Klan.

So this was the first time Roscoe had seen the sheets, felt the heat of the flaming cross, run with the fear of being killed.

That woman, he thought bitterly. The KKK thought he'd murdered Daisy Doe.

Roscoe forced himself to sit still, huddled tight between two thick stalks. The corn closed around him, a shield. If he ran, they'd hear. He caught his breath, his hands clutching the earth beneath him, his thoughts a desperate prayer of salvation. As he listened, they passed him, still too far to the left, then circled back, this time too far to the right.

By now, a flashing red light had joined that of the flames. Sheriff JoeLee Wilkes was no friend of blacks. He wasn't fond of the Klan either, but he was too smart to cross them too hard. Then, as Roscoe listened, he heard the sound of true salvation: the voice of Reverend Billy Mitchell, which boomed out over all other shouts and catcalls. JoeLee had apparently stopped for reinforcements. He wouldn't stand up to the Klan, but Reverend Billy, the white preacher of the Pine Grove Baptist Church, despised the Klan with every fiber of his being. Everybody knew it, and everybody knew the good reverend could call down the angels of heaven and the brimstone of hell when he got riled up. Nobody crossed Reverend Billy, not even the Klan, not if they valued their eternal souls.

Roscoe's fear slipped away as Reverend Billy moved into full-blown preacher mode, calling down the wrath of the Lord on the men. Within seconds, all Roscoe could hear was the pastor and the crackling of fire-ridden wood.

Still, he remained on the ground, waiting. There he stayed until the flames died, the red light vanished, and Reverend Billy hushed. Finally, his daddy called his name, and Roscoe returned home.

Daisy Doe's killer remained a mystery, but Roscoe never again doubted God's ability to answer the desperate prayers of young boys.

CHAPTER FOUR

Pineville, Alabama, Present Day

THAT AFTERNOON, I returned to the studio apartment over the drugstore and took a long, hot shower. Serving for the six-hour morning shift left me grimy, with a thin film of smoky bacon grease on my skin and a scent of stale biscuits and grits in my hair. Sometimes more than the *scent* of grits clung to the blond locks. Grits, I'd decided some time back, could easily be used in the absence of rubber cement.

Thoroughly scrubbed, I propped open the ancient windows and sprawled across my bed, letting a brisk spring breeze waft over my damp body. I massaged my scalp again and pulled my wet hair up and back, getting it off my neck and splaying it like a halo around my head.

This was the quietest, most pleasant moment of my day, and I cherished the silence and cool air. Although the drugstore was on a street corner overlooking the Pineville town square, early afternoon was a time when most folks were huddled away in their offices and plants, or they tooled along on giant tractors on distant fields. Several of the shops on the square closed at one for an hour or so. Sometimes longer, when July and August brought a smothering afternoon heat that made trees limp and hair spray useless. Early April still held a gentle freshness in the wind, which raised a few goose bumps as my skin air dried.

I stared at the ceiling, counting the water stains and thinking about my mother, especially the art, photos, and letters that had cluttered her tiny apartment, remaining for me to clean out after her death six months ago. I grew up with this eclectic collection, often coming home from dates to find her poring over crumbling cardboard boxes and endless notebooks of memories, tendrils of her still-blond hair escaping her scarf and slicked to her soft, creased cheeks by silent tears.

By the time I reached my teens, I hated her, hated my father for dying in the way he did, and hated God for the life he'd left us with by raining these murders down on us. So I tried to destroy the evidence. When my mother caught me trying to burn a box, I found myself on a plane for Birmingham, where I lived with Gran and Papa, my mother's parents, while my mother pulled herself together, stored the boxes, and finished a nursing degree.

But the boxes never went away, not for her, and—eventually—not for me either. They destroyed my family. They got my father murdered. They had helped destroy my marriage and my faith. They led me to hide my heritage behind my maternal grandparents' last name. They estranged me from my own mother, and they killed her before she turned sixty.

But they also made me a cop. They made me a cold case detective. Now I had to finish it. Before they destroyed me completely.

I slid off the bed and into a pair of shorts and T-shirt. My damp feet made soft padding sounds on the hardwood floor as I headed for the card table that doubled as office and dining room. Old and wobbly but serviceable, it perched under the window next to the bed. The files I had brought with me were in a carry-on bag underneath, and I pulled out the one closest to the front, just as I had almost every day since I'd arrived in Alabama. I'd handled it so often that its edges were soft and foxed, like an over-read book.

When I'd rekindled this investigation, I'd narrowed Mother's collection down to one box, but this file was the heart of it, and I went through it daily, even though its contents lived in my head like old friends. I'd also studied Pineville inside and out, poring over history books, online archive sites, and joining social media groups. Once I'd put together as much information as I could from the boxes and the web, I knew the next step meant injecting myself into Pineville.

And it was the good citizens of Pineville who made it all possible. The Pineville pharmacist, a lanky man in his late seventies who still carried the Taylor name, had been thinking about closing down the century-old soda fountain after the previous waitress retired. The community set up a protest that rattled the windows, and he relented. When my web wanderings turned up the job notice in the Gadsden paper, I called Gran.

"Timing is everything, Gran."

"God's timing always is, sugar."

I sighed and pressed my hands down on the file. God and Gran had this tight-knit relationship that I respected but didn't quite understand. Not for any lack of trying on her part. Gran belonged to a denomination that took Christ's instructions on spreading the Word more seriously than most. It wasn't that I didn't believe in God—I did. So much so that I felt betrayed by the way he'd abandoned Daisy Doe and my father . . . and me. Gran, however, had hopes for her last remaining relative, and I knew I was the frequent topic of her prayers.

After spending a few days in Birmingham with Gran, I moved to Pineville and took the job at the drugstore. She told me that once I got settled, we'd clean out the Overlander so I could have a more permanent place. Well . . . as permanent as a silver egg-shaped house on wheels could be.

Since then, I'd studied the files and continued the research while I got to know the folks of a small town that was almost straight out of Faulkner, quirks and all.

Starting with Miss Doris. Everyone called her "*Miss* Doris," although she'd been married to Mr. George Rankin for more than fifty years. He was the younger man she'd fallen in love with on a dance floor a few years after World War II, and at eighty-four and seventy-seven, they still danced, although they had given up competing in ballrooms all over the world. Their five kids had been born in five different countries. Their friends and the church they attended seemed to have forgiven both the dancing and the rather short time frame between their wedding anniversary and the birthdate of their oldest child, a boy who now was senior pastor at a megachurch in Dallas. I suspected the megachurch connection did a lot to smooth over that unfortunate time shortage.

Miss Doris had become my gentle gold mine and as big an advocate for God in my life as my grandmother. She'd been in Pineville all her life, save the globetrotting trips, and her memory of the forties and fifties made my remembrances of last week sound awkward and vague. She was also head of the women's group at Pine Grove Baptist, and her collection of friends, her "girls," hailed from some of the most historical and society-entrenched families in Pineville. They had owned businesses and run charities and could lay a burn on an errant child or wayward spouse with a scald that would have made the most dominant of Southern matriarchs pleased as punch.

They loved to talk, each and every one. After all, it wasn't as if I learned all that about Miss Doris and Mr. George from the internet. But I decided caution should still reign, especially when nosing into a topic that wasn't likely to come up much over afternoon tea.

Returning to the bed, I stacked the pillows against the white iron frame, brushed my feet off, and crawled back up, sitting tailor fashion. I took five deep breaths, let them out slowly, and snapped open the file.

My ritual.

For almost thirty years, Mother had collected every snippet about my father she could find, almost as if it would somehow keep Daddy alive. Until his death in 1984, he'd done the same about his mother, and some of the clippings and notes in those boxes dated back to the fifties.

But I'd been so young when he died that I barely remembered Daddy. A few stark days stood out—my first day of preschool, times when he carried me on his shoulders, a picnic, my first ride at Disneyland—but mostly I remembered a slight scent that was part tobacco, part cologne, and a fuzzy recollection of a dark-haired man who grinned every time he looked at me.

That face, however, bore little resemblance to the photos Mama had left behind, and even less to the shots of his crime scene.

Which was the first photo in my file . . . and the reason for those deep breaths.

Two bodies this time, at the edge of the same cornfield where Daisy Doe had been dumped, this time discovered by two farmhands who showed up for work. My father and the investigator he worked with, both resting on their sides, their hands tied behind them with duct tape. Their belts were still around their necks, their faces distorted by strangulation. Standing around them were the law enforcement officers at the time, including aging, rotund Sheriff JoeLee Wilkes, who had closed the case quickly, unsolved and unsolvable. Sloppy procedure stood out even in the still photo, and I could only imagine what limited efforts Wilkes had taken to "solve" the crime. The bodies had been packed up and shipped home the day after the coroner ruled on the cause of death.

My mother never stopped gathering information about Pineville, and my own research had added mounds of information as well, all in preparation for me to return to this town that had changed our lives forever. I knew this town—at least on the surface. Wilkes had died a few years after my father, the last sheriff to reign alone over Pine County. The area grew rapidly in the late seventies and early eighties, and Pineville had turned municipal, hiring a police chief and a small staff of officers. The sheriff and his office moved to another city, maintaining authority over the rural areas of the county.

I ran my finger over the details in the picture. Next to Wilkes stood two deputies who must have been only in their twenties. I'd had an artist age them, and one I had already spotted around town. Dean Sowers, a haunted-looking man in his late fifties, spent most of his time in a patrol car, late at night, his shadowed gaze moving from one empty store to another. It was a killer shift, playing security guard for a town with a crime rate almost in the negative numbers.

Dean was number three on my interview list, right behind Roscoe and Doris.

My fingernail scraped relentlessly at a dry patch on the side of my foot, showering the bed sheet with minuscule bits of skin. My anxiety showing. I needed to get to work. I'd inherited Daddy's sense of patience—Mother had always said it was nonexistent—and the waiting wore on my nerves. Yet whenever I got the urge to dive into the investigation, confronting witnesses and opening old wounds, I reminded myself that his exuberant impatience had gotten Daddy killed.

Not exactly what I wanted to achieve this time around.

You're afraid.

I leaned back against the pillows, stretching my legs out and putting that dry spot out of reach of my twitchy fingers. The word echoed a bit in my head. *Afraid.*

Well, yes and no. I definitely didn't want to wind up with a belt around my neck. But I'd spent more than a decade as a cop and a year as a private investigator, and the prospect of a new investigation usually put a tingle on my skin, not a clammy sweat. I knew how to protect myself.

I turned the picture over. Underneath was a pencil drawing my mother had done of my father, in one of her "find myself with art" phases. It was a loving rendering of Daddy as a bad boy, wearing leather and straddling a Harley. Copied from a photo taken during his early law school days, it showed a trim, wiry man with a daring glint in his eyes. He was smiling, hands on hips, thick ebony hair down around his shoulders, tossed by a wayward breeze. This was the man that my mother talked about for the rest of her life. The wild boy she'd fallen for, not the driven lawyer who'd so frequently abandoned his wife and daughter for the one cold case that consumed him—and eventually took his life.

I slid my fingers under the remaining documents in the file, pulling out the one that had started it all, had given my father his ambition, his zealous drive.

Another crime scene photo. Daisy Doe to the citizens of Pineville. Esther Spire to me and the son who'd loved her enough to die for her.

Same field. Same cause of death. Clippings from the Alabama papers at the time had compared her death to the Black Dahlia case in LA. The young beauty dumped. The mysterious young boy she'd left behind. In my files, the clippings gave way to page after page of my father's memories, scribbles he'd started as a teen, trying to hold on to the last bits of memories he had of his mother. They continued into his twenties, stopping abruptly about the time he'd entered law school. What emerged was a portrait of a temperamental, loving woman who'd doted on her only child but who had loved to grab handfuls of adventure. She collected unusual friends, soldiers, artists, musicians. She'd survived World War II in France, where she'd been part of the Resistance. A Jew who'd survived the Nazis only to die in a cornfield in Alabama.

To my mother and me—the two people who'd loved them the most—

Esther Spire and her son had been cut from the same romanticized cloth. As a cop, I knew all too well that the truth had a dark side.

My eyes watered. Maybe that was it. I knew that solving the murders would turn everything I knew about them upside down. Right now, they were tragic, golden people. But in murder, there was no gold, and tragedy could take a twisted path.

Maybe what I was afraid of was losing them all over again.

I stood up, wiped my eyes, and walked to the window. I inhaled, letting the air out slowly, as my eyes scanned the street below. I could stop now, before the investigation really began. File everything away. Go back to Nashville, to my life, to all I'd left behind to pursue this case. These cases. Forget about my father's murder. Forget Esther Spire.

Esther. Hebrew for *star.* My father had passed her name and looks to me, along with that apparently irresistible drive of our family to wind up in this tiny Southern town. Unlike them, however, I had no intention of dying here.

But Roscoe had returned home. Now was the moment to decide. Go, or dive into the deep end.

On the opposite side of the street, a delivery truck rumbled away from the curb, like a curtain opening on a brightly lit stage. In front of the hardware store behind the truck, Roscoe Carver sat in an unpainted rocker staring up at my window.

CHAPTER FIVE

Birmingham, Alabama, 1954

THE YOUNG BOY'S face peered up at Roscoe from the newspaper. The sharp cheekbones, broad face, and dark eyes echoed those of Daisy Doe. Mother. Son. The boy's black hair had been parted on the left and mired down with some type of hair goo, but a number of curls had escaped the plastering, drooping over his forehead and ears like sun-darkened vines.

Roscoe picked up the paper, folding it in his lap. Heavily creased by previous readers, it had been left behind on the bench by a man who'd hopped the last bus of the afternoon. Roscoe peered one more time at the store across the street, where his mother and her sister shopped for their husbands' birthdays. His aunt, a flamboyant preacher's wife, had more money to spend today than his father would make on the farm all year, and she was all too eager to share with her sister. They'd already been in there almost two hours.

He sighed and gazed back at the paper, running one finger over the headline: "Do You Know This Boy?" Underneath, a paragraph described how he'd been found at a motel near Pineville, apparently the son of a woman who'd been murdered there. He didn't speak, had no identification, and gave no signs he could even read. They had put him in an orphanage in Birmingham and called him Bobby Doe. The cops would like to find his father, to question him about the boy and his mother. So far, no luck.

"Too bad, kid. Guess they don't know it wasn't your daddy what killed her," Roscoe murmured.

Roscoe wanted to remember the beauty with the daisy in her hair. There were other memories, however, he'd give his eyeteeth to forget.

Across the street, his mother emerged, calling to him. "Guess I'm stuck with them all," he said, tearing the picture of Bobby Doe out of the paper and stuffing it in his pocket.

CHAPTER SIX

Pineville, Alabama, Present Day

THE TWO DAYS between Thursday breakfast with Roscoe and Saturday dinner with Mike passed with little more than my own continued obsession with the files under my table. Neither of the men put in an appearance at the drugstore on Friday morning, and I drove into Gadsden that afternoon to do some light shopping and make copies of a few things in the files. *Be careful* still rang loud and strong in my head, so I made a small, selective list of items to show Mike. I copied them in case he wanted to take them with him after hearing exactly why I had moved to Pineville.

My gut told me that he wouldn't be pleased with the news. Fine-tuned by the streets of Nashville, that instinct had proved more reliable than my head knowledge at times, and I wanted to be as prepared as possible for his reaction. What I didn't want was for him to think that any flirting I aimed in his direction had been solely because he was the police chief and a source for my investigation.

Or was it?

That was when I found myself in an artsy boutique, staring at a rack of designer jeans, wondering how my rear would look in them and if the stenciling on the thighs was too young for me.

OK, so maybe my thoughts about the black-haired Pennsylvania boy hadn't been entirely confined to business. He made me laugh. Not many people had been able to do that lately, and I was always a sucker for any man who could make me laugh. Then there was those eyes, that uncanny blue in an otherwise dark palette. That his intense focus could be unnerving annoyed me. I needed to be stronger than that.

I passed on the jeans. While Star the PI could afford them and wanted a pair so much that her mouth watered, they cost more than Star the counter waitress made in a week. A good fit and fancy stitching across my backside just weren't worth the risk of someone noticing that I was spending far more than I made. I already knew the gossip line had focused on Mike and me. More attention wasn't what I wanted at the moment. I left the boutique and headed for Walmart, where I picked up a couple of cute T-shirts and a serviceable pair of khakis—cheap, cool, and perfect for the day job.

Back in Pineville, I slipped into a tank top, shorts, and my favorite cross-trainers. Time for a good run. When I'd first started working behind the counter, I'd stopped running. Figured I got enough exercise toting breakfasts around the room. My energy level dropped, however, so I started up again, usually after a nap in the heat of the afternoon. This turned out to be a wise move on my part. If I waited late enough, the folks who lived near the square had arrived home. Some puttered about in the yard, watering flowers and plucking weeds. Others just lounged, stretching their legs on an expansive front porch. The more they saw me trotting around the neighborhood, the more they waved or stopped me to chat.

You want to get to know a small town? Walk the streets.

Settled in the latter part of the nineteenth century, the heart of Pineville still looked and felt like a postcard of a Southern community from that time. The drugstore sat on the southeast corner of a pristine square featuring a stark-white Georgian-style courthouse. With twin two-hundred-year-old oaks and a manicured lawn, the courthouse was more park than cityscape. An ornate wrought iron gazebo stood to one side of the courthouse, nestled up against a cluster of stone soldiers. A much-debated statue of a confederate soldier was the oldest, and the town council had finally solved the debate by commissioning statues representing infantry soldiers from every conflict since the Revolutionary War. It had taken most of the city's budget for two years and left folks angry about potholes, darkened street lights, a lack of Christmas decorations, and wild dogs. Of course, now there was a petition, currently tabled, to add a statue of a female soldier, while another had raised the issue of the confederate soldier yet again.

I wouldn't be a small-town politician if you paid me. Brings out the worst in people, I swear it does, being in the public eye.

As I moved from a brisk walk into a slow jog, one of Pineville's most visible politicos, Ellis Patton, waved at me. He stood next to the driver's door of his ancient pickup, keys in hand. On the passenger side waited Dandridge Patton, his grandson and heir apparent. As usual, rumors swirled around the local politicos, as in any small town. One of them had the thirty-something Dandridge being groomed for political office, starting with his grandfather's job.

I love small-town rumors. My research had revealed a lot about the town, but Miss Doris and her girls had been busy filling in the blank spaces with some of the juiciest tidbits.

And everyone in town knew that Dandridge might be waiting a long time to take over for his grandfather. Ellis was nowhere near ready for retirement. He stood tall and ramrod straight despite being seventy-plus, had been mayor for the past twelve years. He lived in an elegant Victorian just off the square, a huge home he'd inherited from his daddy, just as he had most of his income and his political position. Despite being able to pay for his children's and grandchildren's Ivy League educations in cash—a fact one of the local bank tellers still whispered about on occasion—he drove a red ramshackle 1976 Ford pickup with a white topper and a couple of bullet holes. "Huntin' accidents," he'd joke, although his political rivals whispered, "Jealous husbands" behind their hands. Ellis usually wore khakis or jeans and white oxford-cloth shirts to the office. No tie, naturally.

They were his trademark common-folks signatures. Hokey, and the citizens of Pineville knew it was a facade, even as they reelected him three times, with a fourth term likely. No term limits in Pineville. But at least, Miss Doris once confided, he'd never been convicted of a felony. Yet.

Gotta love Southern politics—almost as much as small-town rumors.

Dandridge's—Dan's—father, Thomas, had joined the military after college and had died somewhere overseas, although no one was real sure of the circumstances. That was when Dan came under his grandfather's tutelage, although the local scuttlebutt was that the apple didn't just fall far from the tree but had dropped at least one county over. No one thought Dan was up to the task, at least not yet. Another reason Ellis had most likely refused to retire.

I waved back and shifted my route closer to the pickup. "Hey, Mr. Mayor! Dandridge!"

Dan threw up a hand in a friendly wave, but Ellis paused, grinning. "Hey, Miss Star. You sure do pretty-up things here on the square."

I pranced in place, ignoring his glance below my neckline. "Everything still running safe and sound here in Pineville?"

He nodded once, a gesture of fatherly reassurance. "Always. No place safer."

"One reason I'm here."

"You ready to sell that Carryall yet? I'll give you a good price."

I grinned. He asked me the same thing almost every time I saw him. He'd coveted my 1966 GMC Carryall since the day I drove into town. "Now, you know Belle's not for sale. She's been in the family a long time. Would you trade your truck for her?"

He chuckled. "Nope. You got me there."

"I heard it was your daddy's truck."

"True dat. Well, you know what they say. You'll never get what you don't ask for."

"True that. Have a good evening, Your Honor."

"You too, Miss Star." They slammed their doors, and Ellis backed out of the spot, careful to check for me in his rearview.

I'd think it was to avoid hitting me if they hadn't paused just a little too long, patriarch and grandson watching as I jogged out of the square.

I picked up speed and turned off the square down Maple Street, where the maples that gave the street its name were so old they formed a thick canopy arch overhead. One of the three streets recently designated as "Historic Pineville," Maple ran due north for eight blocks before dead-ending at the city park. The eight houses closest to the square were neat, efficient Federal boxes sitting so near the sidewalk that the front "lawns" were mere strips of wild ginger and silver-gray pussy toes. The back yards, however, were acre-sized refuges, complete with restored outbuildings that had once been slave quarters, kitchens, and smokehouses. Now they were guest cottages, garages, and pool houses.

Farther out, the homes of Maple spread apart, with the houses in the center of the property and surrounded by boxwoods and thick clusters of loblolly pines and ancient oaks. Federals gave way to Georgians, Victorians, Greek Revivals, and Tidewaters, with the sole exception being an elaborate Italianate mansion four blocks from the square. This one, safely lodged on the historic register, featured an ostentatious cupola and a band-sized gazebo, which occasionally did, in fact, hold a forties swing band, hosted by the owners, George and Doris Rankin. When not a location for rollicking music, the polished red cedar deck of the gazebo supported a tasteful selection of wicker and rattan furniture and an old-fashioned double glider.

Miss Doris waved at me from the glider and motioned at me with a tea glass glistening with moisture. I slowed to a walk and took my time crossing the lawn to the gazebo. As I did, Miss Doris plucked a glass from a selection of crystal on a table near the glider and filled it with tea from a matching pitcher. Four or five glasses stood waiting, one already used. The entire town knew that Miss Doris held court in her glider every afternoon—at least while she was in town. Sugar cookies on Revere silver and dark sweet tea flavored with mint in Waterford glasses waited for any guest who happened to drop by. I once asked her why she used such priceless items in the front yard. She'd looked at me over the top of her reading glasses and announced that she was old and it made her happy. Good enough.

She brushed off the opposite side of her glider. "Sit, girl. Cool off." She handed me the glass, which I took as I sank down on the thick cushion. She didn't offer the cookies—I had turned them down enough she knew I wouldn't accept. Holding tight to the glider, she swung into the other side and pushed off gently.

We slid back and forth in the calm evening air, the slick motion of the glider creating enough breeze to dry the little bits of sweat I'd worked up on the short jog.

"You'd think you get enough exercise at the drugstore." Her voice had the soft curves of a prim, Southern charm school.

"Jogging helps me keep my energy up so I don't give out in the mornings."

She nodded. "I understand. George and I still have more energy when we dance than when we don't." She grinned. "And at our age, that makes a difference."

I considered Miss Doris a marvel of nature. At eighty-four, she was still trim and fit, with firm arms and legs, a sweet shock of red hair, and an infectious grin. While most of her peers walked slow and moaned more about their ailments than their next trip, Miss Doris moved about her garden as if on a mission. She let the ballroom dancing take credit for her good health, along with "a few good genes." Her husband, George, was seven years younger and still moved with the grace of a ballet company's *prima danseur.* His dimming eyes had stopped him from driving but not from leading his lady around the dance floor.

Part of me wanted to be Miss Doris when I grew up. The other part knew I had all the grace of a deer on ice.

"Are you and Mr. George heading out again?"

She let out a long breath. "No, I don't think we'll be doing a lot of dancing this year."

"How come?"

She leaned back in the glider, and it eased to a halt. "Carly."

"What about her? Is something wrong?"

A slight movement of her head sent one of her curls astray. "No. And I appreciate you keeping her this weekend."

"Not a problem. Did Mike explain that he'd be coming over for a bit while I'm here?"

Her smile became sly. "You two make such a cute couple."

"Now, don't get carried away, Miss Doris. Right now we're just friends."

"Doesn't mean I can't hope." She patted her curl back in place. "You know I don't mind him being here. He's a good man, even if he is a Yankee."

"Now, Miss Dori—" The sparkle in her eyes stopped me. "Tease."

Her thin, high laughter rattled the leaves. "You are too easy, girl."

I sipped the tea. "What about Carly?"

Miss Doris nodded. "You know her mama is my granddaughter Ellen, who belongs to my girl Charlotte. The middle one. Carly is named for Charlotte."

I didn't know, but I nodded as if I did. All five of Miss Doris's children had married and produced a slew of kids of their own, including two who had married twice and had stepchildren. Several of her grandchildren were following the same pattern. Keeping up took a flow chart. Most of the time, I just nodded and listened.

"Well, Charlotte and Dean still work. He's out most nights. She can't take her."

"Her? Carly."

"Right. She called me—"

"Charlotte called . . ."

"Right. Ellen and Kevin are having a few . . . problems. Young couples always do, but most work them out. It seems to be getting worse for them. So they wanted Charlotte and Dean to take Carly for a few weeks, but they really can't. They live way out, hard to get sitters, and they work—"

"So they asked you to watch your great-granddaughter."

She sighed. "Carly's a sweet girl, but she *is* seven."

"Been a long time, huh?"

"It hasn't been safe for a seven-year-old to live here since 1970. And I'm just a little old to be a soccer mom."

"So you're thinking longer than a few weeks."

She didn't miss a beat. "That's why I like you, Star. You get it."

"What can I do? Other than sitting on the occasional night out with your girlfriends?"

She reached over and took my hand. "Thank you. Let's start with the babysitting. If you and Carly get along, we'll talk. I'll pay you for the time."

"Now, Miss—"

"Hush. I know you can use it, and you know we can afford it. Just look around!"

I did, mostly to notice that the light was fading. "Miss D, I need to go. Finish my jog before it gets dark."

"Well, I need to get back in as well. There's this pesky mosquito who's been annoying my shins like they were ribs on a spit. Let's go in before she makes supper out of my calf."

I picked up the tray of tea and cookies and followed her up the Italian tile path to the back door, picking my steps carefully. Dropping a cheap white mug at the drugstore could be forgiven. Centuries-old crystal and silver . . . not so much. But I loved Miss Doris's house. The warm industrial-sized kitchen was one of the most welcoming I'd been in, with generous smells of cinnamon, basil, and sage blending easily. Black cast-iron pots and skillets hung from ceiling racks, waiting patiently for suppertime. I set the tray on a pine table in the middle of the room, well away from the edge.

I gave Miss Doris a quick peck on the cheek, then beat a hasty retreat, closing the door quietly behind me. I had a lot of thinking to do, since my world had just shifted slightly.

Carly, Miss Doris's great-granddaughter. Ellen and Kevin. Charlotte and Dean.

I picked up speed and hit the street, remembering suddenly Gran's words about God's timing and how things flow together as they are intended to.

Dean was Dean Sowers. The deputy who'd once stood so still and white over my father's corpse.

CHAPTER SEVEN

Cam Ranh Bay, Vietnam, 1969

ROSCOE WATCHED THE young officer stop outside the USO and speak for a brief moment to another soldier, his actions as crisp and pristine as his uniform. Roscoe had been watching him for weeks now, since the lieutenant's arrival at Cam Ranh, convinced that either God had a twisted sense of humor or the world had indeed become a very small place.

Roscoe, who had carried Bobby Doe's picture in his wallet for fifteen years, knew immediately that this was the adult version of the abandoned boy. He'd stared at that face—those black eyes, sharp cheekbones, and unrestrained curls—often enough to see it, even in the man whose hair had been cropped to within one-eighth inch of his skull. Roscoe had followed the officer frequently, his position in the Security Police allowing him to move randomly among the troops. Not that Lieutenant Robert Caleb Spire, his real name, had been hard to spot. The man who had been Bobby Doe took military precision to a new level with his behavior and uniform, standing out in the bay like a new penny in mud.

Yet Roscoe had hesitated to approach him. Exactly how did you tell an officer like Spire that you'd been carrying his picture in your wallet for fifteen years? Not a great opening line, no. And with the segregation of the races, any approach to a white officer of his rank would be suspect.

As the two men saluted and separated, Roscoe took a last, long draw on his cigarette, slid out of his jeep, and stubbed the butt out under his boot. He'd waited long enough. He had to make a move, no matter what the outcome. Obviously Lieutenant Spire was off duty, ready to visit the USO. Roscoe strode toward him, reaching Spire just as the lieutenant headed into the building.

"Bobby Doe." Roscoe intentionally directed the firmly spoken words at the officer's back. To anyone else, they'd mean nothing. Amid the raucous noise of the street, an officer looking away would not even notice the words had been said.

Lieutenant Robert Caleb Spire, however, froze. He completed a slow, steady, strictly defined about-face. The black eyes narrowed with a laser intensity that took in the man before him, examining every pore, every drop of sweat. Roscoe had sometimes debated his buddies about which was hotter in August, Vietnam or Alabama, but in that moment, Vietnam felt infinitely more searing.

Silence reigned between the two men for a full excruciating minute. Roscoe could almost see Spire's brain separating fact from speculation as the muscles in his face at first hardened, then slowly softened in recognition.

"You're the one who found my mother." Unlike his face, Spire's baritone held no hint of emotion.

Roscoe had thought the lieutenant would only react to the name with curiosity. But the leap across the years, the rapid calculation separating Roscoe from among the people who would have known that name, startled Roscoe. He'd heard that the lieutenant was sharp, destined for JAG, but hadn't seen the evidence until now. He stood a bit straighter. "Yes sir."

"Roscoe Carver."

Again, Roscoe tried to suppress his surprise, and he took a deep breath, resisting the impulse to snap to attention and whip a salute to follow the path of the lieutenant's crisp words. "Yes sir."

"No need to be surprised, Carver. I know who you are." Spire paused. "Or at least I know your name. I've collected evidence on my mother's murder for years. I know the names of everyone involved. And I knew when the Pineville paper listed you as one of the men going to Vietnam. And I knew you were assigned here in Cam Ranh. I just haven't had the chance to look you up. I want to talk to you."

"You do? How did you know I was here?"

"It's not that hard to find out. And I may have been a child, Carver, but a boy never forgets how his mother was murdered. Or who was involved. It's why I joined the military, to pay for law school. I will never forget. You can help."

In that moment, Roscoe knew that, while he'd made the right decision in approaching Spire, the murder of Daisy Doe had not only changed his childhood. It had altered the rest of his life.

CHAPTER EIGHT

Pineville, Alabama, Present Day

MIKE LUINETTI STARED out one of Miss Doris's bay windows, focused on the shadows that danced in grays and blacks on the sloping front lawn. The back of his neck remained as red as a bad sunburn, and in the night-darkened window, I could see the reflection of his narrowed eyes and tense jaw. He clenched his fists at his side, and his lips had paled almost to invisibility.

I perched on the edge of the Queen Anne divan, motionless, resisting the urge to gather the papers scattered across the coffee table in front of me or pick up the remains of the take-out containers clustered at my feet. The faint scents of roast beef and chicken still clung to the air, but moving at that moment didn't seem like the wisest idea. I was grateful that being at Miss Doris's home had given us a private place to talk, but in that moment I also prayed that sweet little Carly stayed in bed and didn't need attention from her babysitter.

"You should have told me sooner." His calm, low voice held a hard edge.

I took a deep breath. "All I knew about law enforcement in this county is in those files. It didn't exactly engender—"

"This isn't 1984, and I'm not JoeLee Wilkes."

Good point. "Mike—"

He finally turned, and his eyes flashed with irritation. "We're friends. Or I thought we were."

My gut clenched. This wasn't going well. "We are! I mean, I did not just befriend you because of"—I waved my arm over the files—"this." I stood up. "I like you. I would have liked you had I come here on vacation or moved here for a job. In fact, I waited this long because I was afraid of exactly this reaction."

I stepped from behind the coffee table and moved closer to him. "Look, I'm a cold case detective. This is what I do for unforgettable cases in small towns. I move into town, get to know the people. Eventually I figure out which member of the local officers I can trust. Someone always stands out. But I don't *date* them to get their trust. I wanted to date you because I liked you. A lot. That I feel I can trust you with all this meant—"

"—meant I was a friend . . . with benefits."

I stopped, staring at him, not believing that he'd crack such a joke. Then I recognized the amused gleam in his eyes, and a suppressed laugh exploded from me, a sound that was a cross between a hairball-retching tabby and a frightened lynx.

"You walked into that one, girl."

"You set me up." I took one of his hands and held it in both of mine. "But the truth is, if this goes the way I think it will, I'm going to need your help."

"You think my department was involved."

I nodded. "JoeLee's, anyway. Not yours. If not in the murders, then in the reasons why they weren't solved."

"A cover-up."

"Yes."

He squeezed my hands lightly, then pulled away, returning to the divan. He perched on the very edge of it and focused on the paperwork. "It does seem odd that no one followed up on your father's claims in 1984. And you're sure the files he brought with him vanished?"

"I'm not really sure about too much of anything right now. They never sent the files back. Were they destroyed? Archived? What happened to them when the departments divided?" I sat next to him and pulled two sheets of paper from the splayed files on the coffee table. "Look, in his notes he made frequent references to 'MW1,' which my mother explained was his designation for his first material witness. She'd seen it in a lot of his trial work, which she'd helped him proofread."

Mike's eyebrows arched as he peered at me. "He'd found a witness to his mother's murder?"

A familiar tingle of excitement shot up my spine, and I straightened. *He's catching it. The fever.* "Possibly, if not an eyewitness, then someone who knew a great deal about it. We thought so, my mother and I. My dad did two tours in Vietnam, and the second time he came back, he attacked the case files with a new resolve."

Mike's eyes narrowed, shifting from surprise to disbelief. "You think he found out something in Vietnam about a murder in Alabama?"

I stood up and started pacing in front of Miss Doris's big window. "Yeah, I *know* how it sounds. But in 1969 he started sending home packages full of his journals, asking Mother to keep them safe. He was in 'Nam until late seventy-two, then he still had to honor his long-term commitment to JAG. But he was crazier than ever about the murder after he got home. Late nights going over papers, military reports from World War II, personal histories, stuff that didn't have anything to do with Pineville or his mother."

"So he was looking for cross connections."

"Or someone to confirm a story he'd heard while overseas." I dropped back down on the divan and clutched his arm. "I think he crossed paths with someone from Pineville who filled in some blanks. He needed corroboration."

He glanced down quickly at my hand on his arm, then refocused on my face. "Did your mother ask him what he was looking for?"

"She asked, but he never told her. Even worse, he never put it in writing except in one place, one file, and he had that file with him in 1984 when he came back to Pineville."

"The files that disappeared?"

"They weren't returned with his body or his personal effects. Mother made repeated requests, but the only answer she ever received made it sound as if they were part of an ongoing investigation. She stopped asking after five years."

"So you think they're stored somewhere in the archives here or over in the sheriff's department."

I leaned a little closer to him and whispered, "Y'know, one of the things I love about you is your unflappable faith in the Southern justice system to work exactly the way it's supposed to."

His scowl told me he'd gotten the point. "You think they were destroyed."

"Almost immediately. Probably before the bodies were cold. If not, browsed through to see what he'd found out, then destroyed."

Mike turned cop on me, even more than before, eyeing me closely head to toe. I fought the urge to shiver. When his gaze settled on my face again, he leaned back. "So your plan is to find that witness again."

The crucial moment had arrived. I stiffened my spine. "Yes."

"What have you done so far?"

"Mostly just get to know folks. Find out what the town is like now. What it was like then."

"Miss Doris."

"Yes. Getting to know her has been great on all sorts of levels. But I need to start the next step, and I know if I just start asking around, life could get a little dicey."

"Meaning you don't want to wind up one morning with something cold and painful around your neck."

"Precisely. Obviously I'd like to talk to Roscoe Carver."

"He found your grandmother's body?"

I nodded. "And he was in Vietnam. I'd also like to talk with some of the Vietnam vets who might have been around during the time of my grandmother's murder. See who else from this area served over there. One of my biggest hopes is that whoever my father talked to over there didn't die over there."

Mike picked up the photo of my father's murder scene and gestured toward the deputies. "Well, Dean's too young to have been around for Vietnam. This is 1984, and he couldn't have been more than twenty or twenty-one. He might have been in the military—"

"—but not in Vietnam."

"Picked out any of the vets here in town?"

"There's a couple that I've heard about—"

"Hal Prentiss and Trapper Luke Davidson."

"Right. Trapper Luke hangs out at the hardware store, but I couldn't even get him to go there. Trapper is . . . um, a little, um—"

"Bat-guano crazy."

"I was going to say reticent."

"Very PC of you. But no, he really is bat-guano crazy."

"And I haven't been able to find Hal. Everyone seems to know about him, but not where he is. Like a recluse, but with no set address."

Mike shrugged. "Rumor is there's still a warrant out for him, for something he did years ago. Even without that, I've heard he was a very reticent character. Vietnam was just his first war. He became a professional soldier and didn't come back to Pineville for years. And not a talkative person even then."

"So that leaves Roscoe."

Mike dropped the photo and leaned his elbows on his knees. "Humph." He templed his fingers and pressed them to his lips.

I waited, watching as his gaze wandered to some far place only he could see. He stared out the window and down the lawn, and I knew he was cataloging people and possibilities one by one.

I slowly took in, with gratitude, that he intended to help. After all, if this got ugly, it could put his entire department on trial.

He straightened. "Tomorrow I plan to sit with you at church."

I wondered if I looked as confused as I felt. "Beg pardon?"

He grinned slyly. "Allegiances, Star. It'll declare two things. One, that I intend to court you . . . officially. Two, that I'm behind you."

"And that will help because . . ."

"You're right to move slow on this, get people to trust you. Monday, we'll go over to the museum. I'll introduce you to the Hall sisters, who work there, and tell them you're bored in your off hours and would like to get to know Pineville better. Volunteer to help them with filing, sorting, cataloging, anything they need."

"And this will help *because* . . ."

"You'll get to ask them about the statues on the courthouse lawn. *Who served.* Who didn't. My guess is that they don't yet have a list of the vets of the recent wars. The Hall sisters run the museum but are still pretty much stuck in 1864."

This time the light went on over my head. "And I can volunteer to go through all the newspaper and public records and pull together the lists of new vets without raising undue curiosity."

"All official museum business. Start this on your own, and by Tuesday you'll be answering questions from everyone in the drugstore. In the meantime, I'll see if I can find any records from the 1984 or 1954 cases."

I stood up. "I can't believe we have a plan of action."

He rose as well. "I can't believe you're going to let me kiss you to celebrate."

I froze, my eyebrows somewhere close to my hairline. "You want to kiss me?"

"Are you this slow as a detective or just as a date?"

"Do you really think I'm the kind of girl who kisses on the first date?"

"Thought I might try and find out." Mike stepped closer and cupped my face in both hands. Their warmth and his closeness sent a sliver of desire down my spine, and my chest tightened. I wanted to kiss him.

But it had been a long time since I'd kissed any man, and, apparently, not long enough. An image flashed through my head, a face I had not thought of in months. One that drove any thoughts of a kiss out of my mind.

I couldn't bridge the gap. I put my hands against his chest. "Mike, I—"

A soft rumble under our feet signaled the raising of a garage door, and Mike released me. Saved by Miss Doris.

I paused and swallowed hard. "So this courting thing . . . it's not just a cover?"

He grinned, then stooped to gather up the take-out containers. "OK if I pick you up at about 10:30? Sunday school starts at 9:30, but we'll skip it tomorrow. We'll make more of an entrance if we show up first to the main service at eleven."

Looked like my presence at Pine Grove Baptist would be a bit more permanent than I planned. Miss Doris—and my grandmother—would be pleased.

*

Pine Grove Baptist Church wasn't the largest church in town—that distinction belonged to the newly built First Baptist out next to the interstate—but it was by far the oldest. Located on the outskirts of town, in the bend of a US highway headed into Gadsden, Pine Grove had been around in one form or another since 1846, and it claimed the town's oldest families for members. It sat in a sloping valley between two mountain ridges, the final "toes" of the Appalachian foothills of northern Alabama. The latest incarnation, a white clapboard chapel backed by a pink stucco-covered fellowship hall and Sunday school wing, faced the highway like a spiritual gateway into the city.

Apparently, Pineville's Baptists fell into the same two categories as the rest of the town: locals and commuters, aka "the drive-ins." Drive-ins attended First Baptist, finding Pine Grove too conservative and cliquish.

In the South, small-town religious life bore a remarkable resemblance to small-town politics.

Mike, a deacon at Pine Grove, also served as one of the ushers. When the other ushers would join their wives in the pews during the service, Mike would stand at the back, in a crisp at-ease pose, so he could observe both the entrances to the sanctuary as well as the congregation. The church had not only gotten used to his standing guard, they had embraced it, as if the town's police chief had become their personal guardian angel.

Thus a groundswell of whispers began in the parking lot as we arrived together in Mike's personal car, a long, lean 1978 Jaguar XKE, rescued from a salvage yard and restored by his mechanic father. The twelve cylinders of the white car purred softly, making the engine hard to hear. Most of the men in town knew that Mike owned the car, but he seldom drove it, preferring to tool around town in his police cruiser.

"Nothing like making a statement," I mumbled, not entirely happy with the head-turning attention we garnered as we pulled up next to the church.

Mike grinned. "Trust me, city girl. By this afternoon, everyone in town will know that you have my ear and my trust."

"A philosophical bulletproof vest."

He chuckled. "Something like that. Even though I'm still an outsider here, after this, you'll be less of one. Now wait and let me get your door."

"My mother taught me the proper way for a lady to get out of a car, thank you very much." I grinned. "Even if I never do it."

I waited as he walked around and opened the passenger door. I'd dressed carefully for today, in a simple rose-colored shift that made the highlights in my blond hair stand out and my blue eyes shine. Beige pumps and a beige bolero jacket complemented it, and a beige-and-rose scarf pulled everything together. Conservative but eye-catching.

I swung both legs out of the car at the same time, pressing my knees cautiously and firmly together. I took his hand to pull myself up. The two-inch heels on the pumps put me close to Mike's six-two height, so we made a noticeable couple even without the Jag. His navy-blue suit fit him snugly, and I took his arm as we entered the sanctuary.

Miss Doris faced the altar when we first walked in, but one of her girls spotted us and whispered in her ear. She spun around, her face lit by a wide grin. Mike led me down the center aisle but stopped at only the third pew down. He seated me on the right side of the church, directly opposite most of the ushers' wives. As he went back up the aisle to assume his duties for the morning, I scooted over to leave room for one person. I placed my rose clutch purse on the seat beside me. And waited.

Miss Doris arrived first, dropping in beside me with a wicked grin. "So tell me what's going on? I thought y'all just watched a DVD last night."

I forced back a grin and brought out my best Scarlett O'Hara accent. "Why, Miss Doris, whatever do you mean?"

She smacked my arm. "Now, don't you play coy with me, young lady."

I arched my eyebrows. "I'm serious. There's really nothing to tell."

"Humph. You're holding out."

I hesitated, then relented, leaning toward her with a conspiratorial whisper. "We just talked. Decided to start going out some. But, really, nothing serious."

She grabbed my hand in a surprisingly strong grip. "Good for you. At least it's a start." Miss Doris patted my arm with her other hand and giggled, as if she were fifteen and Mike were the captain of the high school football team. "Just in time too. Now you'll have a chance to show off some of your cooking on Decoration Sunday."

Apparently, I looked as confused as I felt. This was becoming a habit.

"Oh, honey, don't your people have Decoration Sunday where you're from?"

"Um, I don't think so."

"First Sunday in May. That's just a couple of weeks away. Haven't you noticed it in the bulletin?"

"Um . . ."

"Dinner on the grounds right after church. Big potluck. All the women bring their best dishes. After lunch we all put the new flowers for the year on our people's graves. If you had folks buried out there, you'd want to clean off the gravesites a few days ahead of time. Y'know, kill off the weeds, maybe put down clean sand or chips."

There were a few things about small-town life you just had to take as they came and figure them out later.

"It'll be a good time for you to show him you know how to cook." She peered over her shoulder at him again. "You have no idea how we've been praying for that boy. He needs a woman. A good woman."

Right. I could hear Mike's laughter at that statement. "Now, Miss Doris, I'm sure he's—"

"Especially after what happened to the last girl."

A tiny red flag popped up in the back of my head. OK, maybe not really red. More yellow. Maybe orange . . . "What happened to the last girl?"

"And it wasn't his fault. That girl Jessica had always been on the wild side. We'd tried to warn him, but men, you know, they always think they know best. And they hadn't been together long. But my guess is he'll never leave Pineville because of it. Wouldn't be able to."

My stomach tightened. This was turning more ominous by the second. "What happened to her?"

A lone chime from the organ signaled the start of worship. Miss Doris straightened. "Oops. I have to get back." With another pat on my bicep, she scooted away and back to her pew with the girls.

I glanced around at Mike, but his solemn chat with another deacon kept him occupied. I faced forward again, staring at the empty wooden cross at the front of the church, a sick feeling spreading from my stomach up into my throat.

What in the world have I done?

CHAPTER NINE

Pineville, Alabama, 1969

Roscoe Carver shed his uniform as soon as he hit US shores. His second tour ended a few weeks after he'd connected with Robert Caleb Spire, and he hit home ground just before Christmas. Roscoe remained grateful for what he'd learned . . . and that he'd survived. But unlike the first soldiers who'd returned from Vietnam, he knew what kind of welcome waited in the US, especially in his own community during the year following Martin's and Bobby's assassinations.

Which was why he'd told no one of his pending arrival home, and Roscoe stepped off the Greyhound wearing jeans and a sweatshirt. The only remnants of his time overseas were the boots and his service jacket, worn because they were the only items of their kind that he owned.

He waited until the bus roared away and the smoke and diesel fumes had wafted up, dispersing in the cutting winter cold. Roscoe hunched his coat tighter around his shoulders and shoved his hands into the pockets as he glanced around at the small town, the drugstore, hardware store, the bank, courthouse. There was a new beauty salon for white women, and one of the dress shops had closed. The owner, Miss Libby Bowlin, had been ill when he'd left; Roscoe wondered if she'd passed away.

Not much else had changed in Pineville, a small town frozen in time. His mother's letters had mentioned no protests, no riots, no unrest at all. The rest of the country might have been coming apart, but Pineville?

Not so much.

Yet, Roscoe thought. *Just wait.*

Turning east, Roscoe took a long deep breath of the crisp winter air of home and set off on the four-mile walk to his daddy's farm.

Just wait.

CHAPTER TEN

Birmingham, Alabama, Present Day

"A FLAMINGO? IT had to be a pink flamingo?"

"You know your granddaddy loved those birds."

"Yeah, so did Tony," I murmured.

Gran puckered her lips the way she always did whenever my ex-husband's name came up. Ten years after the fact, Anthony B. O'Connell was still persona non grata where she was concerned, and I half expected her to spit and mutter a curse on his head. Gran had always been petite, and age had made her more so. But the one time Tony had dared visit, she'd put a finger in his face and threatened to seriously damage his ability to sire children if he hurt me again. Tony stood six three and had a running back's build. To his credit, he had not laughed, although he had appeared incredulous at the thought of a five-foot-tall, silver-haired grandma doing damage to him.

That was, until she'd murmured, "Smirk all you want. Eventually, you'll have to sleep."

We'd stayed at a hotel that night.

Gran nodded at big pinkie, her short hair shimmering in the sun. "Well, Johnny fell in love with them when we saw a whole flock one year down at Busch Gardens."

"Yeah, I remember the slides from that trip. I just didn't know he loved them enough to paint a giant one of the side of his RV."

"Travel trailer, dear. It doesn't have an engine."

Right. I circled the *travel trailer* one more time. The 1969 Airstream Overlander had been my grandfather's second love. Bought after he retired in 1995, it became his hobby, and he'd renovated it twice before he died in 2009. The last renovation apparently include neon-pink and tropical-green pinstripes that circled it and the six-foot-tall pink flamingo that graced the right side.

"It'll certainly go with Belle's bright blue."

"Oh, you'll just be . . . what is it the kids say?"

I looked around at her. "What?"

She snapped her fingers. "You be stylin'!"

"Gran."

"What?"

"Don't. You're more likely to break a hip than be a hipster."

She laughed. It was a running joke with us, with her insisting she should "stay up with the times" and me reminding her she was just fine with her own times. She always had been. Gran, at eighty, kept her snowy white hair in a pixie cut that sweetly framed her thin face. She wore classic clothes with simple, elegant lines.

"Well, go on in. You need to take a look around, then we'll go shopping and outfit it with all the stuff you need. I do wish you could stay the night."

"Can't. Have to work in the morning, so I need to get this beastie back in time to get it parked in Doc's yard before dark."

I opened the door, expecting the usual trailer décor, since Papa's first renovation had basically restored the old trailer to its original state. I had not seen this latest version, and I stopped just inside, my mouth gaping. "Wow. Trailer life has changed a bit."

Gran nudged by me. "Told you."

Originally, a flip table and a couch that converted into a double bed had dominated the front living area. They'd been replaced by a set of custom walnut shelves with a drop-down desk, a hunter-green swivel office chair, and a matching recliner that converted into a single bed. The dark laminate wood floor stretched into the galley, which Papa had modernized with a new fridge, mini-microwave, and hunter-green countertops and appliances. Three gas burners lined the cabinet next to the tiny double sink. Underneath, a small oven would be perfect for at least two casseroles for Decoration Sunday. Near the front door, a small bistro table waited with two of the smallest swivel stools I'd ever seen.

Whereas the front of the trailer was all dark wood and green, in the bedroom green gave way to a rice-paper look in the shades and the three-panel pocket door that led to the bath. The couch/full-size bed unit on the right side of the room had a soft gray upholstery that I'd need to slipcover, probably before I got it out the driveway. Opposite the couch was a wall of storage—closet, floor-to-ceiling drawers—along with a small vanity table, mirror, and a flat-screen television.

"Well?"

"This thing has more storage than my house in Nashville."

Gran chuckled. "Johnny liked souvenirs. Never enough room for all the things he wanted to buy." She tapped my arm. "Come on. I got dumplings on the stove. I'll show you the technical stuff later."

"Technical stuff?" I followed her outside and toward the house. Gran's chicken and dumplings had the same drawing power as a pied piper or a fountain of hot chocolate.

"You know, the generator, waste control, gas, that kind of stuff. The air conditioner and the solar panel are on the roof."

I glanced back at the trailer, really noticing for the first time the cluster of equipment on the top. "Not exactly a pup tent, is it?"

"Certainly a sight more expensive than a pup tent." She held open the door that led into her enclosed back porch. What had once been a concrete patio was now a comfy sitting area with cushioned rattan love seats, jalousie windows, and a plethora of plants.

The trailer wasn't the only thing Papa liked to tinker with.

"Ever wish he'd have put the money into a nicer house, maybe something over in Mountain Brook?"

In 1963, Gran and Papa had bought this bungalow in a cozy Birmingham neighborhood not far from where US 11 became First Avenue North. There they had stuck through all the changes in Alabama's largest city, good . . . and not so good. A Korean War vet, not much disturbed Papa, with the exception of bad manners and wasteful habits. Twelve years older than Gran, he'd helped her raise three kids in that efficient little three-bedroom: my mother, born two days after

Gran's eighteenth birthday, and two sons. Uncle Brad had died in the first Gulf War, and Uncle Jake up and turned survivalist on us in the late nineties and had moved to Alaska with three cats, four dogs, six months of food, and a trunk full of ammunition. For some reason, Jake had never married. And we'd never heard from him again. After twenty years, Gran assumed bears had eaten him.

So it was just Gran and me. We just didn't mention that part much. No need, really. But Gran had been thrilled when, after the divorce, I dumped Tony's last name not for my maiden one—Spire—but for hers. She'd raised me. It made sense that I would become Star Cavanaugh.

Gran picked up a wooden spoon and dug deep in a pot bubbling with thick chicken broth and bouncing dumplings. "Well, we talked about a new house a few times. Usually when one of the neighbors complained about us having that giant flamingo in the back yard."

"Can't imagine why that would bother anyone."

"Anyone ever tell you that your mouth will keep you single?"

"You. My last four dates."

"We'd look, but we'd never find a place that we liked as well as here. Besides, we fit here. We knew all the flaws and strengths, what we'd need to fix right away, what could wait. Would be like leaving an old friend." She spooned soft dumplings and tender chunks of chicken into large bowls.

My mouth watered. I set out the silverware and poured two tall glasses of milk. We sat, and I waited as Gran said the blessing, then dug in.

"We can start shopping for the trailer in the attic."

I swallowed a savory bit of dumpling. "Beg pardon?"

"I stored a lot of the containers and dishes we used up there. No use in duplicating what we don't have to."

"Sounds good."

She went silent for a long time, and I knew she really wanted to ask me about how things were going in Pineville. After all, I was investigating the death of her son-in-law. Following a few minutes of silence, I cleared my throat. "I'm getting settled in nicely up in Pineville, but I still have a long way to go. I'm just getting to know folks. I've made friends with the local police chief, and I think he'll be a big help."

"Good." But she didn't look up.

After another moment, I said, "Gran, I'm not Daddy. I don't have his lawyer's arrogance or sense that justice must be served right now and out in the open. I'm a cold case cop. I know that things like this take time. A lot of it. Some of the cold cases I've worked on have taken months, even years, to unravel. I also know that most murders occur because of either passion or greed, but I don't think money was the issue in this case. Neither Daddy nor my grandmother had that much. Passion's dangerous. I'm going to be extremely careful."

She reached out and grabbed my hand. Tears dropped from her eyes into her bowl. "I just don't want to lose you too."

I squeezed her hand. "You won't. I'll get through this so I can bring the pink beastie back to your yard and annoy the neighbors."

She grinned. "I do wish you'd known your daddy better." She released my hand and went back to the dumplings.

"Me too."

She shook her head slightly. "No, I don't mean that in just a general way. You were so young—I know you get most of your impressions of him from your mama."

I wasn't sure where she was going. "And?"

She chewed thoughtfully for a second. "Now, don't get me wrong. I loved your mama with all my heart. She was my baby. My first. But she lost sight of a lot of stuff after he died, and she resented the time he spent trying to find out who murdered his mama."

"I knew that part."

"But did you know he was a really good man? I mean a *good* man. Sweet and kind, and when your mama brought him home the first time, Johnny and I couldn't have been more thrilled for her. After his mother died, Bobby was never adopted. At first they thought he was mute, but that was because he didn't speak English. He spoke French, and his mother warned him not to talk to strangers. So he didn't for a long time. But he grew up in that home, learned English, and became a kind of leader among the boys. Encouraged them to do more things at school, get skills that could help them in the long run. He was old enough when his mother died that he had to have gotten that determination from her." She paused. "Did you know that he and Susie met because they were both volunteering at a tutoring program?"

I didn't, as a matter of fact.

"I think Susie left you with the impression that your daddy was either a driven, unrelenting lawyer or this untamable wild child."

That did kind of sum it up.

"But he was so much more. And he doted on you. Lord have mercy, how he played with you and loved on you. He'd snatch you up when he got home at night and threaten to 'steal all your sugar so you wouldn't be so sweet.' And then just smother you with kisses. You giggled and squealed like mad."

She sighed. "He couldn't even bring himself to punish you. When you acted out, Susie had to put you right. You'd stand in the front door, every day, waiting for him to come home."

OK, *now* I didn't like where this was going. "Gran . . ."

"After he was murdered, for weeks you'd go to the front door and just stand there. Waiting. It just about killed your mama."

My eyes began to sting. "Gran . . ."

"And you are just like him."

I blinked. The stinging stopped. "What?"

She took a deep breath. "Honey, I know you need to do this. I know it better than my own life. But this wasn't a real obsession with Bobby until after he went to Vietnam. Sure, he collected information, but it was more like a hobby. After the service, he changed. Something happened to him over there."

"I think he met someone who knew about the murder."

She nodded. "Susie thought that too. But my point is that this was *not* a lifelong thing for him. While it was always there, in the back of his mind, he didn't obsess until later, after the war. And I firmly believe that if he'd not found what he was looking for in Pineville, he might have let it go, if that clue had led to a dead end. So I want you to put that in the back of your head. You're a good cop. You've got a marvelous life ahead of you. If this thing grinds to a dead halt in Pineville, let it go. Treat it as any other case. Walk away. It ate Susie alive and caused her to ruin her relationship with you. And we both know what it did to you and Tony."

Now I *really* didn't like where it was going. "Gran—"

She didn't even slow down. Determination ran in both sides of my family. "But I really believe Bobby could have lived with knowing what happened even if he couldn't have proved it. He could have lived with answers, even if justice didn't come with them."

Something in her words triggered one of my red flags, which popped to the top like a cork in water. I stared at her. "He found out, didn't he? Before he died. He found out who killed my grandmother."

Gran bit her lower lip for a second, then nodded.

"Who was it?" I couldn't stop the demand in my voice.

She shrugged. "He never said. The day before he died, he called Susie, told her that it was about over, that he'd be home that next weekend. The next day she got the call from the sheriff."

My heart broke one more time for my mother. "She must have become convinced she'd find the answer in his papers. And why she was so devastated that she couldn't get hold of the ones he had in Pineville." I stirred the chicken and dumplings in my bowl idly. It was getting cold.

"And that mudhole of a town has done enough damage to this family."

I looked up, choking back a laugh when I saw how bright her eyes were with anger.

"So I mean it. You do this, but you be like your daddy, not like Susie. Solve or let it go."

"Yes ma'am."

"Is that cold?"

"Yes ma'am."

Gran stood up and snatched up both bowls. "Mine too. But we've eaten enough. Don't want either of us to get fat. You'll never get another man if you do, between getting fat and that mouth of yours. What about that police chief in Pineville? He a prospect?"

"What do you say we go upstairs and pick out stuff for the trailer?"

"Your love life off limits?"

"Don't have one to put limits on. Besides, you still haven't forgiven

Tony like you promised to someday. You think I'm ready to bring anyone else around?"

"Maybe someday ain't here yet. God's in the forgiving business, so I don't have to be."

"Attic?"

"Sounds like a good idea."

We spent the rest of my Sunday visit prowling through Gran's attic, pulling out stuff for the pink beastie and frequently getting distracted by a pack of letters or a forgotten photo album. Gran gave me three new pictures of Mother, Daddy, and me. Just so I wouldn't forget.

Oh, I definitely wouldn't. And most of all, I wouldn't forget that I now knew, with certainty, that someone in Pineville had been helping my father. MW1 wasn't just my mother's assumption. Someone knew, without a doubt, who had killed Esther Spire. I just hoped they were still alive to tell the tale one more time.

CHAPTER ELEVEN

Pineville, Alabama, 1972

"BREMER, YOU FOOL. You go to jail and that racist becomes a martyr."

The fuzzy gray figures on the television moved about in a silent puppet play, with photos of Arthur Bremer and George Wallace punctuating the announcement of Bremer's sentence for his attempted assassination of Alabama's most well-known governor.

"Like that would make a difference anywhere to anybody," muttered Roscoe as the figures shifted to news about the dying war in Vietnam. "What y'all gonna talk about when there ain't no more body counts, huh? Make it up?"

Nah, there's always something bad to talk about. Just over a week ago, the news about the Tuskegee Experiment had broken, and folks were still buzzing about that. Roscoe looked down at the latest letter from Bobby Spire. Always something bad going on. Roscoe had been exchanging letters with Bobby Spire since they'd met in Cam Ranh Bay. The letters were sparsely written and infrequent, and Bobby never put his name or return address on his. *Smart boy.* Roscoe always mailed his on the way to work, at a drop box far from anyone who knew him. He always made a copy too, which he kept tucked, along with Bobby's, in a cigar box on a high shelf at the back of the pantry, where not even Juanita would look, much less the kids.

Now there was cash in there as well, sent in Bobby's latest, urging Roscoe to get a post office box in Gadsden. "This isn't an in-country mission, Roscoe," Bobby had written, "but I well know it could be more dangerous. Be careful, and never take anything or anyone for granted."

Given what Roscoe had written in his last note, Bobby was probably right. Time to be more careful.

> *Like I told you back in the Bay, I saw more than one that night. Two, at least, probably three. Thought I knew their voices, but I was a kid and not around many white folks much. We stayed to ourselves back then. Just safer that way. Ain't much different now, even after Martin came and went. Too easy to get killed just for being black, much less going up against people like them.*
>
> *I went hunting last weekend, just me, quiet, because most things ain't exactly in season right now. Turns out I wasn't out there alone. Not going to mention names, just in case. But we need to talk soon.*
>
> *Anyway, I perched in a big oak, looking out for anything we could eat, mostly deer or turkey. Had settled for a few squirrels. Two old boys came wandering through. Father and son. I knew them right away. These ain't the kind of people to be messing with lightly. They got some serious power in this town. And outside of town too, so I hear. Stuff neither one of us want to be messing with. Federal. Both were carrying shotguns, but they weren't looking for game. The old man is walking with his head down, and the son, he is giving his old man a world of hurt, cussing and fussing. If I talked to my daddy like that, you'd find me in the woodpile with a blistered behind, even at this age.*
>
> *Then I heard this. "That was eighteen years ago! JoeLee buried it for us, just like they buried her. Don't you go digging either of them up just because you feel guilty. It was an accident. Over and done with. Let this bone go!"*
>
> *Then they got out of earshot. Bobby, eighteen years ago was 1954. They had to be talking about your mother. We both know it wasn't no accident. But maybe the old man didn't see how it happened, so they got him convinced it was. Nothing certain. But now I know who to start digging around. Now I know what sheet and pointy hat to look under.*

Roscoe folded both letters together and put them back in the cigar box and closed the lid. Dangerous, all right. More than either of them realized. Maybe more than in-country. 'Cause that was just you against the enemy. You knew who would be doing the shooting. This was home. Neighbors. Family. Especially family that lived in this house.

"Roscoe?"

He looked up. Juanita leaned against the doorframe, her nightgown limp from the heat and humidity that hung in the air. "Why don't you turn off that nonsense and come to bed? It's always the same."

He shook his head. "Can't sleep with William snoring like that."

She crossed the room and ran a hand along his shoulders. "It won't be long. He'll find something, then he and Maybelle can get their own place. Come on, I'll turn on the window fan. It'll help drown him out."

Roscoe snagged her hand and kissed the back of it. What would he do without this woman? "In a minute, baby."

She leaned over and kissed him, then smiled sweetly. "Don't be too long. I might actually go back to sleep."

"I won't." He took a deep breath as she headed back down the hallway, then he stood, watching the flickering television. They'd switched to local news, and he could tell the report was about the new gas line going in on the other side of the ridge. Lots of jobs. *Yeah, if you're white.* William hadn't been able to find a job after coming home from the war, and so far, Roscoe had not been able to help his brother. Lots of folks hated the vets, especially the black ones. Life seemed to be changing in other parts of the States. But not here. Here, Martin Luther King Jr. might have never led a march. Here, white men could still kill white women and get away with it. A black man would just vanish into the mist. Or up a tree.

He turned off the set and picked up the box. "Bobby, it's about to get real ugly around here."

CHAPTER TWELVE

Pineville, Alabama, Present Day

BLENDING IN AND being inconspicuous was no longer an option. And in hindsight, that might not have been the best plan of action anyway, especially in a community like Pineville, where everybody's business was everyone's business. What I could tell you was that there was something about living in a twenty-six-foot-long silver egg with a big pink flamingo on the side that made people want to show up on your doorstep for a chat.

It started before I even got the thing parked.

Doc Taylor and his wife, Maude, had this gorgeous Victorian just off the square and behind the drugstore. Doc and Maude are Jack Sprat and his wife—Doc once told me they weighed exactly the same, even though he was six four and Maude barely topped five one. But I'd never met two people who seemed more like two halves of a single unit. I went out to dinner with them one night, and you would have thought they had one plate. She ate off his and he ate off hers in a rhythm that would have made an assembly-line architect jealous. He was more of a talker than she was, and he once told me they had grown up together, gone to school together, and except for his time in the military, they hadn't slept apart since the day they'd married. They thought so much alike, they hadn't had a fight since the presidential election of 1960—they were both Democrats, but apparently he was a bit more anti-Catholic in those days.

Call me a rebel, but such a life felt like a confining prison to me. For them, it was heaven on earth. God bless 'em.

Anyway, the Victorian sat on almost an acre of prime downtown property. At the back right corner sat a small barn that Doc had mostly stuffed with gardening equipment. He wanted me to snug the beast in next to the barn so that the trailer door faced the back of the house. I knew all too well that there were two reasons for this.

First, Maude's nosy. She'd been driving him nuts with questions about me. This would give her access, and she could see my comings and goings firsthand.

Believe it or not, I didn't mind this. Maude was one of Miss Doris's girls. I could use it.

Second, it faced the flamingo away from the Victorian and directly toward his backyard neighbor, Jacob Beason (father of Vic, the newspaper editor), with whom Doc had been feuding for close to thirty years. It started over a fence that separated their yards, a fence that had been gone since 1990.

Now, while I'd never really thought about a six-foot flamingo as being akin to dropping your drawers and mooning your neighbor, I could see where Doc and Jake might. Jake appeared on his back porch as I pushed and pulled the pink beastie into place. Once we were satisfied with its location, Doc helped me unhook Belle and anchor the trailer. I was still chocking the wheels as Jake marched across, raising a ruckus about it. Doc reminded him that the historic section was on the other side of town, and if he wanted to start a homeowner's association, he was welcome to try.

Maybe Jake would come to like the flamingo. It was certainly starting to grow on me.

The neighbors trickled in not long after. Doc and I set out the awning, which was the size of a small patio. I pulled out two lawn chairs, a small table, and a charcoal grill. Jake had retreated, fuming and threatening to "call codes on this!" by the time Doc started a fire in the grill and dragged over two more lawn chairs. I got out hot dogs and the fixings and popped open Cokes for both of us.

I flipped the hot dogs, then plopped down onto one of the chairs. "How long do you think it'll take?"

Doc sat, stretching out his long legs and running a hand across the few gray tendrils that slicked across his red scalp. "Look down the driveway."

I could just barely see the edge of the street. A long boxwood hedge stretched from the back of the barn down the drive, blocking most of the view. His drive, an old-fashioned one-car access with twin strips of concrete running in the tire tracks, barely left enough space between the hedge and house for the beast and Belle. So I could see, maybe, a five-foot sliver of pavement.

Two men, three women, one child, and a dog stood there, peering at the beast.

I waved, then motioned for them to come on in. They all waved back, but one couple moved on, smiling. Ah, two down. They were probably old hands at this and knew they could find out what they wanted to know at church without getting involved.

The other four, a couple with a four-legged powder puff on a tether and a young mother with her son, headed up the driveway. When a motion to my right caught my eye, I saw Maude coming down the back steps with a tray loaded with more wieners, paper plates, cups, and condiments.

"We're going to need another table," I muttered.

Doc scrubbed his hands together. "I love a good picnic!" He launched out of the lawn chair and headed for the barn. On the way, he motioned at the man. "C'mon, Brady. Help me with this!"

Brady handed the puff's leash to his wife and veered toward the barn as Maude, laughing, greeted the women and started introducing me. I knew Maude would give me a refresher lesson later, so I just shook hands, nodded, and said "Nice to meet you" a lot.

The puff's name was Precious, aka "Demonspawn" (according to Brady), and she pranced around, exploring all feet and the occasional tire. I gave them a tour of the beast, to plenty of oohs, aahs, and questions about, um, waste management (from the nine-year-old boy).

When we emerged, I paused in the door. At least eight more people had joined the party, and Doc had dragged tiki torches, more chairs, and several citronella candles out of the barn. Maude gave a little bounce when she saw me, her eyes sparkling. "There are more hot dogs in the freezer!"

Two more people wandered down the drive. "How about a side of beef?" I called back.

Word spread through the neighborhood like beets through a baby's backside. Around six, I stopped giving tours of the beast and just left the door open to all comers. I hadn't moved anything important in yet, and all curiosity would be resolved. I still had plenty of questions to answer. I would say that I might never understand the infinite fascination of young boys with the elimination of human waste. The good news was that people who asked questions tended to be a little more open to answering some, in the name of making the new neighbor welcome. This was especially true after the cooler of longnecks showed up around seven.

The impromptu party went on until well after dark. My little charcoal grill gave way to Doc's big gas monster. No side of beef was to be had, but someone showed up with three slabs of ribs and five pounds of ground beef. Misses Betsy and Claudia Hall, the two women who lived next door on the other side of that big hedge, brought over more buns and chips. Tagging along at their heels trotted a loving, oversized, half-blind tortoiseshell mama cat who decided that Demonspawn was one of her long-lost kittens and that my legs were the perfect place for circle eights. I wound up having to check for her every time I stood up.

And a good time was had by all.

Too good a time, as it turned out. Around ten thirty, maybe closer to eleven, Mike Luinetti arrived with two of his officers in tow, including Dean Sowers. Maude greeted Mike with a strange sound that was half guffaw, half squeal, which told me that she'd overcome her Baptist reluctance to the longnecks in the cooler. Mike, a bit startled to find a sodden seventy-something hanging around his waistline, peeled her off and faced her forward, with his arm around her shoulders. He spoke softly and kindly to her as he escorted her to where Doc and I were plucking the last ribs and burgers from the grill.

"I take it you two are responsible for upsetting Jake Beason's evening."

Doc snorted. "That stick-in-the-mud wouldn't know fun if it wrapped itself around his neck and screamed 'Howdy!'"

"That may be." Mike rotated Maude toward Doc and gave her an encouraging push. "But he does know what time it is."

I looked at my phone for the time. "Oops. Noise ordinance?"

"Yep. All quiet in the city limits after ten, Sunday through Thursday. After eleven Friday and Saturday."

Doc took a deep breath. "Right. I helped get that passed." He turned off the gas on the grill. "I'll start funneling people out."

"Would appreciate it, Doc." Mike motioned for his officers to help. As they started to round up folks, he looked pointedly at the trailer. "That yours?"

"More private than the room over the drugstore."

"Jake asked about that too. Said it was an eyesore."

"What did you tell him?"

"As long as it wasn't a permanent structure, not much I could do."

"Want to see what's really bugging him about it?"

Mike raised an eyebrow, and I motioned for him to follow me to the other side of the Overlander. That side, away from the house lights and tiki torches, remained in dark shadows. Mike pulled his flashlight from his belt and turned it on the trailer. Pinkie shone like a sunrise.

Mike burst out laughing. "This was your idea?"

"Trust me, no."

He gazed at it a few more moments, both of us silent. As the sound of the party moved away, he said, "Find out anything during this shindig?"

"Most everyone over sixty thinks you are infinitely better to have around than JoeLee Wilkes."

"That's reassuring, considering the general consensus is that ongoing corruption kept him in biscuits and gravy."

"At least four of the younger women have a crush on you. They're not real happy with my presence right now. Three of them are even single."

"About the case."

"Oh, that. Well, gossip does run deep around here. I told a couple of the older folks I was interested in the museum and got a complete rundown of the town's history. Including a few of the 'dirty little secrets' that turn out to be common knowledge. Did you know that JoeLee was in business with a bootlegger up near Fort Payne?"

"I've heard the rumors."

"Fellow by the name of Buck Dickson. And apparently Mr. Dickson had some deep connections in Grundy County, Tennessee. Maybe even Dixie Mafia connections."

Mike hesitated. "Hadn't heard that part."

"Apparently, the shine ran downhill in more than one way. It gets better.

"How much better?"

"Dickson apparently ran the overall operation up and down the Highway 11 corridor before the interstates were built. He contracted local politicos to run business in their towns, keep everything under wraps. No trouble equals no feds looking over their shoulders. Ever wondered why the civil rights movement that cracked open Alabama never wormed its way into Pineville?"

Mike stared at me. "You're joking."

In the distance, I heard my name mentioned.

"There's more, but we'd better get back, before Doc starts to worry that Jake has taken his own action."

"I need to go to more parties."

"With booze."

Just before we wandered from behind the trailer, I rubbed my lips hard with the back of my hand. Grinning, Mike's hand gently took my elbow. He too knew how to keep up appearances.

We needn't have bothered. Standing under my patio awning, twisting their hands and bowing in tandem, the ladies from next door greeted me eagerly. "Miss Star!"

"Ah, I see you've already met," Mike said.

I looked from him to the ladies, whose anxiety escalated. "Please help Miss Snopes!"

I looked back at Mike.

"Museum," he said softly.

I still didn't get it, so I looked back at Doc's neighbors. "Please," they begged in tandem. "She's under your trailer."

Light dawned. "Your tortoiseshell."

They nodded. "We think she went under there after Precious, but she hasn't come out."

I looked back at Mike. "You're the first responder on scene."

"Nope." I could tell he was fighting a grin. "Cats are below my pay grade. Besides, I just had these pants cleaned."

"Please!" Their voices sounded as one.

I touched one of the women on the shoulder. "Don't worry. Some of us know more about being heroes than others." I looked back at Mike. "At least give me your flashlight."

This time he did grin, broadly, and handed it over as if it were a surgical instrument. Then I knelt and shined the light back and forth under the trailer, examining each section. No pussycat. With a long sigh, I pulled my phone from my back pocket and passed it to Mike. Then I lay down and scrambled under the trailer. Once under it, I rolled onto my left side to look toward the back. Scanning each section carefully—which gave me time to get familiar with the plumbing and other underworks—I found the wayward Miss Snopes on top of the wheel well, tucked away, tense and wary. She blinked at me owlishly, none too thrilled to have been discovered, and swished her tail furiously. I knew then that she had not sought out shelter under the trailer out of curiosity or in search of Precious. And I was about to do battle.

"Now why would you do this, worry your ladies so?" I spoke softly, scooting closer to her. No good. In her half-blind state, she had no idea who I was by sight, and any smell of mine she'd garnered from her rubbing my legs had no effect. "Miss Snopes, I'm not going to hurt you."

She wasn't a very believing cat. She jerked right, making as if to leap over me and bolt, but she bumped a pipe and froze, backing into position. She couldn't see well enough under the dark trailer to run, even with the bouncing beam of the flashlight. I frowned. "How long have you been under here, baby?"

Her upper lip curled, and she let out a low warning hiss. I inched closer, holding my hand out so that she could sniff me. The hiss became a deep-throated growl. Then she slapped my hand.

I jumped, hitting my head on the bottom of a pipe, and she yowled. Muttering ugly things about Miss Snopes and at least two generations of her mothers, I rubbed my head briefly. My hand showed no marks. Miss Snopes, apparently, had no claws. "Why in the world would they let you out with no claws?" I whispered at her. This time I moved closer and, with one sudden grab, snatched her by the nape of her neck.

A piercing scream shattered the air around me as I dropped the flashlight and pulled her to me, holding her tightly against my stomach. She twisted furiously, trying to bite me, fighting me with her clawless feet, but I grasped her head with one hand so she couldn't latch those teeth into my flesh and wrapped my arms around her, pulling her head against my chest, whispering to her. I could feel her heart racing; I wanted her to hear mine. She continued to freeze, then buck suddenly, trying to escape, for several minutes.

"Miss Snopes, shh. Miss Snopes, shh." I whispered it over and over, absolutely certain at this point that she had not come under here willingly. This was a dark and scary place to her. She'd come under here to get away from something that had terrified her more than the underside of the trailer. "Miss Snopes, shh." I rocked her, repeating it, holding her tight until she calmed.

Without moving, I called Mike. He peered under. "Yeah?"

"Get one of the big towels out of the bathroom."

"Sure." He disappeared, and I heard his shoes clunking the floor over my head. He returned shortly.

"Can you drape it over my leg? I think I can get it from there." He did, and I drew my knee up slowly. Every move except a breath seemed to make Miss Snopes jumpy, so I took care to move in gentle inches and stay calm, breathing regular. Once the towel was in reach, I moved it over her, holding her with one hand as I wrapped her with the other. Thus confined, her tension eased, but I knew she'd launch free at the first opportunity. Rolling to my back, I held her against my chest, put the flashlight onto my stomach, and pushed out from under the trailer with my heels.

When the light first hit her, Miss Snopes jerked, but I held on. The two ladies bounced nervously and tried to reach for her, but Mike held them back until I was well clear of the trailer. "Listen to me," I said softly to them. "She's terrified. You both need to be calm. Very calm. Stop bouncing."

They looked at each other, nodding, and both inhaled deeply.

"Good. She needs to feel safe. Leave her wrapped in the towel as you take her home. Now one of you reach down and take her firmly but gently by the nape of the neck, just behind my hand. Press down at first, then wrap her with your other arm as you feel me push up on her. She's going to jerk, but don't let go. We'll never find her in the dark, not as scared as she is."

"Poor Miss Snopes," one whispered.

The other one reached down, and I felt her hand move in behind mine. We made the transfer with only a few sudden jerks from Miss Snopes. They cuddled her, cooing and stroking her as they headed across the yard, disappearing through a small gap in the hedge.

Mike took his flashlight and helped me to my feet. "I didn't realize you knew so much about cats."

"It's a gift."

"I'm now really glad you went under there. I would have just snatched her out by the nape of the neck and handed her out here. You're sure to have a job now."

I brushed cat hairs off the front of my T-shirt and grass from my butt. "What?"

He motioned toward the hedge with his flashlight. "Miss Betsy and Miss Claudia."

"What about them?"

He chuckled. "I get it. Doc didn't tell you who they were."

"Just told me they were Betsy and Claudia Hall from next door."

"They're the museum curator and director. The ones I wanted you to meet tomorrow."

Now it all came together. "I see, said the blind man."

"They'll love you for this. By tomorrow afternoon, you'll be the local hero."

I gave up on brushing off. Between the cat and the grass, everything I had on would need a good soak. I crossed my arms and looked around the yard, Miss Snopes still on my mind. Maude and Doc had disappeared with most of the detritus of the improvised cookout. Most everyone had gone following Mike's arrival. Doc still chatted with one of the officers next to his back porch.

"What's wrong?"

I couldn't put my finger on it. Everything looked . . . normal. But something was . . . or had been . . . amiss.

"Mike," I said softly. "Something had absolutely terrified that cat, and I don't think it was a tribble on stilts named Precious."

He grew sober and a bit more alert. "What do you think it was?"

"No idea. She has no claws, so I don't think they would have brought her unless they believed she'd be safe. She had to know everyone here. So either some critter came into the yard that we didn't notice . . ." It was his town. I didn't really want to say it.

I didn't have to.

"Or someone here has terrified her before."

We were silent several minutes. "I guess that sounds silly. Worry about who terrified a cat."

Mike didn't answer immediately. When he did, his words sounded official, even though his voice was so low I barely heard it.

"Star, everyone in Pineville knows how important that cat is to Miss Betsy and Miss Claudia. If the cat doesn't like you, they don't. They would never trust someone who Miss Snopes didn't trust."

"This wasn't about the cat."

"It was about you. They couldn't have known your gift with felines would make it backfire. Someone tried to make sure Miss Snopes was terrified enough to turn the Hall sisters against you."

CHAPTER THIRTEEN

Pineville, Alabama, 1972

ROSCOE LIT ANOTHER cigarette, blowing the smoke out slowly. He sat at the kitchen table, watching William. Dusk had settled heavily in the kitchen, but neither Roscoe nor William turned on a light. Standing at the counter, William wrapped biscuits and leftover ham in wax paper and thrust them into a paper sack. He moved jerkily, as if his muscles occasionally touched an electric wire. In the remaining light, sweat gleamed on his dark skin, trailing across the contours of his well-defined arms and soaking his T-shirt.

They had long since finished dinner, and Maybelle and Juanita had washed the dishes in a sullen silence as both men sat at the table, fidgeting with their cigarettes. Finally, the women retreated to the front porch. Maybelle, having said all she could think to say, sat in the dusk with her Bible on her lap, praying, her soft lips moving wordlessly. Juanita had settled on the steps, although her gaze focused somewhere along the horizon. For a while, Roscoe had stood in the living room, watching them through the screen door, taking comfort in the cool evening breeze and chewing on the end of a matchstick, thinking about the night to come. Finally he returned to the kitchen and sat, his weary gaze on his brother.

"You don't want to do this, William."

William stopped packing food, pulled a chair out, and dropped heavily into it. He glared at his brother, then suddenly rubbed his face and head vigorously, nervously. He finally placed his hands on the table, palms down, spreading his fingers wide. His voice was harsh, with a bitter edge to it.

"You're right, Roscoe. I don't. I don't want to drive to Gadsden tonight and meet with a bunch of cracker white boys and convince them I'm loyal to their lawless, draft-dodging selves. I don't want to drive up to Fort Payne and pick up a car full of shine and beer and bootleg tapes, then drive it back down to these parts. You're right. I don't want to do any of that. But you, all heavenly mighty Roscoe-with-a-job, you tell me how I'm going to make money to feed my family. You know what it does to a man to depend on his brother? Don't you? I can't keep living here. We need a place."

"Mr. Teague offered—"

"—a tenant house. A farm. Roscoe, you know this ain't the forties and I ain't no farmer. I never was, even before I went overseas. I'm not Daddy. Or you. I'm a driver. I was good before I left. The army made me a better one."

William stood again and took a quart jar out of the cabinet, filled it with water, and capped it. He paused, then spoke more quietly. "It's only for a few months." He took a deep breath. "I been talking to the bank over in Carterton. The manager knows Daddy, knows us. He cares more about green than black. If I can get the down payment put together, he'll help me finance a truck, a used big rig. It would be hard getting started, but independents can make decent money. It would be a good way to support myself, giving Maybelle and Jeshua a regular place to live."

"And if you get killed?"

"I'm a good driver. Told you that."

"What happens to your truck loan if you get arrested?"

William snorted, looked down a moment, then up at his brother. "You really don't know what this is about, do you?"

"Tell me."

William shook his head. "Let's just say that once drivers get out of DeKalb County and back on our side of the line, they don't have to worry about the local law. JoeLee sees to that."

"JoeLee? What's he got to do with it?"

"He and Buck Dickson." William held up two fingers pressed tightly against each other. "Why do you think JoeLee keeps winning elections after more than twenty years? As long as towns and counties are dry, as long as Baptists keep voting down the drink, JoeLee will keep winning and Buck will keep running booze like it was still 1925."

In silence, Roscoe and William looked at each other a few more minutes, then William reached out and took Roscoe's cigarette, taking a long draw off it, pulling it down to the end. He ground it out in the ashtray. "I got to go. I'll be back in the morning."

He picked up the sack and quart jar and headed out the back door, letting the screen slam behind him. After a moment, Roscoe heard William's old Ford pickup growl to life, saw the reflection of the headlights as he headed down the drive.

The cigarette smoldered a bit longer in the ashtray, a long tendril of smoke rising in the last of the day's light.

"Brother, you don't even know the half of it. JoeLee Wilkes and Buck Dickson ain't even the tip of it. And you are going to get us all killed. Like lambs to the slaughter."

CHAPTER FOURTEEN

Pineville, Alabama, Present Day

AS USUAL, THE farmers showed up at the drugstore fountain between five thirty and six Monday morning. Office and retail folks showed up a bit later, sometimes as early as seven, but a few didn't drag in until almost nine, still looking for hot coffee and plenty of gravy with their biscuits and eggs. Monday was one of Miss Doris's days as well, and she and the girls showed up about eight thirty, their normal time. Maude Taylor held court this morning, and their table fairly spun as they laughed and chatted about last night's get-together. Miss Doris seemed a bit miffed that she hadn't been invited. Apparently word had never made it that far down Maple Street. But she melted when one name came up: Miss Snopes.

Mike had been right about one thing: the rescue of Miss Snopes was a hot topic, and the fact that I obviously knew and loved cats had turned even the most reluctant of Miss Doris's crew in my direction.

What was it about cats?

I couldn't eavesdrop as much as I wanted to, however. The regulars kept me hopping. Ed Walker's hardware store two doors down opened at seven, although if you had a special need, like a tractor part so you could get your day started, Ed would meet you as early as you needed. Every farm and contractor in town had Ed's cell phone number. But if Ed's wasn't busy, the boys would show back up around nine thirty for coffee and any biscuits we had left. Today, apparently, was a really slow day at the hardware store.

But truth was, I liked being busy. It gave me plenty of customers to get to know, and on days like these, it kept me from thinking about things like how stupid I felt for being that concerned about a scared cat. Despite what Mike said, I couldn't shake the idea that it was just dumb. It wasn't part of some grand conspiracy to scare me or make sure I felt unwelcome in Pineville.

It was because I have a weak spot for cats. Always did. Gran used to scold me for bringing home every stray in the neighborhood. But she'd feed them, and I'd nurse them back to health, then find them homes. Papa was allergic, so they were relegated to the back porch and we never kept one for long. Being a serial adopter was my way of satisfying my love of cats. Even Tony had tolerated the habit, although his philosophy on felines normally consisted of "So many cats, so few recipes."

Mike was the one regular who didn't show for breakfast Monday morning, but I didn't really expect him. Around seven fifteen, I saw his cruiser barrel through the square with the blue lights going. A few minutes later, two fire trucks followed suit, so I figured I wouldn't see him till after my shift.

To be honest, I appreciated having a normal morning. I still hadn't moved anything into the trailer, so after work I headed upstairs. A cold shower and a short nap later, I took the first boxes of clothes and toiletries over. I paid Doc rent by the week, so I didn't have to be out of the room until Friday. I wanted to take my time, however, settling into the pink beastie.

Adjusting to life in what was essentially an elongated walk-in closet was not as easy as you might think. Back in Nashville, I had a twelve-hundred-square-foot cottage with two bedrooms, two baths, and a nice-sized living room. Even the room over the drugstore was large and airy, about twenty by twenty, with a high ceiling. The Overlander was basically my cottage stuffed into a twenty-six-foot-long aluminum sausage. As Gran used to say, "Not only can't you swing a cat in there, if you turn around too fast, you can say hello to your behind."

You weren't going to acquire a large art collection if you lived in a travel trailer or enjoy a big-screen television, but it had all the essentials: stove, fridge, more storage than you'd expect, bathroom, comfy bed. And with the way Papa had refurbished the beastie, I had a nice office space for my laptop and a recliner to develop bad habits in. I decide to move in back to front, saving the more sensitive office files for last. So I went to work, putting away my clothes and setting up the bathroom.

"Ahoy the Overlander!"

Ah, the unmistakable Yankee baritone of Mike Luinetti.

"In the back. Come on in."

He ducked and stepped inside. "Are you putting away your underwear?"

"Nope. Already done. You're safe."

"Actually, I was going to offer to help."

I grinned and closed a drawer on a stack of T-shirts and shorts. "Sorry. What's up?"

"We had a fire this morning."

"Yeah, I saw the trucks. Where was it?"

He dropped down into the recliner. "Out on the old highway heading for Pell City."

I sat on one of the bistro stools. "Anyone hurt?"

"Nope. It was an old shed that should have been torn down about forty years ago." He grinned.

I took the bait. "And you're telling me this because . . ."

He grinned a bit longer, incredibly pleased with himself. "The Pell City Highway runs right past the archives where the old sheriff's records are stored."

I got it. "So when you left the fire, no one had any reason to suspect a side trip."

"Yep. The archivist is a lovely lady who is a stickler for protocol, but she's also glad to see a friendly face. She got to tell someone new about her two new grandbabies, and I got to poke around to my heart's content." He leaned forward and winked at me. "She was also curious about the new woman in my life. And the big flamingo that has Jake Beason in a kerfuffle."

"I beg your pardon."

He grinned. "News travels fast. Small town."

"Did she really say 'kerfuffle'?"

"As my grandma lives and breathes."

"Love it. What did you find out?"

"That you, my dear Star, are not always right."

My eyebrows shot up. "They still had files on the cases?"

He nodded, then shrugged one shoulder. "Not extensive files. Just the basics, the way you'd expect on a case that old. Mostly it was the same paperwork you already have." He stood up and then sat down on the stool next to mine. "But I did get you this." Mike pulled a folded slip of paper out of his shirt pocket. He leaned against my arm as he handed it to me, and the strength of his presence had a calm reassurance to it, something I was not used to.

I leaned back on him with a mischievous smile before I unfolded the paper. "You haven't started stealing for me, have you? Is this a copy, or did you raid the files?"

"A copy. I knew it would raise too much suspicion if I actually checked the files out."

I unfolded it and scowled. It was a copy of my father's autopsy report. I looked back up at Mike. "I have this."

"Not this one. Remember how the signature is blurred on yours? You can't tell who did the postmortem?"

I looked down again and flipped the paper over. There on the back, the clear signature of the doctor who did the exam. I stared at it a moment, not really believing it. I stood up, staring down at him. "This can't be right. Andrew Taylor. My Doc Taylor? He's a pharmacist!"

Mike still hadn't lost that possum-eating grin. He took my hand and pulled me back down to sit on the stool, closing his fingers around mine. "Star, you still have so much to learn about this town. Doc inherited the pharmacy from his father. In the seventies and early eighties, our current Doc Taylor was a practicing physician. Samford grad, UAB med school. Board certified in 1978. Practiced here for a long time before his father became ill. But then old Doc Russell Taylor became so determined to have his son follow in his footsteps that Dr. Andrew Taylor went back to school and changed professions, from doctor to pharmacist, out of respect for his father. They worked together as pharmacists for a couple of years before the old man died."

"That's serious family loyalty."

"Well, it did mean no more house calls and late-night interruptions. Being a small-town GP is not exactly easy street. He gave up his practice, but not his license. I'd still trust him to set a leg in an emergency."

I had a new appreciation of the man who'd given me a job and a place to park my life. "And how do you know so much about my new employer?"

"You do know that Dean Sowers is Miss Doris's son-in-law, right?"

"Ah. Right. Cops gossip more than town matrons do."

"Yep. Anyway, it's not much, but I thought you might be able to talk to him some as this starts getting out. What else did you find out last night?"

I pulled my hand from his and crossed my arms, leaning against him again. "Enough to think that the corruption may not have stopped with the sheriff's department. Did you know that Buck Dickson employed mostly black drivers to run his shine? Hired a lot of the black vets who couldn't get work otherwise, dating back to the first involvement in Vietnam in the early sixties."

Mike's eyes widened, and he let out a long breath. "Very progressive of him."

I coughed. "Yeah . . . it was hardly altruistic, much less progressive. Mostly he considered them expendable and easily replaced, but they helped him build trust in the black community. It also funneled enough money into this town that the local politicians made sure Buck had a good employment pool. The locals, who were apparently deep in the till with Dickson, put pressure on business owners not to employ the black vets."

"That's insidious. Who told you that?"

I nodded toward the house. "Doc. He'd consumed enough beer that when I asked how you compared to previous sheriffs, all kinds of stuff came rolling out. And politics and civil rights had nothing to do with it. All Buck cared about was business. Employing the black vets satisfied the community and made for good business relations, since he ran shine and other illegal stuff to both whites and blacks for forty years or more. Paid good money for the best drivers, then charged them with keeping the peace around here. Sit-ins and protests interfered with business. When the shine market dried up, he switched to bootleg music and movies, expanded into Birmingham, where having black drivers drove business even farther into the black communities. JoeLee and his cronies made sure they didn't get caught. If they did get caught in other counties, the local politicians worked it out. Drivers who caused trouble had a habit of getting into bad car wrecks. Continued for a while under the new sheriff after JoeLee died, then the internet started taking over."

Mike nodded. "I remember some of the tales about Buck when he tried to go legit in the late eighties and failed miserably. He died in the early nineties, I think."

"And Doc said you didn't dare cross him. People who did up and disappeared."

Mike looked at me closely a moment. "You think Buck killed her?"

I paused, then shook my head. "I considered it, but I can't see a reason why he would. She'd been in Pineville less than forty-eight hours. Besides, Doc said Buck never got his hands dirty. Something had to be taken care of, the local guys did it. Even when the feds did get wind of something going down, the locals took the heat. That was the reason Buck was able to retire and die a rich old man."

"How about your dad?"

I shrugged one shoulder. "That's more likely. Maybe whoever killed my grandmother was involved with Buck, and my dad was killed to protect them." I shook my head again. "An interesting theory, but unless I can turn up a connection, it's just that. A theory. Truth is, all of that corruption might not have had anything to do with my grandmother's death at all. She was Jewish in a town thick with the KKK. Or maybe she was just in the wrong place at the wrong time. I need to know more." I took a deep breath and leaned back. "How long before you think it'll happen?"

"That everyone will find out about the real reason you're here?"

I nodded.

Mike slid his arm around my shoulders and pulled me closer, sending a calming warmth through me. His voice was low. "Not too long. I had to sign the files out, but she didn't really pay attention to which ones I pulled. Sooner or later, she'll get bored enough to check. She's county, not Pineville, but eventually she'll say something to one of her friends." He made an explosion gesture with one hand.

"I can probably talk to Roscoe without anyone knowing. After that . . ."

Mike pulled away from me and stood. "Let's walk over to the museum. I'll introduce you to the Hall sisters all over again. See what you can find out without talking to anyone just yet."

I changed into a pair of slacks, then locked up the beastie. Mike slid his hand into mine as we headed toward the square. The growing affection between us had begun to feel more comfortable, even natural, and I realized that I hoped nothing during the case would cause Mike a lot of pain, physically or emotionally. Getting involved with someone during a case was usually a bad idea all the way around. I knew that from experience. But I'd have to be a complete sociopath to ignore the camaraderie we had developed, even in such a short time.

The walk over to the museum, which was housed in a storefront facing the square, took all of ten minutes, but the afternoon sun had begun to show promises of summer in its heat. A light breeze kept the temperature pleasant, however, and Mike set up a running patter about the people in passing cars, as if I'd remember all he said an hour from now. He waved at each one, and most of them waved back and smiled. The citizens of Pineville had, indeed, adopted their Yankee chief.

The museum storefront, a three-story building with an aged redbrick federal front, had once been an Elmore's Five and Dime, as evidenced by the remaining "more's Fiv me" that hadn't quite been scraped off the window. A large hand-lettered sign had been taped to the window: "New Home. Pineville Musuem and Historically Archives. Come In."

Well, at least the lettering was neat.

Mike caught me staring at it and chuckled. "We only have one guy in town who letters windows. The art teacher at the high school. He's scheduled to do their window after graduation."

"Hope he knows spelling and grammar. They couldn't hire someone out of Gadsden or Birmingham to do it?"

"They wouldn't dare."

"I love small towns."

A small bell dinged as Mike pushed open the door. Cool air rushed over me, and the dust of a thousand artifacts tickled my nose. I sneezed.

"Miss Star!" Two voices sounded as one.

One of Elmore's former checkout stands had been converted into a small reception area. Behind it, rows of display shelves that had once held trinkets and household goods were lined with tidy stacks of papers, books, boxes, and glass cases. Twenty feet over our heads, wooden ceiling fans circled lazily.

One sister stood on a ladder, arranging something on a top shelf. The other had been lifting old books from a box, but stopped, wiped her hands on a thick bibbed apron, and headed my way.

Mike pointed at the sister on the ladder. "Miss Betsy Hall."

The other sister reached us first, as Betsy began her descent. "And I'm Claudia. I had a feeling you wouldn't remember from last night. It was pretty hectic, what with Miss Snopes and all." She held out her hand.

I shook it, a little surprised by how warm and firm her grip was.

"Two of the five most beautiful sisters ever to grace Pineville." I couldn't tell if Mike was being gallant or slightly sarcastic. I hoped gallant.

Claudia blushed a bit. "Pshaw. Such a flatterer."

I glanced at him. "Five?"

Betsy joined us, and in the light of day, I could tell she stood a bit taller than Claudia. "He means Abigail, Beulah, and Dinah. Our sisters. We're one of the local stories, Miss Star, if you haven't heard by now."

"Um, no."

Claudia touched my arm again. "We can tell you that later. Is there something we can help you with?"

I glanced again at Mike. He cleared his throat. "Star's looking for a way to know Pineville better, and I know y'all have had a lot of work getting the museum moved from that old house. Thought you could use a volunteer, and she could learn the town."

Their faces brightened. "Truly?" Betsy asked.

I nodded. "Yes ma'am."

They both pressed their palms together and looked at each other.

The sisters nodded simultaneously, and I wondered if they'd somehow mastered telepathy.

Betsy looked to me. "We'd love to have your help. Can you start now?"

"Absolutely."

"Excellent," Mike said. "I'll leave you to get to know each other." He winked at me, and the bell dinged again as he left.

The three of us looked at each other for a moment, then I spoke suddenly. "Oh! How is Miss Snopes today?"

They beamed. "Back to her perfect self," Betsy explained, then she looked around, glancing behind me, as if Mike had not really left. "And we figured out what spooked her."

"I thought it was the dog," I said, a bit wary.

Claudia leaned closer, her voice dropping in volume. "No, not at all. Precious—"

"—Demonspawn—"

Claudia flapped an annoyed hand at her sister. "—Precious is sweet. Miss Snopes never showed any fear of her. The dog can be a pest but not terrifying. Anyway, after we got her home, we remembered the last time Miss Snopes had acted like that."

"Last year," Betsy put in, her words just as sotto voce, "we had a break-in at the house."

"Oh, I'm sorry!"

Claudia sniffed. "Horrible people. They took some of Mother's prized jewelry, some cash, a box of papers we were cataloging for the museum—"

"—a few other items. Terribly invasive. We found it when we got home. Called Michael right away—"

"—and he was there in just a few minutes . . . but . . . Miss Snopes took a distinct dislike to one of the responding officers. We couldn't prove it, but we think—"

"—we think he kicked her during the investigation. They were all over the house, examining everything, and Miss Snopes was always so friendly—"

"—like she was with you. We think he got tired of being pestered and booted her. She hid for a day after they left. Now she hates him. Gets like that every time he's around." Claudia paused and looked around again, as if someone outside could hear her.

"How horrible! Have you told—"

Betsy waved away my words. "Oh, we could never tell Michael. We have no proof to cast such aspersions on one of his men. And people would hate him if they thought he hurt Miss Snopes."

"Folks around here adore Miss Snopes."

A cold chill settled over me as I recalled the two officers who had arrived with Mike last night. "Who . . ."

"Dean," Betsy whispered.

Claudia closed her eyes. "Yes. Dean Sowers."

CHAPTER FIFTEEN

Pineville, Alabama, 1973

CIGARETTE SMOKE DRIFTED throughout the kitchen, wisps and tendrils stirring in the faint afternoon breeze and vanishing through the half-inch opening in the windows. The heat of dinner slid out as a mild moistness of the March wind freshened the air. William poured another cup of coffee from the pot Juanita had left simmering on the stove. He sat down at the table again, pushing his plate back. Roscoe toyed with his pork chop bone, even though it was bare of meat and sucked dry of juice.

Both of them tried to ignore the soft sobbing of Maybelle in the adjacent bedroom and the quiet voice of Juanita as she comforted her sister-in-law.

Roscoe cleared his throat. "Didn't think y'all were going to have any right now. I thought you were going to wait till you were out of this mess."

William sipped the scalding coffee and flinched. "This was an accident."

Roscoe looked up at him. "A preventable one."

William shrugged. "You hear that Bull Connor died?"

"Finally. Good riddance to bad garbage." Roscoe put the knife down and pushed away the plate. "I saw Isaiah at the bank in Carterton last week."

William sat quite still. "And?"

"He asked me if you were still interested in that big rig."

Roscoe watched as William stared, unmoving, at the steam rising from his coffee. In the bedroom, Maybelle's sobs had quieted, although Juanita's voice remained a soothing drone.

"What did you tell him?"

"That you had taken a job making deliveries for a man in Gadsden and would have to see where that went."

William snorted.

"Fortunately, he didn't ask any more than that. But I think he knew. They all know, all the old men who run these towns. They just don't talk." Roscoe took a pack of unfiltered Camels out of his shirt pocket and shook one out. "But make no mistake. I won't lie for you if someone asks specific."

"I don't expect you would."

Roscoe lit the cigarette. "You said it would be a few months."

William pointed at the bedroom door. "I can't quit now. I got too much riding on the money."

Roscoe nodded. "Maybelle still liking the new place?"

"Yeah. She's fixed it up real sweet-like on the inside. The baby will have his own room. We'll have y'all over soon."

Roscoe hesitated. "Who's the landlord?"

William looked away a moment. "Chris. Pass me a Camel."

Roscoe slid the pack across to his brother. "Chris? As in Christopher Patton? Didn't know he'd branched out into real estate. His daddy must be proud."

"I'm sure he is. And, um . . ." William paused to light the cigarette. He inhaled deeply and let the smoke trail out slowly. ". . . his daddy has him riding with me on the runs."

Roscoe leaned back in the chair, fighting the surprise and the fear. "You have lost your mind."

"What am I supposed to do? Tell 'em how to run their business? Old man Patton wants Buck to teach Chris the business. Buck ain't much keen on it, but they're making it work."

"Why in the world . . . I thought you said business was off."

"Shine business, yeah. More and more places have liquor by the drink. Less demand. But plenty of folks still need cheap booze. And we've started running . . . other things."

"Drugs?"

William flicked the first clump of ashes into his abandoned dinner plate. "Nah. Buck doesn't want any dealings with drugs. There's a couple of other groups already running them, don't like competition. One right there in Fort Payne is particularly nasty. Buck doesn't want to fight the feds *and* other organizations."

"So what are you running?"

"Cassette tapes."

Roscoe didn't get it. "The kind you can buy anywhere?"

William shook his head and sipped the coffee. "Nah. These are live concerts, back door copies, stuff like that. We run 'em into Gadsden, Birmingham. That's why they want Chris to go with me. Learn that side of it, where to sell. Kids mostly, suburbs, projects—doesn't matter. White kids buy from him. Black kids buy from me. Money's good."

"For cassettes of music."

William shrugged and looked out the window.

"So. Not just cassettes."

"Don't ask about this, Roscoe. Just don't."

"Sounds like you're more likely to get caught."

William took a long drag, nodding. "Another reason for Chris to come along. Baby boy gets caught, Daddy pays all the bills."

"So he says."

"Well, I know you won't."

"Got that right."

William looked around the kitchen. "Juanita got any of her fried pies tucked away?"

Roscoe pointed at a Hoosier cabinet on the back wall of the kitchen. "Top shelf. Hand me one while you're at it."

His brother stood and pulled open the door on the cabinet's hutch. He prowled about a few seconds, then pulled out two half-moon-shaped pastries. He handed one to Roscoe. "So why were you over to Carterton talking to Isaiah?"

Roscoe sniffed, twirled the cigarette between his thumb and forefinger. "I did it."

William froze, then dropped slowly back into the chair, a wide grin slowly spreading over his face. "You for real?"

Roscoe couldn't hide the pleasure anymore and grinned. "Yep. I signed the lease this morning. Made the first payment."

"Like you said, on that place next to Ed Walker's hardware?"

Roscoe nodded. "Yeah. Isaiah's giving me the loan on the first stock inventory, which will ship in this Thursday. Appliances in the front, repairs in the back."

"Well, you been slaving for old man Holland so long, it's about time. You got savings to back it up?"

Roscoe took a short drag, then stubbed it out on his plate. "Enough to tide me over in an emergency, but not much else. I'll be working harder than I ever did for Mr. Holland."

"You think they'll accept a black man on the square?"

"I reckon so. I talked to Ed. He seemed OK. The pols over to the courthouse may not like it too much, but I been in their houses aplenty, working on their stoves and fridges. They know what I'm about."

William laughed. "I'll tell Chris to keep 'em off your back. His daddy ought to be good for something besides bailing his kids outta jail." When Roscoe didn't respond, William's laughter faded, and he clapped his brother on the forearm. "Seriously, man, I wouldn't involve you with this stuff."

"Just don't get yourself killed."

"Doin' my best, brother. Doin' my best."

CHAPTER SIXTEEN

Pineville, Alabama, Present Day

I STAYED SO long at the museum that afternoon that dusk had settled on Pineville before I made my daily jog. Misses Claudia and Betsy had been more than eager for me to gather the names of Vietnam veterans for their records, but just a few hours prowling in old newspapers and record books had told me that I'd already mined that field. Most of the vets had moved away or passed on. Miss Betsy said the rest didn't even acknowledge there had been a war, much less their part in it. That left the three I already knew about: Hal Prentiss, Trapper Luke Davidson, and Roscoe Carver.

As I stretched, then set out on the run, I found most of Pineville deserted. The dinner hour had passed, and everyone had already watered the flowers, traded all the latest gossip with the neighbors, and burrowed in for the night before my feet slapped their way down Maple Street. All that was left were random clusters of children chasing fireflies. I loved the fact that in an era of video games and smartphones, kids still loved chasing dancing lights at dusk.

I was glad, too, for the time alone. As much as I wanted another chat with Miss Doris, I also needed to plan to decide exactly what I would do next, who I would talk to, and how I'd react when the news leaked out about why I'd truly made Pineville my new home.

I tried to clear that thought out of my head. Pineville most certainly was not home, and it would become even less like one shortly. Pineville had destroyed my family. As much as I liked some of the people here, it would never be home.

Which, of course, made me think of my real home, that cottage in Nashville with hardwood floors, Craftsman trim, and knockout roses ringing the brick walls outside. It was cozy and I adored it, my refuge from the world. I'd bought it after the divorce from Tony, who had kept the furniture and the house we'd bought together in Brentwood, that nouveau riche area south of Nashville. I didn't fight it—I hated that house and the overpriced antiques he'd peppered it with in order to impress his clients. I especially hated the big four-poster king-sized bed in the master suite.

The rhythmic sound of my feet on pavement sped up as an image of that monster flitted through my head. With its posts as thick as my thighs and a heavy wooden canopy, it anchored a room that reminded me more of a movie set than a bedroom. I had despised it even before I caught Tony in the middle of it with two of his high-profile clients, a power couple under investigation for mail fraud. The woman he'd been caressing had invited me to join them.

I had walked out and not seen him since, so my last memory of him was a freeze-frame of those wide, sensuous brown eyes, cunning and smirky underneath a shock of silky hair as thick as any I'd ever had my hands in. Eyes cloudy with desire and satisfaction as he'd assumed he would pull me into his world.

He later blamed my obsession with Daisy Doe as the reason he'd strayed, but Tony's affairs had been about money, not passion. He loved manipulating people much more than he loved taking them to his bed. Even me. And when he'd learned he couldn't manipulate me into giving up my family—including Gran—he'd turned everything he had against me. He'd planned for me to discover him in that tryst, and he never really believed I would be willing to walk out and leave it all behind. Tony believed that because the trappings meant more to him than I did.

That part I'd never told Gran about. She despised him enough just thinking he'd cheated on me—and that he had a punch like a Golden Gloves boxer. Gran had grumbled that any man who'd hit a woman who carried a gun for a living had to be a few sandwiches short of a picnic. When she suggested that she could make a connection between his manhood and her pinking shears, I reminded her that not even Tony O'Connell was worth going to prison for, for either of us.

But the rest, the truly evil rest of it, the reasons that Tony still lived like a bore worm in my heart, that was between me and God.

God. I glanced up, almost involuntarily, as if I expected to see an old man's face hovering in the sky. I knew better. Gran had taught me a lot about God. What she hadn't taught me, though, was how to forgive God for Tony and Daddy and Mama . . . and all the other pain my family had been through. For no good reasons, at least none I could see.

I left Maple Street at the park and made a circuit around the grassy square, breathing hard, the sweet scents of honeysuckle and wild onion tickling my nose.

The pain Tony had left in me made sure I wanted nothing out of that house. His alimony payments made up the difference. They paid for my cottage, allowing me to finally make the leap in careers that had brought me here. I had left the Nashville Police Department and Tony behind and had been working for my father's former law firm as an investigator when my mother died. The timing had been right to finish this. To end the horror that had hovered over my family for more than fifty years.

So maybe that's why. All the pain. To bring you here.

No! I pushed the thought away. I refused to believe that God would allow so much pain to come to people, just to push me to this point in time, to this place.

For a time such as this.

That quotation from the book of Esther hung in my head like smoke. I ran faster, trying to clear it. No. Nothing could be worth what we'd been through.

I circled behind a set of swings, where a lone father pushed a giggling girl, repeating a singsong rhyme as she squealed and begged, "Higher, Daddy!"

"Higher, Daddy!"

I stumbled over an uneven clump of grass and almost went down as a sharp memory flashed through my mind, almost blinding me. *"Higher, Daddy!"* I slowed and then stopped next to a towering oak tree.

I pressed my hands against it and stretched my legs, then prowled back and forth in front of it so that my muscles wouldn't cramp.

I couldn't have been more than three. We were moving out of the only home I knew, and I'd been crying most of the day. The huge moving truck appeared like a dragon to me, rumbling and consuming our stuff. I clung to a stuffed bunny and kept hiding in one closet after another. Finally, my father had pulled me out and carried me to the back yard. He'd cuddled me, whispering. What his words were I couldn't remember, except that he made me laugh. Then he'd set me in one of the swings on the playset we were leaving behind. He pushed me higher and higher until my mother called us. Until it was time to go. Exhausted, I'd slept in the back seat all the way to Tennessee.

I paced in a wider circle, not wanting to cool down yet. Finally, enough of the memory passed that I could run without tearing up. *Focus on the case. On the here and now.*

As an adult, I knew our move had been a shift from the military JAG office to a civilian position in Nashville, but as kid, it felt as if my life was ruined. My friends, gone. Daddy had made it OK by showing me he was still there, still taking care of me. It was just the reassurance I needed at that age. My mother told me that life had been great during those first months in Nashville, but it was a short-lived reprieve. Slowly the obsession returned, until in 1984 he felt he had enough evidence to force a confrontation with Esther Spire's killer.

Apparently, he did.

But I did not. I had remnants of his files and a few hints that might mean nothing. A cat disgruntled with a deputy who had worked my father's murder. A pharmacist who had signed my father's autopsy report. And Roscoe, who had found the first body and might or might not remember something from that time. I had gathered as much physical evidence as I could. It was time to start asking some specific questions. That was what solved most cold cases. Not physical evidence. Questions. The right questions to the right people at the right time. Buried memories solved more cold cases than DNA. DNA just made better news reports.

Where to start? The minute I pressed Miss Doris harder about those years and her son-in-law in particular, she'd get suspicious . . . and her network of "girls" was no place to drop a secret. Roscoe might answer without spreading the word, given what I knew of him from my father's files. Doc . . . maybe.

I exited Maple and rounded the square again, my feet drumming a steady rhythm as I passed the last open shops. As the lights winked out, I spotted a sign that seemed distinctly out of place to my city-bred mind. There, taped to the window of the florist, a bright-green poster board held the message SADDLES NOW AVAILABLE.

My feet slowed and I stopped. Saddles? In a florist's shop?

Then it all came back. Floral saddles. Sometimes called clips. For the tops of gravestones.

So . . . there might . . . just be a way to get the town talking about Daisy Doe again without me completely dropping the veil. There was something I could do, if I could do it without anyone finding out, that might just start tongues to wagging.

After all, Decoration Sunday was coming, and I knew a grave that definitely needed tending.

*

It took a couple of days. I didn't want to break my daily routine of work, shower, nap, run, supper too much, or Maude would notice. So I let her think I was shopping for date-night outfits in Gadsden for two days just before Decoration Sunday.

The graveyard at Pine Grove was unlike any of the city cemeteries I'd known. Each family's plot stood out for its unique border, ground cover, and headstones. Between the graves, the sandy ground shifted underfoot, occasionally dropping grains into any passing shoe. Patches of grass marked unused plots, but those were few and far between. The cemetery dated back to way before the founding of the church, and some of the earliest graves were from the 1700s. A dirt road circled through the middle of the cemetery, and on the far side of it, some plots had become so overgrown that they had reverted back to the forest that encircled the area. Broken primitive headstones could be seen among the trees, covered in lichen and pocked by two hundred icy winters and roasting summers.

The sadness I felt over the forgotten, abandoned graves surprised me. Especially since I had come to tend just such an abandoned grave.

I parked in a curve of the dirt road and slid out, my gaze taking in the full view. Wind, forced into a stiff breeze by the parallel ridges on either side of the valley, stirred my hair, and I pulled it back into a ponytail. The air felt hot and dry, and everything smelled of mown grass and damp earth. I dragged my duffel of tools from Belle and headed past a few of the older plots.

Daisy Doe's grave was near the back of the cemetery. No borders or flowers, just a sandy plot with a tiny headstone. Wilted dandelions sprouted from beneath the granite, and dried spikes of ragweed poked up through the red sand. Someone had spent the money to have four lines engraved on the stone:

DAISY DOE
UNKNOWN FEMALE
DIED 1954
BELOVED MOTHER

I stared at the last line—an obvious nod to my father, the boy abandoned by his mother's death. I wondered if they knew exactly how beloved she'd been. "Bobby Doe" supposedly had not talked at all after he'd been found. Who told him she was gone? Old JoeLee or one of his minions? A social worker? I'd read a lot of my father's diaries, but he'd never discussed that part . . . or his silence, beyond noting the fact that he'd remained mute until he'd learned English and a new resident at the group home had befriended him about a year later.

I'd made a few of those painful notifications as a cop, but none to a child left behind. Thank God.

I took a deep breath and slipped on a pair of leather work gloves. Time to make a difference. I wasn't sure why, but I said a quick prayer before starting. Maybe I thought I needed all the help I could get. Whatever was about to happen, however, I did hope God was in it somehow.

I set down the duffel and extracted my supplies. The sand over the grave had turned clumpy, scattered, and pocked from rain. The granite had patches of lichen growing on the corners and base. I started with a small shovel and dug out all the weeds, then raked the sand, breaking up the clumps and spreading it more evenly. I added a bag of fresh sand and blended old with new, then used the back of the rake to even the edges up. I'd made a weed killer and cleanser from Epsom salts, vinegar, and dish soap, and the gallon jug I'd brought sufficed to clean the lichen and pour around the edges of the sand.

Finally I took the saddle of flowers and bent the wires so that it perched securely on top of the headstone. I gave it a few tugs to test it, then stood back to admire my handiwork. The red silk roses, white camellias, and green fern fronds shuddered in the breeze. It was a subtle move, this cleaning of the grave, but it would definitely be noticed.

"You look like her."

I screamed, jerked around, and stumbled backward over the duffel, landing hard on my butt. Gasping for air, I stared up at Roscoe Carver.

He leaned heavily on his cane, his head tilted to one side, watching me. His slacks and dress shirt hung loose, as if he'd lost a lot of weight, but sweat stained his underarms, chest, and neck. "Am I that scary?"

I found my voice. "I . . . I didn't hear a car. Or footsteps."

He pointed back toward the church with his cane. "I was already here. Back side of the church. I saw you buy those flowers. Knew you'd come here before Decoration Sunday."

I swallowed hard and pushed up off the ground. "You've been waiting every day?"

He braced on the cane again. "Not much else to do. I'm an old man. Waiting is easy. Done a lot of it in my life."

"Why?"

He gestured at the grave. "Her. Took me a bit to figure it out. Your hair's blond. Didn't used to be, did it?"

I shook my head.

"I knew it. You can dye the hair, but I never forget a face. Especially when I see 'em die."

I brushed off the back of my pants. "You found her."

"I did." His lips pursed. Something else was on his mind.

"You knew her son. You're the one Daddy found in Vietnam."

"Yep."

"Did you get to talk to him before . . . before he died?"

Another nod. "He told me about you. Thought you hung the moon. Couldn't wait to get this over with and get back to you and your mama. You were, what . . . five?"

"Two, almost three."

"He told me a lot. We had a few good meetings before—" He sniffed, staring at the headstone. "My daddy did that. The headstone. Not right away. Too expensive. But eventually. He felt we owed her that much."

"Why?"

His lips pursed again, and his shoulders hunched as he looked north over the ridge. "Because we didn't stop it. Daddy thought we should have stopped it. We knew what was going on, what was happening up and down US 11, even then. Knew that she was about to step into a mess she didn't know was there. If we'd stopped her, maybe it would have stopped everything. But we were too scared. We had to live here. Keep living with those demons."

Realization tightened my stomach. I took a step closer. "You saw it? You saw who killed her?"

He held up a hand. "Not me. But Daddy knew who killed her."

"So you knew as well."

He grew still. "No proof."

"But you told my father. He tried to find the proof."

"And it got him killed. It'll get you killed too."

"I'm not my father."

"The men what killed them won't care. They won't care about that cop you're sweet on either, if they find out he's helping you. They don't care about nothing but green. You get in their business, they'll kill you too."

I glanced back at the grave. "You said you owed her. So do I. And my father." I faced him. "Help me."

He examined me, head to toe. "You got kin here? For real."

"No lie. Just my grandmother in Birmingham."

"She live here long?"

"All her life."

"She remember Bull Connor? The Dixie Mafia? Buck Dickson?"

"Connor's goons arrested her brother once. For vagrancy. Just because he had no ID on him. Beat the crap out of him."

"Sounds about right. She know you're doing this?"

"She found the notice of the job at Doc's in the paper. She took it as a sign it was time."

"So she knows you could die."

"Not her hope. But she knows what this means to me, to find the answers."

Roscoe hesitated, then inhaled as if he needed to catch his breath, and I realized his eyes gleamed with tears. "You should put her real name there."

I glanced back at the grave. "Her name was Esther Renee Spire. Daddy kept diaries once he was old enough to understand what had happened. He wrote down as much as he could remember. She was French. She didn't speak much English."

Roscoe dug a handkerchief out of his pants pocket and wiped his face. "French. And Jewish."

I remembered all too well the strange mumblings of my mother about Esther Spire, mumblings that made sense only after I'd begun my own investigation in earnest. "She worked with the Resistance in World War II. That's how she met my grandfather. Her mother was French."

He nodded and tucked away the handkerchief. "Her father was Jewish too, a jazz singer who worked in Paris in the twenties. When the war was done, she tracked down your grandfather here. KKK didn't like Jews almost as much as they didn't like blacks. Your daddy knew all this. He didn't put it in those papers?"

"Not the ones we have. The papers he had with him here disappeared. My mother told me Esther had been in the Resistance. That she was Jewish. But nothing more." The tightness in my chest put a hitch in my voice. "But I didn't think about the KKK at the time." I swallowed. "She should never have come here."

"A Jewess with an illegitimate son. Claiming the father was one of Pineville's own heroes. No."

I crossed my arms. "It's a wonder she made it off the bus alive."

"That's why my daddy felt guilty. We should have stopped her. But he didn't want to expose her." Roscoe hesitated. "But truth is, that's only half of it. It wasn't just about her being Jewish."

I frowned. "Then what? You know who killed her."

He coughed and gasped for breath. "Did Bobby's papers not contain who his father was?"

"Please tell me." I stepped closer to him. "Please."

He cleared his throat, then turned his head and spit into the dirt at the foot of the grave. The spittle was red and foamy, and my gut clenched. "Roscoe. You need a doctor."

He held out his hand to stop me, shaking his head. "She could have been lily white and Christian. It wouldn't have mattered. Showing up with a boy who could claim part of an inheritance. No. This was about greed. Reputation. But mostly greed. Green is always the harshest color. Not black. Not white. Green. You know what they say. Follow the money." He turned. "No doctor. I just need to get out of this sun. I'm going back to the car. I'm parked next to the church."

"Wait for me? I'll put this stuff in the truck, then meet you there."

He nodded, waving his hand in an affirmative gesture as he walked away. "I'll tell you everything, but you need to come to the house. I got some stuff I need to show you. We're about to stir up a lot of trouble, Miss Star."

An understatement.

I should have gone with him.

When I pulled the Carryall up next to his sedan, Roscoe Carver sat, his head back against the seat, eyes staring up. A dozen spiderwebbed cracks spiraled out from a neat, round hole in the windshield.

"No!" I'd barely braked when I bolted from Belle. I had heard no shots, but Belle's engine would have masked just about anything. I ran around to the driver's side of Roscoe's car and reached for the door handle. But I froze, my fingers twitching, my brain screeching *Don't touch it!* Through the window, I could see a tight circle of blood staining his shirt, a small round hole in his sternum. CPR would be useless.

He was gone.

"No!" My scream echoed off the wall of the church. I wanted to grab him, yank him from the car, and pump life back into him.

A second shot ricocheted off the roof of the car and slammed into the church wall behind me, as the report echoed around the cemetery.

Instinct made me drop to a squat beside the front tire of his car, grateful Roscoe had parked so close to the church. I twisted, trying to get a good look at the surrounding woods beyond the graves, and a third shot shattered his left headlight and thudded into the engine block. I flattened myself next to the wheel well in a weak attempt to stay hidden, and my gut churned as I called 911. After a few moments, I heard the grinding of gears and the roar of an engine, but I couldn't tell the distance or direction, not with the way the sounds bounced all over the cemetery.

I didn't move until I heard the sirens in the distance. I sat up, leaned hard against the tire, and sobbed.

My one living connection to two murders was beyond caring about Esther Spire, his father's guilt, or the danger that came from nosing into past crimes. Another good man had died.

"Rest in peace, Roscoe," I whispered. "You deserve it."

My trouble, however, had just begun.

CHAPTER SEVENTEEN

Pineville, Alabama, 1974

ROSCOE LEANED AGAINST the doorframe between the kitchen and the hallway, a Camel burning down between two fingers. He watched as Maybelle emptied a second ice tray into a muslin cloth and tied it into a bag. She exchanged it for the one William had pressed to the left side of his head. Her husband smiled up gratefully at her, but Maybelle's expression could have curdled milk.

In the bedroom next to the kitchen, a gentle mewing grew into a wet fuss, threatening to become a full-blown wail. Maybelle handed the limp and soaked cloth to Juanita and headed for the bedroom, one hand pressed hard against the side of her breast.

Juanita had to turn sideways to get by William, with her swollen belly ready to deliver their first. She opened the bag, dumped the half-melted cubes into a bowl, and pushed the bowl into the freezer. She wrung out the cloth and draped it over a rack behind the sink. With a fierce scowl at Roscoe, she followed Maybelle into the bedroom, closing the door with enough force that the dishes in the Hoosier cabinet rattled and shifted.

Roscoe stepped to the table and tamped ashes from his cigarette into a tin ashtray. "What happened?" He took one more draw from the cigarette and stubbed it out in the tray.

William lowered the ice pack and gingerly probed the puffy and bruised skin around his left eye. "Some of the Dixie Mafia boys thought we might be running drugs after all. Took a notion to show us that wouldn't be a good idea."

"Even though Buck's made it plain—"

"You know what they say. 'No honor among thieves.'"

"I thought JoeLee was supposed to take care of this."

William replaced the ice pack. "Me too."

"Chris get the same?"

William hesitated. "Worse. I'm just his n—" He coughed, set the ice pack down, and wiped blood from the corner of his mouth. He motioned for Roscoe to hand him a cigarette. He lit it, his fingers trembling. "I'm just the driver. Chris is Buck's right-hand man these days. They wanted to send a message." He took a long drag on the cigarette, staring at the table, his gaze distant. "Roscoe, they messed Chris up bad. Broke ribs. Maybe his arm. Maybe more. He's in the hospital. His old man's fit to be tied. Abner Patton went off on Buck like nothing I never seen. I thought it was going to be World War III."

Roscoe pulled out a chair and sat. "What happened?"

William picked up the ice pack again and returned it to the side of his face. "Two old men hollering. Too old to come to blows, I guess. They screamed and pushed and screamed some more. Then Buck said that he had a line on a product that would get them out of everything else, out of the line of fire, and make even more money."

Roscoe huffed. "That got the old man's attention."

William gave a half smile, then winced. "Sure did. Then Buck started blabbering about needing Abner's influence, that he had more power than JoeLee ever thought about. Flattered the old man till I thought he was going to purr like a lap cat. They disappeared into Buck's office, and I was told to go home and wait for a call. Might be a few days."

"What's the product?"

William sniffed, rearranged the ice pack, and looked toward the bedroom door. "Roscoe, you take care of them if something happens to me. Right?"

Roscoe lit another cigarette. "You know I will. Don't even have to ask."

"I know. But if something does happen, it'll be bad. Really bad. You got me?"

Roscoe released a long stream of smoke. He watched as it drifted toward the ceiling, dissipating into the filmy blue cloud that already hung there, left by too many cigarettes and Juanita's fried chicken and okra. He sniffed. "What's the product?"

William rolled his shoulders, then ground out his cigarette, stood up, and tossed the ice pack into the sink. It landed with a heavy thud. "You only do business with Isaiah over in Carterton, right?"

Roscoe's eyes narrowed. "I do. I think Juanita's daddy still has an account at Abner's bank here in Pineville. Why?"

"Make him move it."

"Why? We already know the old man's a crook. Whole town knows it."

William shook his head. "All that, just normal small-town-crook stuff. This . . . this is something . . . an entirely different animal. If it goes south . . ." He stopped and took a deep breath. "Just keep all your business with Isaiah. And keep your head down and focus on that store of yours. Don't let anyone bully you. Not anymore. You gonna need it." He jerked his head toward the bedroom door, then crossed his arms over bruised ribs, wincing. "Gonna need it for them. Don't let nothing happen to them. And don't ask me about this ever again. OK? You don't know anything. OK?"

Roscoe hadn't seen his brother this terrified since they were children. He nodded. "OK."

"I gotta go." With a nervous jerk, William strode out the back door.

CHAPTER EIGHTEEN

Pineville, Alabama, Present Day

ONE RULE OF thumb in law enforcement was the person who found a body usually had a part in how the deceased ended up that way, either through direct action or influence.

"What were you doing here?" Michael Luinetti glared at me, knowing that truth in this case. He'd pulled me away from the church, away from the ears of the crime scene unit that he'd called in from Gadsden. They currently scoured the two cars and the surrounding area for evidence. Roscoe's body had already been removed by the coroner and taken to the morgue in Huntsville for processing. Two of Mike's deputies, including Dean Sowers, stood near them, making notes.

I wiped the tears from my eyes, crossed my arms, and tried to explain. Mike listened without expression . . . well, except for that unrelenting glare. "What I don't know is how anyone knew we were here. I wasn't followed, and you can't see that grave from the highway. Unless they followed Roscoe . . . but why would anyone do that?"

"You said Roscoe saw you buy the flowers?"

I nodded. "He's been watching me. I knew that. Was glad for it, actually. I thought it might give me an opening to talk to him."

"But if someone noticed him watching you—"

"—they might have put two and two together." I wiped my eyes again, annoyed that I couldn't stop the tears. "Which still leads to me getting another good man killed."

Mike had no sympathy. "Do you have a gun?"

I glanced back at the cars. Two of the crime scene specialists shot occasional glimpses at us. So did Sowers. Mike needed to follow protocol—and to get in front of this quickly. "I do. A nine millimeter Glock. But I left it at Gran's in Birmingham. I didn't think I'd need it this soon."

He cleared his throat. "Let's assume for now you won't need it at all."

"You don't think I can still be Star O'Connell the soda jerk after this, do you? It'll take the town about five minutes to figure out that I found the body because either I was out here taking care of a grave or I had planned to meet Roscoe. Either option doesn't end well, given that I'm supposed to be a stranger in town."

"Or you're the one who killed him."

I stared at the ground. "Yeah, I've already thought about that. If that were true, then the question is why, and that leads back to the same place. That I have a connection with Daisy Doe." I looked up the slope toward my grandmother's grave. "And that I came to town under false pretenses. Or tried to hide. Deceive. I didn't expect it to come out this soon. And definitely not in this way."

"So are you really Star O'Connell? Without the soda jerk part."

I focused again on his face. The glare had not changed.

"Because the only Star O'Connell I could find associated with Nashville was married to a sleazy lawyer with the reputation of having most of the city's corrupt elite in his back pocket. And she vanished about ten years ago, left the Metro Nashville PD, completely disappeared off the grid."

"I told you it was a long story."

He held up his hand, palm toward me. "Don't. Not now. I need all the truth you got."

I swallowed. "Cavanaugh. Star Cavanaugh. And yes, O'Connell was my married name. After the divorce, I took my mother's maiden name, started completely over. Gran is the only relative I had left, so it made sense. Being married to a crooked lawyer with dirt on about half of the major players in town is not a great place to be if you're in law enforcement. I'm not exactly proud of having Tony O'Connell as a part of my past." I stood straighter. "But everything else I've told you is the absolute truth. Right down to what happened today."

He glared at me a few more moments, then nodded, as if confirming something to himself. "I called a PI I know in Nashville. He told me you were probably Star Cavanaugh. Said you were building your business word of mouth instead of hanging out a shingle."

I shrugged. "With the kind of work I do—cold cases—it's not always a good idea to be too high profile. And I've worked hard to clean the internet of any trace of Star O'Connell. But Tony is a stench that's harder to shed than a skunk's spray."

"And the internet is forever."

"So what now? Are you going to arrest me?"

He drew in a deep breath. "I should. But I am going to have you tested for gunshot residue. Unless they find some immediate evidence connecting you to Roscoe's death. . . ." His eyes narrowed. "Did you touch him or the car?"

I replayed those last moments in my head. Again. "Possibly the front fender." I wiped more tears away. "I was pretty stunned when I saw him, and my first thought was that I'd be next. That's when the other shots hit."

"That's why you can't stop crying."

"What?" I scowled at him.

"Fear. Anger. Grief." He stood a little straighter. "They all have the tendency to force tears from us. Especially when they hit us unexpectedly. You'll grieve more for Roscoe later. Right now, you're more angry and afraid."

"I'm more numb."

"You're in more denial than feeling numb. Otherwise you wouldn't be crying. I'm glad you don't have a gun, because you would have fired back, which really would have messed things up."

"I don't usually go around firing at things I can't see. I'm not that insane."

"No, but in this state of mind, if you knew who was behind this, you'd probably leave here and go kill them." He paused. "Did he tell you who killed her?"

"No. But he was going to."

"But they don't know that. And I'm not convinced those last shots were just to keep you pinned down so they could get away. You need to be prepared that they may try again."

It was my turn to glare. My brows came together, and I crossed my arms so tightly that I hurt a rib. But he was right. Anger about this ran bone deep. "I'm definitely aware. Any suggestions about getting in front of this? You know all the players."

The glare was finally gone from his face. "Go home. Start by having a sit-down with Doc. Tell him all of it. Everything. He's a good man, the heart of this town. You'll know right away what the primary reactions are going to be."

"Good idea, and I need to apologize to him. What about you?"

His eyes narrowed. "We will keep an eye on you, but you can't be in this part of the investigation into Roscoe's death."

"I know. I'm a witness, if not a suspect."

"And I haven't ruled you out. I *do* have to do that first."

"Please don't forget the skin I do have in the game."

"Not likely. But you have to stay out of this . . . and away from me."

My chest tightened. It made sense. I knew that. Didn't mean I liked it. "I know. It would taint everything."

"Or worse. Now, let's get your hands swabbed. I'll have one of the officers take you home. I'll get Belle back to you as soon as we clear her. Just don't leave Pineville."

"Are you kidding? My feet are glued here until they toss me out."

"Or I have to put you in jail."

It wasn't a joke. Mike might not have been glaring any longer, but the tight skin around his eyes told me he seriously considered that as a possibility. He liked me, maybe even more than *liked* me. But he was first and foremost the head law enforcement officer of the town. And because of me, he had to find Roscoe's daughter, Imajean, and deliver one of the worst messages a cop ever had to.

The officer—not Dean Sowers, unfortunately—got me home about the same time that Doc closed the drugstore. I caught him before he went in to supper and asked if he could join me under the awning afterward. I had something I needed to tell him.

I did feel a little regret that I deceived a man who had been so open and welcoming to me, who had introduced me to so many of the people in Pineville who had become important to my investigation, including Mike and Miss Doris. He'd accepted my cover story of trying to start over after an abusive marriage—sticking close to the truth is always a good basis for a cover—even though I knew he couldn't have found much in a background check. In some ways it was like betraying my grandfather, and I hoped he'd understand why I had taken the steps I had.

Dusk had settled long before he emerged from the house. Dew brought a pleasant coolness to the evening, and a soft air stirred the hedges and shrubs full of lightning bugs. I waited, going over in my head a dozen times the words I wanted to say. Doc brought a beer with him, settling into the lawn chair with a deep exhale and solemn expression. Before I could say anything, he asked, "Is this about Roscoe?"

I tried not to be astonished. I don't think I succeeded. Whatever words I'd rehearsed vanished.

He took a swallow of the beer. "Don't be so surprised, Star. That you had called 911 made it around the square before Mike could get in his car."

"The small-town grapevine."

He nodded, then cleared his throat. "And before you start, I should probably tell you that I know you aren't Star O'Connell." He stopped and pointed at me with the bottle. "Or at least, you aren't Star O'Connell any longer."

"I wasn't sure if you had run a background check on me. There's not much to find on Star O'Connell."

"Yep. Before I even called you back from the application. It made me curious, this woman with a new name applying for a teenager's job, moving to a small town from a big city. When I found out you were a PI, the curiosity level shot through the roof."

"So you didn't think I was just trying to get away from the aftermath of a bad marriage, to find solace in a small Southern town?"

He chuckled. "No. That only happens in cable TV movies."

"Why didn't you ask?"

"I wanted to see how it played out. You had something going on. But you did a good job, made some friends. I figured you'd tell me sooner or later." He paused and contemplated the label on the beer bottle. "I didn't realize you'd get one of my favorite people in this town killed."

The tears sprang to my eyes again. "I'm sorry."

"I'm sure you are. So . . . tell me what this is all about."

I did. Starting in 1954.

He just listened at first. I took a breath shortly after Bobby Doe was delivered to the children's home, and Doc spoke up. "That would have been during my dad's time at the pharmacy. Are you sure that was the last time she was seen?"

"As far as my father could figure out. Obviously her killer—or killers—found her later. But the missing hours are a puzzle. Roscoe found her the next day."

He nodded. "I remember that. I was in high school. My folks talked about it. Pretty much everyone did. Big news, a stranger getting killed like that. The Klan almost lynched Roscoe and his father over it. Ebenezer was a good man, would never have been caught up in something like that. But the Klan was ruthless at that time. Didn't take much to push them into slaughtering a black man. The Pine Grove Baptist preacher put a stop to it. What was his name?" He looked up at his roof, staring more than sixty years into the past. "Can't remember. Go on."

I continued, through my father connecting with Roscoe in Vietnam and his eventual arrival in Pineville and death in 1984. Doc didn't interrupt again, but he nodded at all the right places. I touched on my own history with the cases, my mother's death, and the general obsession of my family with the death of Esther Spire. Daisy Doe. When I finished, he remained silent a long time, staring into the darkness of the big hedge. Then with a lurch that startled me, he straightened in the chair and set the bottle on the table between us.

"Your father's murder shook up things around here for a while. The other man . . . what was his name?"

"Alex Trawler. He'd worked with my father in some fashion. I found where he'd been with the government. Not sure how, but my father seemed to hire him for something else. Not sure what."

"No idea what else he did for a living?"

I scowled. Odd question. "No."

"I did the autopsy on both men."

"I know. The reports are in my files."

"Of course. Public record." He shook his head. "The way they were killed . . . JoeLee Wilkes . . . he wanted me—" He stopped.

"Doc?"

He faced me, his cheeks reddening. The skin around his eyes tightened to a shiny white. "Do you have any idea what kind of wounds you're about to rip wide open in this town? Do you know how dangerous this is?"

"It got my father killed. And Roscoe."

He jerked from the chair and paced back and forth in front of me. "Oh, it goes way beyond a few murders."

That was a phrase I never expected to hear from a kindly old pharmacist. "A *few* murders?"

He stopped, towering over me. "Yes. A few. More than a few. You have no clue how deep this goes. Neither does Michael Luinetti. He hasn't been here long enough to know the nasty reach all the tendrils have. You're about to root into the very heart of power in this town. Political. Financial. And anything that threatens the established power structure is dangerous."

"Will you help me?"

He stopped, then scrubbed his face hard with his hands. "I'll . . . try. There are some things I will *not* talk about. You can ask. I won't say. I can't say." He clenched his fists, closed his eyes, and took a deep calming breath. Then another. He relaxed and opened his eyes, but he focused on the kitchen window. A single light revealed Maude washing the last of the dinner dishes. "There are some things I just can't risk." He paused, then looked to me, his voice quiet. "You need to talk to Imajean and Maybelle Carver. Start with them."

"Maybelle? . . ." Her name wasn't in any of my files.

"William's wife. Widow. William was Roscoe's brother."

Another name not in my files.

He started pacing again. "After William died, Maybelle took the kids and moved in with William and Roscoe's aunt and her husband. Seemed odd since Ebenezer still worked the farm, but they were pretty terrified. The uncle was a preacher in Birmingham. They are probably still down there. Her oldest kid would be about Imajean's age. Um . . . something biblical . . . Joshua . . . Jesus . . . no, Jeshua!" He grinned suddenly, pleased at the memory, then the grin vanished, and he dropped back in the chair and snagged the bottle. He took a long swig, draining it.

He looked at the back of his house. Inside, Maude moved around, tidying up the kitchen. "Keep Maude out of this. Can you?"

"I'll do my best."

"You ever survive a direct hit from a tornado?"

"No. But I've seen the aftermath."

He nodded. "You are about to walk directly into the core of one. Remember that storms have no minds, no intentions, no feelings. They only grind up whatever happens to be in their path. Maybe, just maybe, you'll be the one to survive it."

With that, he stalked back to the house. Through the window, I watched him pull Maude into a tight hug and kiss her fiercely.

My cell phone buzzed, the first of many calls that would go on until almost midnight. Vic Beason was the first, wanting a comment for the paper. I told him I wouldn't comment until Mike's investigation concluded. A long silence followed, then Vic said quietly, "Star, I'm not talking about Roscoe Carver's murder. I'm talking Daisy Doe. And Star's real name—Cavanaugh. There's a picture circulating on social media, a shot of you working on that grave. I'll text it to you. You'd better get in front of this before the information that leaks out gets all messed up. Call me when you want to make a statement."

I stared at the phone. *A shot of you working on that grave.* My eyes burned, and every muscle in my body tensed as the text tone sounded. I opened the picture. There I stood, placing flowers on the headstone of Daisy Doe. In the foreground of the picture, Roscoe picked his way among the graves toward me. The whole town knew his connection to Daisy Doe. What was mine?

My head spun as I studied the photo closer. The rear of Roscoe's car stuck into the frame from the left. This photo had been taken by the shooter. Or someone with the shooter.

Doc was right. Whatever control I thought I had on my presence here had all been an illusion. The debris was about to start flying.

CHAPTER NINETEEN

Pineville, Alabama, 1983

ROSCOE SAT BEHIND his desk in the small office at the rear of the appliance store. He fidgeted with his favorite fountain pen, pulling the top on and off, twirling it between his fingers. He craved a Camel so badly he could have bitten into a pack and swallowed half of it whole. Definitely the wrong time to quit smoking.

He should have known it was all too good to be true. William had been right. *Keep your head down. Focus on the business.* And Roscoe had. For several years, he'd worked long, hard hours to become one of the most successful businessmen on the square. Not just a successful *black* businessman. Against all odds and expectations, the white folks had accepted him on the square. He ate at the drugstore, right up front with the other square business owners. In the early days, Miss Doris Rankin had adopted him, had him fix all the appliances in that big house on Maple. It was the approval he needed, and other customers followed, some of the richest in town. The store thrived. Good money. They'd moved out of the rental house on the farm and bought their own place, which had thrilled Juanita. She was happier than she'd been in a long time.

But good money attracts attention—and not always the right kind. Roscoe replayed today's visit from Abner Patton over and over in his head.

> *"It's simple, Roscoe. Every Friday, my boy will drop by. You give him all your tens and twenties, and he'll replace them with new*

ones, plus two hundred dollars extra. You take the deposit over to the bank, use them for change, whatever. That's all there is to it."

"But, sir, I don't use the bank here. I use the one over in Carterton."

"You'll need to back off that. Slowly. You can make deposits there for now. Just open an account here. Start small. Do things slowly."

"But I don't see—"

"It's time you came on board, Roscoe. Like everyone else. Your brother . . . he's protected you long enough." The old man stood up, looking around. "This is a real nice store, ain't it, Roscoe? You've worked hard. People like you. All kinds of people like you. But they've started to wonder why you're not with us. What makes you special?" He looked at Roscoe. "I'd hate to see all the progress you people have made go bad." He tapped the edge of Roscoe's desk. "I'd hate to see your brother get caught up in something bad." He examined Roscoe's face carefully, then nodded. "I thought so. My boy'll be here Friday at noon."

Roscoe didn't have to ask what the old man meant by all that. Loss of customers. Rejection. Suppliers drying up. Fire. All of it. Abner Patton's power ran all the way to Montgomery and beyond. No one stood up to him. And William. William would always be vulnerable to the old man's whims.

The pen shattered in Roscoe's hand, spreading ink all over his palm and desk. A shard of the plastic embedded in one finger. Roscoe yanked it out, then opened a drawer on the right side of his desk and pulled out a towel. He wiped up ink and blood, then pressed tightly on the puncture. The ink made the wound burn like a match flame had been held to it.

His eyes watered. *God almighty, why?* he prayed. *Show me what to do now.* How had he let this trap close around them when he wasn't looking? Had he really thought William could keep this at bay forever?

Roscoe pulled the towel away from his hand. The bleeding had stopped. The ink had dried. Not too bad. But he needed advice. Not from Juanita. Not from anyone else on the square. They apparently had gone along with this scheme. When had William told him things were changing? Back in 1974?

No. Roscoe needed sound advice. A lawyer. He needed a lawyer. *But where would he find—*

He started to drop the towel back into the drawer when he noticed an ancient newspaper clipping in the bottom, one he'd once carried in his wallet. The curly-haired boy whose mother had been murdered.

Roscoe smiled slowly. "Thank you, Lord." He opened the middle drawer and pulled out his second favorite fountain pen and a notebook.

Dear Bobby . . .

CHAPTER TWENTY

Pineville, Alabama, Present Day

THE NEXT DAY wasn't the worst day of my life—Tony O'Connell had the lock on numbers one through seven of that scale—but it definitely fell in at eight. The soda fountain was only open for breakfast on Saturdays, and, as usual, this Saturday brought a packed crowd. But they were quiet and subdued, all staring at me.

Make that glaring at me.

Orders were given in clipped voices, and a low buzz of rumors circulated. I had a feeling no tips would be forthcoming. Doc had offered to close the drugstore entirely, but I knew I'd have to face this sooner or later. And at about eight thirty, I had to. I delivered a plate of biscuits to a table of guys from Ed's hardware store. As I set it down, one of them grabbed my wrist.

"Why aren't you in jail?" The question came through clenched teeth.

Whatever murmurs had been buzzing through the room silenced. I looked down at his hand on my arm, and he tossed it away as if I had mange. I straightened and faced the crowd. "That's why you're all here, isn't it? You want to know about yesterday."

A few heads nodded. Miss Doris looked down at her hands in her lap.

I went to the counter and perched on one of the stools. I cleared my throat. Out of the corner of my eye, I saw Vic Beason set his phone next to his plate and press one of the buttons.

"My name is Star Cavanaugh. O'Connell was my married name, but I gave it up about ten years ago. And as much as I like working for Doc and serving y'all, I'm actually a private investigator. I've wanted to chat with Roscoe for a long time, but he's the one who sought *me* out at the cemetery. I did not ask him to meet me there. It would not have been my choice as a meeting place. I know that by now most of you have seen the photo that's been making the rounds. If you'll look closely at it, you'll see part of Roscoe's car in the picture. That's the angle from which he was shot. I believe that picture was made by someone who either knows—or is—the person who killed Roscoe."

I looked at the guy who grabbed me. "To answer your question, the reason I'm not in jail is because there's not enough evidence to suggest I shot Roscoe. And I had no motive. In fact, I had all the motive in the world to keep him alive. Roscoe was the one remaining witness to the cases I'm investigating."

Miss Doris's head shot up, her eyes wide. Obviously she got it. She'd put the grave, Roscoe, and me together and suddenly understood. A few people looked around at her, then back at me.

"So the last thing I wanted was Roscoe dead." My voice softened. "More than that, I really liked him. We'd chatted enough in here that I'd wanted to know him better. I am cooperating with the police department, and they are investigating me, just as they would anyone else who finds a body. They checked me for gunshot residue. I have agreed to do nothing that would interfere with their work. If they find reason to arrest me, they will."

"Even though you and Mike are dating?"

I couldn't make out who said that, so I answered to the crowd. "We've had one date. We like each other. But what relationship we might have had is on hold until this is done. We won't be seeing each other socially, even in here, until it's resolved."

"You're not going to keep working in here, are you?"

I shrugged. "That's up to Doc. And y'all. Tell you the truth, I like working here. I liked getting to know everyone."

"But you're just investigating us."

"Not really. I admit it helped me to get to know Pineville, your history, what makes the town tick. Most of the people I've met and spent time with, however, have nothing to do with the cases I'm looking into. I just liked spending time with you."

"What are the cases?"

And there it was. The question of the day. I looked at Miss Doris. Her eyes had turned red, and tears glistened on her cheeks. But she gave me one nod. I glanced at Doc, who did the same.

"The murder of Daisy Doe. And the murders of the men who came here in 1984 to try to find out who killed her."

A buzz shot through the crowd, and one of the older farmers stiffened in his chair. "That was almost seventy years ago!"

"I'm a cold case detective."

"So who are you working for? Who's got you poking around in our business?" That was the guy from Ed's again. Another moment of truth.

"I'm working for myself this time." I straightened my shoulders. "Daisy Doe was my grandmother. And one of the men who arrived in 1984 was her son. My father."

The silence felt like a late-summer humidity. Heavy, cloying. Unending.

I pressed on. "So this is personal. And I need your help."

A few of the murmurs picked up again. One of the men I'd seen at church spoke up. "Most of us weren't even alive then."

"I know. That's the reason most of my work will be in the archives or the library. Cold cases are far more about research and conversations than anything you'd see on television." I slid off the stool. "Look, I don't blame you if you hate me right now. Hate that I lied about my name or if you feel I deceived you about being here. Truth is, before yesterday, I'd only told one person why I'm here—Michael Luinetti. I haven't discussed it with anyone else, one way or another. Last night I told Doc everything. Roscoe figured it out because he recognized me."

My eyes stung, and I swallowed hard. "He said that I looked like her. Like Daisy Doe. He wanted to help me. That's why he was in the cemetery yesterday—to talk to me. He told me some things but needed to go back to the car for the air conditioning. I was going to join him, to talk more. Obviously, someone didn't want that to happen."

The guy from Ed's stood up. "Are you saying it could be dangerous to help you? Why? That woman's been dead since 1954!"

I focused on his face. "Yes. And *why* is the exact question. I don't know. Not yet." I scanned the crowd again. "Most of you can't help me. Others won't. But if you have any information at all, I hope you will."

I let the room go silent. After a few tense moments, Rafe coughed. "Order up, Star."

I picked up the plate and a fresh pot of coffee and faced the room again.

Some people had left. Some even edged out without paying their tab. Others focused on their plates, and gradually . . . gingerly . . . conversation resumed. They eventually finished eating, and the room emptied.

Except for Doris Rankin. As Rafe cleaned the grill and I bused the last of the cluttered tables, she watched me. The tears had dried, and I expected her to be angry. But her expression had softened even more, her eyes wide and curious. I washed the final plate, hung up the apron, and dried my hands. I pulled out the chair next to her and sat down.

"You remember, don't you?"

Her eyes narrowed with intensity. "Of course I remember. I was eighteen. Had just graduated high school and was about to head off to nursing school in Birmingham. I was going to be the next Florence Nightingale. Maybe even go on to be a doctor. I loved helping people." She paused and fluttered her hand in front of her, as if pointing to a far destination. "The future was bright . . . glittery . . . hopeful." Her hand dropped back into her lap. "Then she came. They killed her. And all my dreams."

I leaned toward her. "Why?"

She focused on my face. "Because they killed her! It shocked the whole town. Nothing like that ever happened here. People were afraid for their girls, their children. So no woman under thirty was allowed to leave the house alone for weeks. No one knew if it was some random stranger or if we had a killer living in town. We were terrified, all summer long, way into the fall and winter."

My heart ached for her. "You couldn't go to school."

"Daddy drove into his office in Gadsden every day. An accountant." A small smile flitted across her mouth and vanished. "He used to say, 'I'm an actuary actually.' He thought that was funny. But with him driving in and me bored out of my skull, I started going in with him. Found a job in an investment firm next door. Typist, then secretary. By the time the next term at the nursing school rolled around, the president of the firm wanted me as his girl Friday instead. The money was great. I could afford as much lipstick and home perms as I could handle. So I stayed."

She glanced out the front window of the drugstore a moment, then faced me squarely. "I like you, Star. But I knew you had to be up to something. You had too much going on to be here because you wanted to sling biscuits and gravy every day. Although I didn't expect all this!"

"I sometimes catch people off guard."

"Well, I'd think that would be a good thing in your profession."

I smiled. "Most of the time."

Miss Doris let out a long, slow sigh. "Honey, I will be eighty-five in a month or so. These cracker fools terrified me once. They ain't doing it again. I will help you any way I can. That doll's death has hung over this town for far too long."

I reached out and took her hand. "Thank you. So I have a question."

"Fire away."

"What can you tell me about Dean Sowers?"

Her eyes narrowed. "My son-in-law? That Dean Sowers?"

"Yes ma'am."

Miss Doris frowned, confusion clouding her expression as she thought about why I'd be asking. Then recognition hit suddenly, and her eyes widened. "Oh my goodness," she whispered. "How much time do you have?"

I walked Miss Doris home. We both knew dozens of eyes watched as we crossed the square and headed down Maple. More than a few ears as well. Instead of talking about anything related to the case, she regaled me with her adventures as a girl Friday, which I pointed out would now be called a personal assistant.

She chuckled. "And how boring is that. People took note when they heard who I worked for. And I went all over the world those first few years. Then he decided I needed a degree."

I matched my pace to hers, which was much faster than I expected. "You didn't go back to become a nurse?"

She looked incredulous. "Are you joking? After learning how to conduct my job in Paris and Tokyo? No ma'am. That World War I ditty was right. Can't keep 'em down on the farm after they've seen Paree. He paid for half the degree. Mother and Daddy paid the other half." She tapped my arm. "They still felt guilty about me missing my nursing dreams, but we'd all just accepted that God had a different plan. And sure enough, when I was a senior, that's when I met my George. He was a freshman, but he was hot!"

I laughed, and Miss Doris blushed. "Pshaw! You just see a half-blind seventy-seven-year-old man. I still see the freshman who could flip me over his back without thinking twice about it. He was lean and wiry, and I couldn't wait to marry the man. The age difference was looked down on, of course, me being the older woman. But we knew. Almost from the moment we met. It happens that way sometimes."

"Is that the way it happened with Dean and Charlotte?"

We had left the square and moved under the thickest of the shade trees arching over the street. They cooled the air and muffled our voices, but Miss Doris still spoke more quietly. "Hardly. They got a little too up close and personal after some rock concert. Charlotte had to drop out of school, and George threatened to bury Dean in the back yard if he didn't step up."

"I thought shotgun weddings went out in the thirties."

Miss Doris looked up at me as if I were a child. "Oh, my dear, where do you think you are?"

I had to laugh, and she joined me. We'd reached her house by that time, and we headed up the drive to the kitchen door. She pushed it open and ushered me in. "Would you like some coffee?"

"Would love some."

She pointed to a rack of coffee pods near the stove. "Pick your pleasure. Looks like the maker has enough water." Miss Doris pulled two mugs from a cabinet and handed me one. "Have you ever asked Doc about getting some better brands at the drugstore? That stuff is barely above swill."

"The farmers seem to like it."

"Humph. Their favorite blends fall somewhere between burnt and tar. They just like it strong."

"Truth. And they tip well if I keep their cups full. Or they did."

Miss Doris pulled out a chair and sat at the kitchen table as I popped a pod into the coffeemaker and put my cup under the spout. She watched me, her lips in a tight bow. "They like you, Star. You're the first outsider in a long time who's won their affection. That's why they're so mad at you."

I leaned against the counter. "Do you think they'll get past it?"

She shrugged one shoulder. "Probably, if you stir up their curiosity in the right way."

"How so?"

"Most of them weren't around for any of the murders. The ones that were have avoided talking about it for more than thirty years. Don't make them feel bad about that. You don't remember what it was like under JoeLee Wilkes. Corruption in law and business was status quo. Most people turned a blind eye in order to stay out of trouble. And alive. Your daddy was murdered out in the open. Most people who took a stand against JoeLee simply disappeared."

"And now?"

Another shrug. "I suspect there's still pockets. The sheriff after JoeLee tried to ferret some of it out, but he'd been one of JoeLee's deputies."

"Like Dean was."

Miss Doris paused. "Dean suddenly found himself with a wife and new baby and a need to support them all. The deputy's job was supposed to be short term, while they earned enough money for him to go back to school."

"But that never happened."

She shook her head. My coffee gurgled to a halt, and I pulled the mug out, then slid Miss Doris's mug under the spout. She pointed to a pod she'd set near the maker, and I pushed it into place.

"Spoons are in that drawer." She pointed. "Sugar's next to the Frigidaire. Half-and-half is in the door."

I gathered the items and set them on the table, then retrieved her cup. We dipped, poured, and stirred in silence. After a few sips, Miss Doris peered into her cup as if she were reading tea leaves in the bottom. "Y'know, Dean was never the same after what happened to your daddy. I can't explain it, exactly, but I know that he and Charlotte came close to a breakup after that. She said Dean was just . . . different. Quieter, and in some ways, meaner."

I sat up straighter, my cop instincts firing. The thought of what the Hall sisters had said about Dean and Miss Snopes flashed through my mind. "Mean? He hit her?"

Miss Doris shook her head furiously. "No. Not that way. I'm sure he wanted to sometimes. Charlotte's my own and I love her, but she can be tetchy sometimes. Even as a kid she could try the patience of a saint, and I am sure not one." She paused and sipped the coffee. "No, he just became more impatient. Would yell about the slightest things. He would go off by himself—still does—for two or three days at a time. Charlotte thought he was cheating on her, until George had him followed."

"So. Not another woman?"

"No. He just goes off to a place in the woods next to a creek. Sometimes just sleeps in his truck. It's down an old field road, so George didn't get too close. Once we knew he wasn't cheating on Charlotte, we let it be."

"He sleeps in his truck? For two or three days?"

She sniffed, then wiped one eye. "Yep. As far as I can tell, he's been doing it for the past thirty years."

"Same place every time?"

"As far as I know. Three or four times a year. I guess when Charlotte just gets to be too much on his nerves."

"Isn't he getting close to retirement?"

"Charlotte said he could retire in two or three years. But he wants to work as long as he can."

"And he's never talked about the murders?"

"Not to me. I doubt to Charlotte. I think their marriage has been running on inertia for years."

"What about to George?"

That produced a sly grin. "Oh, my George and Dean Sowers operate on two completely different levels of life. George is opera, champagne, and world travel. Dean is Southern rock, beer, and fishing." She took a sip of coffee. "Not that there's anything wrong or right with either one. It's just that they don't exactly have a lot of heart-to-hearts." She paused, looking thoughtful. "Although he might have talked some to Kevin."

I had forgotten. "Kevin?"

"Ellen's husband. The ones who are having trouble, so I'm getting stuck with Carly for a while?"

Yep, I needed to make a flow chart of Miss Doris's family. "Oh, right."

"With Kevin and Ellen squabbling, the two men might have some common ground."

I had my doubts. "About a murder more than thirty years old?"

Her mouth twisted. "Well, there is that."

"Miss Doris, I have a photo of the crime scene. JoeLee and all his deputies standing around the bodies. Dean was there. Can you think of anyone else who might still be around from the sheriff's department?"

She got up, poured the remainder of her coffee in the sink, then leaned against it, crossing her arms. "Maybe. Could I see it?"

"It's pretty gruesome."

"Right." She looked up at the ceiling, her lips a thin line. "No one from the sheriff's department. But there's Doc and Maude. Oh, and Jake Beason."

I thought about the pink beastie. "Yeah, Jake's not real happy with me right now."

Her eyes crinkled in amusement. "Well, don't let that bother you. Jake's not been real happy with anyone since Jimmy Carter was president. He's a curmudgeon by trade."

"Anything else you can tell me about Dean?"

She sat back down. "Maybe. Ever notice that he limps?"

"I . . . uh . . . no. Why does he limp?"

"Right about the time of your father's murder, Dean got tangled up in a car wreck with some bootleggers. Not sure what happened, but the bootleggers were killed, and his leg got pretty mangled. If you can get him to talk to you about that time, you might want to ask him."

"I will."

"Oh, and Ellis Patton."

I stared at her. "The mayor? That Ellis Patton?"

She nodded vigorously. "He would have been just a boy when your grandmother was killed, but Ellis would have been about thirty-five or so when your daddy came to town."

"And you think he'd know something because . . ."

She leaned back in her chair. "Rumors. Just rumors. And his daddy was mayor back then. The Pattons? They pretty much run this town. Have for more than seventy years."

CHAPTER TWENTY-ONE

Gadsden, Alabama, 1983

"NASHVILLE'S NOT THAT far away, Roscoe."

Roscoe rolled his shoulders and shifted in the booth. They'd chosen the Waffle House off the interstate as being more anonymous. Few locals, more passers-through on the way from Chattanooga to Birmingham. But the server had been eying Bobby's handsome face. She'd remember him, for sure, if someone asked later.

"It's not about the distance, Bobby."

"You know I can take care of myself."

"Yeah, I thought I could too. But this ain't like the violence of 'Nam. Not like facing down the enemy in the paddies."

"So he came by Friday?"

Roscoe nodded. "I didn't have much. An appliance and repair shop is not a big cash-flow business. Mostly credit cards and checks. I had maybe five, ten of each bill. But he didn't blink. Gave me the replacements, plus the two hundred."

"You got 'em?"

Roscoe slipped an envelope across the table. Bobby took it and slid it into a folder beside him on the seat. "Y'know, I can't keep taking this much out of the till every week. I'll go under. Eventually, I'm going to have to let them go into circulation."

Bobby nodded. "Give me a couple of weeks. I'll see if I can't arrange for something else."

The server appeared beside their booth. "More coffee?" They both nodded, and she poured, winking at Bobby. "Y'all's food will be up in a minute." She moved on to the next booth.

Roscoe chuckled. "You get that everywhere you go?

Bobby winced. "I thought it'd die down some after I hit thirty. Usually they check out my left hand."

"Well, they never know exactly how married you are if they don't try."

Bobby's smile vanished. "You think that's what's going on in Pineville? They didn't know how you'd react until they tried? Think they'd take no for an answer after all?"

"Not without leaving some serious damage behind. And it's more than that. It's more about loyalty than actual cash."

"Loyalty?"

"My brother's been tangled up with them for years. He knows a lot about the inside of the business. They probably think he's talked to me, that I know it too. This is about getting me in deep enough that I won't go to the authorities outside of town. That I'll stay loyal to my brother, my family, no matter what."

"Good thing I'm not any sort of authority."

Roscoe leaned forward. "Seriously, man. If you can do anything, thank you. You have no idea how complicated their web is or how dangerous they are. Me and William both. It's like we're sitting on top of land mines. Can't get off, and the wrong move could get us both killed."

They paused as the server set down an array of plates on their table—eggs, bacon, waffles, grits, toast, hash browns. They settled into eating, enjoying the food in silence a few moments. Finally, Bobby paused and wiped his mouth. "About that other thing."

Roscoe pulled a card from his coat pocket and handed it over. "Names and phone numbers. But it won't be easy. They are both"—he paused, and one corner of his mouth jerked—"'fortunate sons.' Now they're pillars of the community, so to speak. They'll close ranks. The older one, he was maybe eighteen when it happened. Get your man to look into him. But he's enmeshed in all of this as well. Not sure about the younger one—he seems legit for the most part, but you never know. The older one, he is. Won't be easy to get him alone, to see what he knows. And he's as deadly as the rest. William says he knows where all the bodies are buried, even if he didn't put them there."

"We'll be careful."

"Y'all need anything else?" The server's infectious grin and happy tone made them both smile. Her grin faded a little as Bobby took the check from her with his left hand.

Roscoe shook his head. "Boy, you are trouble everywhere you go."

Bobby shrugged. "An old family tradition."

CHAPTER TWENTY-TWO

Pineville, Alabama, Present Day

THE NEXT DAY, Decoration Sunday, I went to church alone. Partly to face whatever music awaited, but also to demonstrate that Mike and I weren't a couple after all.

I did not bring a casserole.

I sat about halfway down toward the altar, careful not to sit in anyone else's usual spot. People were creatures of habit, after all. The church was packed for the event, so I saw a lot of unfamiliar faces, not all of which looked particularly friendly when turned in my direction. But a lot of reunions of distant family and friends kept a high chatter going, and most folks ignored me. Placement of new floral arrangements extended beyond the cemetery into the sanctuary, and a row of polished and watered peace lilies stretched along the steps leading up to the pulpit. Daylilies lined the outer walls, their overpowering scent leaving me on the constant edge of a sneeze.

A few minutes later Miss Doris twisted in her seat down front and motioned for me to join her and her friends. I hesitated, then shook my head. I was a spectacle paired with Mike—I knew I'd stand out like a sore thumb among the short crew of eighty-somethings. But Miss Doris's expression became insistent. I finally picked up my purse and joined her. As she and the others scooted over to make room, she patted my arm and whispered, "You need me, dear. You need some solidarity. Especially today."

Miss Doris, as it turned out, was not just the lighthearted party girl who liked being flipped over her husband's back.

"Where's Mr. George?" I whispered back.

"Oh, you *are* new here, aren't you? George hasn't darkened the door of Pine Grove Baptist since our wedding. He's Catholic. Attends St. James in Gadsden. Three of our kids followed in his footsteps."

"Charlotte and Dean?"

She glanced over her shoulder, checking to see who else had arrived for service. "Technically, they are members here, but I doubt they even know who the preacher is." She peered at me closer, then held up her readers in front of her face to magnify the examination. "And, darlin', if you're going to stay up all night crying, you need to invest in a better concealer." She gestured at my face with her glasses. "Roscoe?"

I nodded.

She *humph*ed under her breath. "Just remember. You didn't get him killed. Whoever pulled the trigger did."

I touched the thin skin under my eye. It did feel puffy.

A chime sounded from the organ, and the choir filed into the loft at the front, signals for everyone in the pews to settle down. Miss Doris faced the front again, and I fought a sense of disappointment. I had hoped Dean would be here today to see my improvements to Daisy's grave. I was determined to raise his curiosity about me as much as mine had heightened about him. Given what I knew about him, I had a feeling that the direct approach would never work. He needed to be lured. And if I could draw him out, who knew what other woodwork-dwelling critters might emerge with him.

After the service, Miss Doris invited me to join her crew for lunch, but I'd never be able to eat more than enough to insult them. The area where Roscoe had been killed was still taped off, so most of the gathering had moved up the hill a bit. I did as well, wandering up toward the cemetery, lingering at a few plots to admire the landscaping and new silk flowers. I thought idly about how other cultures honor their dead, and glanced up at the sky once, muttering, "Was this your idea? Flowers to smother the scent of death?" No answer, but I hadn't really been expecting one. My steps halted at Daisy Doe's grave.

This first Sunday in May grew warmer as I stood there, my thoughts circling around the woman who'd started all this. The tawdry glamour that must have encompassed her childhood, the mixture of jazz and religion that probably had confused her as much as it did some children even today. Born between the wars, Esther Spire would have been a child when Hitler rose to power, a teen when the invasion of Poland began. But to have been in Paris in the late thirties and early forties! Her work with the Resistance must have given her confidence, a sense of power.

But nothing could have prepared her for the South of 1954. Her skin might have been white, but her wartime lover would have known the truth. "Is that the sum of what this was about?" I whispered. "Her being a Jew? Please tell me something else was going on."

Not sure why I felt that kind of conflict. Being Jewish would definitely have been enough to get her killed. History proved that disturbing fact. Why did I feel the need for something more to be involved?

I didn't turn when I heard the footsteps and felt the strong presence at my back. "I thought we were going to stay away from each other."

Mike cleared his throat. "The gunshot residue test was negative."

"Of course it was."

He remained silent a few moments, then his voice dropped a bit. "You need to get ready. This may be about to explode."

My chest tightened. "What's happened?"

"Someone broke into Imajean's home last night while they were at a movie. Roscoe lived with her and Charles. Ransacked the place."

My mouth dropped open, and I spun on my heels. "What did they steal?"

"As far as she can tell . . . nothing. But it was clear they were searching for something. All her valuables are still in place, but they pulled and dumped the drawers, cleaned out the closets, upended the beds. They even left two pistols behind."

I frowned. "No one leaves the guns. Even if they don't take the electronics and jewels, they take the cash and the guns."

He shrugged. "No guns, no cash. She had five hundred dollars tucked away in the underwear, and all they did was spread it around the room when they tipped the drawer over."

Roscoe's words popped back into my head. "Roscoe said he had something he wanted to show me."

"Did he have it stashed at Imajean's?"

"No idea. We were going to talk about it when we got back to his car. But I bet someone knows what he had."

"I'll mention it to Imajean."

"I still want to talk to Dean Sowers."

Mike looked away from me toward the woods, his gaze distant. "Ever since I came here, Sowers has been a good, reliable officer. He helped show me the ropes, get acquainted around town. Stood up for me when people thought he should have had this job, not an outsider."

"I'm not saying he was involved, but–"

"–he has to know something."

"Right."

He focused on me again. "I don't want good people to get caught up in this when they weren't a part of it."

"I'm just hoping the good people are who we think they are."

He crossed his arms. "Sowers has put in his papers. He's retiring, effective the fifteenth." Mike must have seen the confusion in my face. His eyebrows arched. "What?"

"Miss Doris said Dean didn't plan to retire for a long time. Basically, his marriage isn't great, so he didn't want to spend long hours at home."

"Explains why he likes the night shift."

"But not why he's suddenly retiring." I filled Mike in on my chat with Miss Doris.

He listened passively, his face calm, then he scanned the dinner-on-the-grounds crowd. A lot of heads looked our way. "Go home, Star. You've got the message across for now. Let things ferment for a while."

"See what bubbles to the top in a few days?"

"Something like that. But keep me posted if you hear anything new."

I looked across the spread of the cemetery, the families gathering around the tables and a few of the stragglers wandering up toward the newly groomed plots. The kids running in groups, chasing one another among the headstones. "Somehow I don't think it's going to take a few days."

Mike nodded once and strode away, all business, back toward the long tables laden with the offerings of Pineville's best cooks. A group of the children, five or six of them, circled around me, squealing. One boy had a lizard, threatening to throw it on the girls, who screeched with glee. A girl scooted behind me to hide. I laughed.

I looked around at her, grinning. "You're not afraid of a little lizard, are you?"

She gazed up at me, brown eyes gleaming. "You're Star, aren't you?"

My eyes widened. "I am. Do I know you?"

She shook her head, dark pigtails bouncing. "Nope. But I'm supposed to give you this." She pressed something into my hand, then scampered back to her friends.

"Thank you," I whispered, but I didn't look at it until I got back to Belle, started the engine and the air conditioning, and locked the doors. It was a folded offering envelope, obviously lifted from one of the special holders on the back of each pew. Three short lines were scrawled across the back:

MEET PANERA
THE SUMMIT
2:30, MONDAY

The Summit was a shopping complex in Birmingham. A busy area, but relatively easy to access from the interstate bypass. At two thirty, Panera wouldn't be crowded, but it was tucked away from the main drag. A good choice overall.

I tucked the card over the sun visor and drove back into Pineville, wondering how hard it would be to find Dean's "disappearing" spot, the one Miss Doris had mentioned. I needed to get directions from Mr. George. I circled the square, noting how deserted everything was. Decoration Sunday drew everyone out to the churches, even the ones who normally spent Sunday reading the paper. I pulled up beside the Airstream and put Belle in park. She dieseled once before cutting off. Ah, time for a tune-up.

I got out, unlocked the door to the trailer, and pulled it open.

Dean Sowers sat in my recliner waiting, a .38 revolver held in his lap. He nodded at me. "Come in and close the door."

CHAPTER TWENTY-THREE

Pineville, Alabama, 1983

"WHAT DO YOU mean, it's not all counterfeit?" William braced his rear against the lowered tailgate of his truck. He pulled a pack of Camels out of his shirt pocket and shook one free. He tucked it in the corner of his mouth and offered the pack to Roscoe.

Roscoe declined the cigarette, then slipped off his suit coat and draped it over one arm. He loosened his tie. He'd closed the store early that afternoon and driven into Gadsden for a parts order. He stopped by his PO box before heading home to find a letter from Bobby Spire.

"Bobby gave the money to a contact he has with the Secret Service."

William lit the Camel and took three strong drags on it. "The guys who guard the president?"

"Yeah. They're the ones who investigate counterfeiting. They said only part of the money was bogus."

William blew free a long trail of smoke, then flicked the first ashes off the end. "Chris said it was all funny money. Why wouldn't it be?"

Roscoe shrugged. "No idea. He said most of the real bills had no trace on them. But one was tracked to a bank robbery in a little town in south Georgia. Another had significant traces of cocaine on it."

William pushed himself up on the tailgate, letting his feet dangle. "Why would Chris lie?"

"Maybe he doesn't know."

William looked down at the gravel driveway, lost in thought.

Roscoe went on. "Bobby said they might be looking at two levels of criminal activity. The counterfeiting and money laundering."

William's head jerked up. "Money laundering?"

"Passing cash from criminal acts through legitimate busi—"

"I know what money laundering is."

Roscoe studied his brother. Since he'd started driving for the old man, William had gone from being fidgety and nervous to comfortable and arrogant about the almost nightly runs through northeast Alabama. In the past few weeks, he'd become agitated again, smoking more, disappearing more.

"What are you thinking, William? What's going on?"

William took another draw of the cigarette, crushed it out against the metal of the tailgate, and flicked the butt onto the grass. He licked his front teeth and stared down at the driveway again.

Roscoe waited. Since he'd been a child, William had taken his time putting any serious thoughts together. Weighing all possible combinations. Roscoe had once teased him that he and Maybelle would have been married two years longer if William had gotten the words together sooner. When William looked back up at Roscoe, it was if all his worries poured out in a stream.

"Chris's been acting weird lately. Skittish. Scared of Buck and scared of his old man. He says that something's going down, and they aren't keeping him in on it. Like they still want him to do these runs, but they no longer want him to know what they're about. When they'll happen. They're starting to treat him like an outsider. They've been depending more on Chris's brother, Abner's youngest. And a friend of his brother. Like they're setting them up to take over. Chris thinks he's being pushed out, but he doesn't know why, what's turned the old men against him."

A chill of fear sank into Roscoe. "That means they've turned on you too."

"Maybe. But I've always known I'm expendable. Just another . . . driver. A dime a dozen. I thought as long as I was up close and personal with Chris, I'd be safe. I just don't know anymore."

"William, you've got to get out of this. Let me help you."

William scoffed. "You kidding? Do you know what would happen to both of us if they knew you'd given that money to the feds? How much have you given them?"

"About two months' worth."

William frowned. "How are you getting by with losing that much?"

"The feds are replacing it."

"That's a sweet deal."

"It won't be if anyone finds out. Brother, you have got to get out of this. If they turn on Chris, they could take you both out."

"I can't believe Abner would let Buck take his own son out."

"Then you'd better believe it. They would both save their own skins at the expense of anyone in this town."

William paused, pulled out the pack of cigarettes, stared at the label, then slid them back in his pocket. "Can I get you to do me a favor?"

"Anything."

"Can Maybelle and the kids stay here when I'm making the runs? I don't want her to be alone . . . y'know, if something goes wrong."

"You know they can. Anytime." Roscoe took a deep breath and crossed his arms. "You think something is going wrong. Soon. Don't you?"

William pulled out the pack of smokes again, but this time he lit up. As the flame of the match cast harsh shadows over his face, he nodded. Slowly. Firmly.

CHAPTER TWENTY-FOUR

Pineville, Alabama, Present Day

"YOU'VE SIGNED MY death warrant. You know that, right?"

I sat down slowly on one of the bistro stools near the door. The man looked as if he hadn't slept in a month. His uniform hung on him, crushed and wrinkled. Even his hat looked abused, smeared with mud and grease. Dean's gun lay loosely on his lap, and his fingers played over the gun's surface as if it were a fidget spinner. I felt every muscle tense as I expected it to slide off and hit the floor.

I cleared my throat and found my voice. "Not my intent, no. Why do you think that?"

He laughed, a harsh, bitter sound. "Well. We know what they say about good intentions and the road to hell, don't we?"

"Dean—"

"Sergeant Sowers. You owe me that."

"Sergeant Sowers. Why do you think—"

He jerked straight, leaning forward, his shout blasting through the trailer, along with the strong scent of whiskey. "Because you stirred all this up again! Why couldn't you let them rest? They're dead! All of them! Let them go!"

The gun did a slip-and-slide on his lap, and I stiffened, bracing my back against the table. Words failed me, and I waited as he sank back onto the cushions of the recliner. His right hand closed on the pistol grip, steadying it.

"I'm sorry. I don't know—"

"Of course you don't. You couldn't. You weren't here. But you got Roscoe Carver killed. And you're going to get me killed."

"By asking questions."

He nodded. "Of course by asking questions." He let out an exasperated sigh. "These skeletons have been locked away for almost forty years. Everybody in town knows they're there. Knows about that grave at the Baptist church. Knows about the other graves at the end of the road. Knows about the lawyer who stuck his nose where it didn't belong, stirring up more than he bargained for."

Curiosity spiked through my fear. "More? What other graves?"

His eyes narrowed. "You really don't know, do you? My mother-in-law thinks you're just here about your grandmother. I didn't think anyone could be that naïve."

"Tell me about the more."

He glanced down at the gun again, his fingertips on the grip. "I didn't know you were really that much of an idiot. They think you know it all, that you're just dragging it out, leading Luinetti down a garden path, wanting all the glory for yourself. Your daddy made over, just waiting for the next 'special agent' to show up so you can expose it all. You'll never make them think otherwise. I certainly haven't been able to convince them. You've been hanging all over Miss Doris, picking her brain, asking about me. Looking for anyone who'd confirm what you know. All the while pretending it's just about that old man's slut. Who apparently didn't know that a Jewess doesn't just show up here with her bastard and expect her soldier boy to step up."

"No one warned her?"

Dean scoffed. "Of course he warned her. Told her to stay away. That he was already married. But no, she believed he was a man of honor, like he'd made her believe over there, that he'd do the right thing by their son, even though he already had two who were half grown. And they certainly weren't going to share their daddy's money with any half-breed."

"Inheritance."

He shook his head slowly, as if accepting my total ignorance. "Not just inheritance. Business. She . . . and that boy . . . would have interfered with business. Brought unwanted attention where it didn't need to be. They'd already killed a half dozen. More would be in the future. They didn't care. Some good people died. Wrong place, wrong time. Buried at the end of the road and forgotten, like nobody should be." Tears clouded his eyes.

A glimmer of light dawned. "That's where you go. When you disappear."

"You mean when I can't stand that witch of a wife anymore? That disappearing?"

"Yes."

"Did your darling Miss Doris tell you that I never wanted to be a cop? That I had bigger plans? I sure never meant to get caught up in all this."

"Why didn't you leave?"

He stared down at the gun. "I'd like to think because I'm not that kind of man. That I'm the one who's honorable. But I am. I'm a coward. I wanted to leave. Even had a scheme to get me the money to do it. But it tangled me up with Buck and Chris and the old man, and I wound up working for them, just like JoeLee did. Then it was too late. Folks who crossed them just disappeared. I didn't want to be one of them."

The sad weariness in his voice sounded like a man who had surrendered. Given up even trying to make things change. He looked up at me again. "Your daddy and that other man—"

"The investigator."

Dean paused and studied me. "Alex Trawler. He was Secret Service."

My breath caught and a deep cold settled into my bones. That information had not been in any of my father's records. My mother and I both assumed he'd been a private investigator with Daddy's law firm. If the Secret Service were involved . . .

"They would have disappeared too, if Roscoe's old man hadn't been such an early riser. Good old Ebenezer was already out, good farmer that he was, running the tractor in the fields behind their house before sunup. They didn't expect that. Had to improvise."

"Duplicating the first murder."

A quick nod. "That's what they told me. Since they couldn't bury them, they'd let Ebenezer take the blame. Those two weren't even strangled like she was. Shot. Chris's brother was still furious about Chris getting killed in the accident. Doc said he had to stop him from torturing them half to death. He shot 'em to stop it. Stripped off their belts to put around their necks. Doc fixed the autopsy reports, and JoeLee processed the scene. Made it all go away. Just like the others."

A deep numbness stilled me. What my father went through . . . Doc's involvement . . . how deep did all this go? "What happened to the paperwork on the case? The files my father had?"

"They burned 'em. Doc insisted we keep the autopsy reports. State stuff needed to get the bodies sent home. Everything else, they said they burned.

"Why are you telling me this now?"

He laughed, low and under his breath. "Because it doesn't matter anymore. We're dead. We're both dead." He pointed at me with the pistol. I flinched, and he laughed, a low bark. "You aren't afraid of death, are you? The way you're courting it, you should be old friends." He pointed at himself. "You and me. They were supposed to kill you when they shot Roscoe, but they missed. And they are not happy they had to bug out before the job was done. You can bet they're going to try again. And they're coming for me too, thanks to you and your big mouth. I'm just not going to give them the chance." His arm draped over one knee, his hand slack on the gun again. A tease, making me wonder if I could get to it in time.

"Sergeant, if they're coming after you, help me. We can stop them. Who are *they*?"

He shrugged. "Everybody. Anyone who is anyone in this town. All of them. Take your pick. And you can't stop them. I can't. You can't. They are the irresistible force in this town."

"But only one pulled the trigger on Roscoe."

"True. But that was probably just one of the hired hands. Like William, Roscoe's brother. Or me. That's who they use and lose. Bury deep in those woods. Secure the base. Protect the family. Save the money."

A fist thudded against the door, and a rough male shout echoed through the trailer. "Open the door!"

I didn't recognize the voice. Mike? No . . .

Dean obviously did. His face lost all color. "This is it then."

The pounding continued, rocking the trailer. I moved toward it, then froze as Dean sat straight, every muscle tensing as he pointed the gun at me. "Sit down!"

I put up my hands, an almost involuntary reaction as fear froze every muscle. "Sergeant–"

Whoever was outside tugged hard on the door, twisting the knob. The sharp jerks rattled the door in its frame.

He took off his hat and flung it at me. I caught it between my palms. "Oh, I'm not going to kill you. They'll take care of that. But I'm not going to let them take it out on me. No one gets that pleasure but me." He turned the gun suddenly, bracing the end of the barrel under his chin.

"No!" I screamed and lunged for him, but I couldn't reach him fast enough.

He pulled the trigger.

For the second time in one weekend, I watched forensic techs swarm over the scene of a man who'd been killed in my presence. For the second time in one weekend, I'd been tested for gunshot residue. I now felt grateful the first test had been negative; even more grateful that I hadn't gotten close enough to Dean to catch much blood spatter; forever grateful that the techs let me change from my church dress to a T-shirt and jeans and walk out with my purse and phone. They bagged the dress, of course, but I'd never wear it again, even if they returned it. One of the responding officers had ordered me away from the trailer but not to leave the premises. I'd taken one of the lawn chairs to the far side of the yard and perched under a thick-canopied beech tree. Mike arrived straight from the church, still in his suit, but he never approached me.

Doc and Maude arrived home right behind him, and after Doc conferred briefly with Mike, Doc and Maude went inside and took up a position at the kitchen window. Watching.

Whoever had been trying to get into the trailer had vanished. The pounding stopped with the gunshot. Despite the ringing in my ears, I had heard a loud string of sharp curses, which had sounded muffled and muddied. Then silence. By the time I'd gotten the door open, the man was gone.

Sitting out in the open, in the middle of the yard, was probably tempting fate, but at that moment I didn't much care. Sergeant Dean Sowers had laid a lot of disjointed, confusing information on me, and I felt blindsided. My brain seemed to slow to a snail's crawl as I tried to sort through where all of his details fit into what I already knew. Nothing seemed to congeal. But two of his statements had struck hard, and I desperately needed more definition on them. One was that Doc had falsified the autopsy reports. That detail had hit like a ton of bricks.

My doc. Doc Taylor. The man who'd welcomed me into Pineville, gave me a job, a place to live and to park my trailer. Who had known my identity and kept it a secret. The sweet man who'd loved his bride since she was a child and who played the town's Jimmy Stewart to her Donna Reed. Doc, who acted as a father/uncle/granddaddy to most of the town. Who often got up in the middle of the night to fill a prescription for a frantic parent with a sick child.

The man who had lied about how my father and his investigator had died. Why would he do that? Why would it matter how they were killed?

And that was the second stunner. My mother and I had long believed that the man who had died with Robert Spire had been an investigator from Daddy's law firm. Apparently not. Secret Service, according to Dean. Why the Secret Serv—

All thoughts again screeched to a halt as a small, dim light bulb went on in the back of my head. I was going to need backup. I shifted in the chair and pulled my cell phone from my back pocket. Darius answered on the first ring, almost as if he'd been expecting my call. His Sam Elliott voice—deep from the heart of Texas—resonated in my phone.

"Why, hello, darling Star. Why are you calling me? I thought you were deep under somewhere in the wilds of Alabama."

He could always make me smile, but I fought the urge. "Deep in Alabama, yes, although the 'under' part didn't work out so well."

"Why am I not surprised? Oh, that's right. You have all the poker face of a toddler at Walt Disney World."

He knew me too well. Darius and I had met during a cross-agency investigation when I was still with the Metro Nashville PD and he'd been on the local Joint Terrorism Task Force, on loan from the Secret Service to deal with the movement of counterfeit money to a sleeper cell. He still worked out of the Nashville field office.

"Thanks, bud."

He laughed. "So how can I help? 'Cause I know you're not calling just to chat."

"What do you know about counterfeiting operations in northern Alabama in the 1970s and 1980s?"

The silence that followed went on for a while. I watched the forensics team work while I listened to Darius tap on his keyboard.

"You know you could search these databases yourself," he muttered.

"Not what I'm about to ask of you."

The tapping stopped. "Oh?"

"Ever heard of a Secret Service agent named Alex Trawler as a part of one of those investigations?"

This spate of silence was followed by a somber question. "Where did you get that name?"

"From a guy who just shot himself in front of me."

More silence. "What in the world have you dug up, Star?"

I took a deep breath. "I think I'm in over my head, Darius. This goes way beyond what I was expecting. I'm finding things I've never seen in any of my father's files."

"You have if you've dug up Alex Trawler's name. Tell me everything."

I did. Darius and I had dated for a few months after the JTTF investigation had finished, so he knew all about my insane obsession to solve the three murders and reclaim Daisy Doe as my grandmother, Esther Spire. He understood it—every cop had a case or two they could never let go of—but he'd tried to stay out of it. Keep personal and professional separate. But eventually he'd listened to all the details. Now I told him about Mike Luinetti, Doc Taylor, Buck Dickson, what Roscoe had said at the cemetery, and Dean's ramblings before his suicide.

About Miss Doris and the anonymous request for a meeting at Panera the next day.

"Are you going?"

"If Mike doesn't arrest me."

"I'm a little surprised he hasn't."

"Thanks."

"Well, you have been found beside two dead bodies."

"I didn't help either of them get that way."

"No witnesses."

"Any ideas, assuming I can stay out of jail?"

"Come back to Nashville before you get killed?"

"Other than that."

Darius paused. "Let me see what I can find out about what Alex was up to down there with your father. I doubt it was official business, but it might have been the start of some. Maybe just a conversation or two as a favor. But I'd be surprised if there's not another autopsy report somewhere. I can't believe they'd accept the word of the local country doctor."

"How did you know Alex Trawler's name?"

Mike had been talking to the first responders. Now he looked at me, frowning. He headed my way.

Darius's voice was even and quiet. "You know the name of every Metro Nashville cop who ever died in the line of duty?"

I got his point. "Like the back of my hand."

"Uh-huh. Keep your head down, girl. I don't want to be adding you to my list."

"Will do my best." I ended the call as Mike closed the distance.

He pointed at my phone. "Who were you talking to?"

"A friend at the Secret Service." I wasn't sure what Mike expected me to say, but that obviously wasn't it.

His eyes widened. "Are you serious?"

When I nodded, he asked why. I told him everything that Dean had said, as much as I could remember. I would make notes later, see if anything else popped out of my memory. "It all happened quickly, and I was primarily focused on that gun."

"If he'd really wanted you dead, you couldn't have exactly dodged it. Not in that space."

"No. I guess I was hoping for a chance to take it away from him. Did all of that make sense to you?"

"We're missing too many pieces." He looked down at me through narrowed eyes. "But he obviously thought it made sense to you."

I put up my right hand, as if swearing in court. "Honest on a stack, Mike. I didn't understand half of it. I wanted to press him, but I was afraid he'd lose it and shoot me."

"He probably would have. Did your friend at the Secret Service know Alex Trawler?"

My eyebrows arched as I waited for him to do the math. He didn't. He waited. I finally cleared my throat. "My friend Darius was born in 1986."

"Oh." Mike paused a moment as he did a different kind of math. "So this means you like younger men?"

"You already knew that part."

The fleeting grin that flashed across his face told me we were all right, even if we needed to keep it totally professional right now. I got it. So did he.

He cleared his throat. "I need you to come down to the station and make a formal statement. On both incidents.

"I will. How about tomorrow afternoon?" He scowled, and I went on. "Obviously I can't stay here tonight. I'll go to Gran's in Birmingham, come back late tomorrow."

He didn't like it, but he finally nodded. "You'll probably be safer down there anyway. Stay in touch. Let me know if your friend turns up anything."

"I will."

"Or if anyone else shoots at you."

CHAPTER TWENTY-FIVE

Birmingham, Alabama, 1983

"THANK GOD FOR an abundance of Waffle Houses."

Alex and Bobby laughed, and Alex motioned to the server for more coffee. Roscoe shook his head. *That boy must have a bladder the size of a watermelon*, he thought. Every time they met, the young agent downed at least ten or twelve cups and always got one to go. The servers didn't seem to mind. Alex, even taller and more athletic looking than Bobby, had a shock of floppy blond hair, which made him look like Robert Redford, and a baritone voice as smooth as butter. And no wedding ring.

This was their fifth Waffle House, their preferred venue because of a proximity to a major highway and a lack of local customers in the middle of the afternoon. As usual, Alex had passed Roscoe an envelope of cash and Roscoe had signed the receipt for it. They'd settled in for a late lunch, with Alex taking notes on Roscoe's latest information.

Alex flipped back a page in his notebook to check something. "So William thinks that a major shipment is coming."

Roscoe nodded. "A mix of counterfeit and dirty money, with some other items they still bootleg, maybe stolen goods. They've been moving the cash in small fireproof cases, nothing more than the trunk and axles of a Crown Vic can handle. Last week, Chris asked William if he could handle a Class 8 truck, a big rig. Apparently a major shift in the upper management is coming up on the Tennessee end of this, and it's making Buck nervous. A new generation is taking over, and his relationship with the younger boys isn't as secure as with their daddies. He wants to move some major merchandise, then lay low for a bit till the dust settles. See who he needs to court and who to dump."

"Early next year?"

"That's what seems to be in the works. The fly in the ointment is that most of this is coming from Chris, who may be on the way out as well. Buck is not happy with him, and he and Abner are fighting a lot over the Pineville runs. Abner's ready for his younger son to move into Buck's business, and Buck is growling about all of them getting too greedy. So Chris's information may not be completely accurate. And scuttlebutt in the ranks is that the turnover up north is due to information being leaked to the feds."

Alex and Bobby remained silent a moment. Bobby cleared his throat. "But they think the information is coming from the Tennessee crowd."

"Oh, yeah. If they thought it was from down here, there would have already been a housecleaning that would make the Jonestown massacre look like a stroll in the woods. They have no loyalty to Buck or any of his guys. They're just a conduit. A means to an end. Easily replaced."

Bobby shifted uncomfortably. "Anytime you want to cool this off—"

Roscoe twisted to look at the man next to him more directly. "Say that again, Lieutenant."

Bobby's mouth tightened in a part grimace, part grin. "Point taken, Sergeant."

"Look, my town has its problems, but it's home to a lot of good folks. If this is not dug out at the roots, it'll bring the whole place down. Hurt a lot of good people, innocent folks who have no clue what their town officials have been up to. We gotta do something."

Alex looked up from his notebook. "How's William taking you working with us?"

Roscoe straightened in the booth again. "Antsy. But he's been that way ever since he started running with Chris. And since it started looking like Chris was getting pushed aside. His baby brother has taken over many of the runs with a new driver. Chris and William are doing more of the distribution into Birmingham, Montgomery, points south. Pay's not as good. And old JoeLee is up for reelection in a couple years, and there's already talk that he's too old to run again. Buck needs to consolidate his organizational contacts before too much else changes."

"How old is Wilkes?" Bobby asked.

"Pushing seventy. He's been sheriff for almost forty years."

Bobby crushed a napkin in his fist. "Was sheriff when my mother was killed."

Alex glanced at the younger man. "Bobby, is this going to be a problem?"

"No." Bobby's voice turned crisp. "But I don't want us to forget why I dug back into this in the first place. I don't want her to get shoved aside because we stumbled over something bigger."

"It won't." Roscoe was a bit surprised at the sharpness in his own tone. "That murder changed my world. I sought you out, remember?"

"I do, but–"

"What if they're tied together?"

Both men stared at Alex, who calmly downed about half his cup of coffee.

"How?" Bobby asked.

Alex set down the cup and focused on Roscoe. "Look, Chris is your central figure in all this, right? He's the source of William's information. He's the older son of the Pineville connection to Buck Dickson. And he was the one you heard talking in the woods that day with his father about the murder. Right?"

Roscoe swallowed hard. He'd almost forgotten about that conversation. "Right."

"So what if Esther Spire's murder wasn't about who she was but what she might uncover? Remember, Bobby, if we're putting all the pieces together correctly, then Chris is your half brother. What if Esther's murder had less to do with shame or inheritance than business? Greed?"

Bobby looked at Roscoe, who nodded. "He has a point, Bobby. These critters would definitely eat their own young for more money. So what's next?"

"Keep the money exchange going," Alex said. "And eyes and ears open about that shipment. You keep us informed. We'll do the rest."

CHAPTER TWENTY-SIX

Birmingham, Alabama, Present Day

BELLE IS HARD to miss. Even in an area fond of and full of classic cars, a 1966 GMC Carryall stands out. Especially a bright-blue-and-white one that sounds like a Sherman tank on the move. When I first started working as a PI, one of my friends still on the police force suggested I might trade her for something a little quieter and nondescript. With a 305 V6, a subtle entrance was nigh onto impossible.

Maybe. Someday. But I could live in her if I needed to, and I hadn't really needed to sneak around much, at least so far. But I did wish that I could be a little less obtrusive when I left Gran's Monday afternoon and headed for The Summit. I took reasonable precautions to make sure I wasn't followed, but anyone in pursuit would have to be blind to miss me on a road, even on Highway 280's normal crush of traffic. I turned into the lower part of The Summit's parking area, hoping all threats had remained behind in Pineville.

But I wasn't the only obvious vehicle around. A bright-red 1992 Thunderbird already sat in the parking lot, announcing who my secretive meeting would be with.

Roscoe's kin.

Imajean Carver Thompson, as elegant as always, sat at a booth in the rear corner of the restaurant, reading a paperback and nibbling on a pastry. Steam rose from a cup of coffee near the plate. Her hair was a neat cap of blonde-tipped curls that nestled in rows against her head. Two loops of a gold necklace accented her soft red shirt, and matching bracelets bumped the coffee cup as she reached to take a sip. Her son, Charles, occupied a two-person table a few yards away from his mother, focused on a computer, his fingers blazing away over the keyboard. The very opposite of his mother, he sported jeans, a University of Alabama at Birmingham T-shirt, a neat goatee, and stylish thick-rimmed glasses.

I bought a chai tea and made my way toward Imajean's booth, approaching slowly. As I neared the booth, Imajean set the book aside and motioned for me to come closer. As I did, she smiled, a sad expression that didn't quite make it to her eyes, which were puffy and shot full of red streaks.

"I won't bite. I promise." She gestured toward the seat opposite her. "I've heard you had quite the weekend."

"Yes ma'am." I sat, pushing my cup of chai closer to the wall. Imajean may have been a generation behind Miss Doris, but I had the same respect and admiration for her. Maybe more so. "But not as bad as yours."

"No. But you do know what it's like to lose a father." Her gaze stayed on me, watching every muscle in my face.

"Yes ma'am. Although I was just a kid."

"Like my cousin, Jeshua. When he was only a child, he lost his father. And a baby brother. I lost my mother at the same time."

Not what I expected her to say, and my eyes widened.

She nodded, as if confirming something to herself. "You came down here to investigate your grandmother's death. Your daddy's. You thought it might be about race or just how outsiders were treated in the Jim Crow South."

"I suspected. I had nothing that proved anything."

"You had no idea you were about to beat a hornet's nest with a stick."

"I knew it could be dangerous, but I thought that danger would be aimed at me, like it was my father. I thought your father would just be a source of information."

"That's because you had no idea how many other people died that week. The week your father and that other man died. It wasn't just them. That's why I wanted to talk to you. In private. Away from all that.

To let you know what you're really in for. You see, they also beat that hornet's nest, and my father handed them the stick."

Her metaphor had started to confuse me. "I'm sorry, but I don't—"

She held up a hand to stop me. "May I still call you Star?"

"Of course."

She took a long deep breath. "Star, my family has lived with a web of secrets for a long time. Decades. We just got involved because it was so hard for black vets to find work after they got home from Vietnam. My uncle, William, couldn't find anything. They wound up living with us until Uncle William started driving for some bootleggers. That's what pulled us into this. Daddy worked the farm for a bit, with my grandfather, but then went to work in a repair shop. Worked his way up to owning his own store right there in Pineville, on the square. Everybody respected him. But they eventually pulled him into it too. Then it all came crashing down. That week."

"What happened?"

She remained silent a few moments, still studying my face. Then she reached down beside her and set an ancient shoebox on the table. "This," she said softly, "is what they trashed our house looking for. There are two others just like it. Almost from the time your grandmother died, my father kept notes. Anything he could remember about her, about how she died, anything his father told him, letters he exchanged with your father, they are all in these boxes."

She placed a hand flat on the top of the box. "He kept them hidden for all these years. My mother didn't even know about them. I only found out about them last year when we moved him in with us, after his previous stroke. When I found out, I made him put them in a safe-deposit box. The other two are still there, along with some other things he had squirreled away. I don't dare give you all of it at once."

"I don't blame you."

We sat in silence a few moments, both of us staring at the box. Finally, she let out a sigh. "No. I haven't read them." She smiled. "I know you're dying to ask. You see, unlike you, I already know too much, and I have no desire to know any more. And I hope to God my family is finished with this. That it's finally over for us." She slid the box toward me.

I accepted the box and placed it on the seat beside me. "Can you tell me about the hornet's nest?"

She pursed her lips a moment. "Not really. I don't know enough details. I heard rumors, gossip, things I overheard when Daddy and Uncle William would talk. Mostly I remember people who died. Enough that it almost took the town apart. Daddy sent Aunt Maybelle—that's Uncle William's wife—and us kids to live with his aunt here in Birmingham. To get us out of it."

"Where's Maybelle now?"

Imajean paused. She took a sip of coffee. "She's in hiding. She doesn't know anything. She insists that William never talked to her about anything. To protect her. He mostly talked to Daddy."

"Where are you staying?"

She glanced briefly at her son. "Charles and I both work down here. He already has an apartment, and I'm staying with him for now. We really kept the house in Pineville for Daddy. Once the police release it, we'll probably clean it out and put it on the market."

"So you're safe."

"As we'll ever be. Until this is over."

Realization dawned, and I leaned back against the booth. "You want revenge."

One elegant eyebrow arched. "Don't you? You don't want to only solve the puzzle. You want to expose all the cockroaches to the light. So do I. Revenge? Absolutely. But this has been going on for more than sixty years. Too many people have died. Too many others walk in abject terror each and every day, looking over their shoulders, afraid of making the wrong move. That's why Dean Sowers shot himself. He'd had enough of the fear. And you are probably the one person with enough guts, information, and determination to end this. Once and for all."

"No pressure."

Imajean gave a small laugh. She pulled a business card out of her purse and handed it to me. "My cell phone is on the back. When you make it through the first box, we'll meet again."

"Be careful. Apparently most people who meet with me about this wind up dead."

She slipped out of the booth and stood up, adjusting the shoulder strap of her purse. "You may have realized by now that I am not most people."

I nodded. "I can see that. And I'm sorry about your father."

Imajean paused and inhaled deeply, as if steadying herself. "Thank you. But we almost lost Daddy three times in the last two years. He coded twice. The last time, we made our peace and said our goodbyes. He loved Jesus and his family, in that order. It hurts, and we'll miss him for a long time. But I'm grateful it was quick. His funeral will be at the AME Zion in Pineville. Not sure when yet. Whenever they release him. You'll be welcome if you want to attend."

"Thank you."

She touched my shoulder in an affectionate farewell and headed toward the door. Charles met her there and opened it for her. I watched as they headed away in the Thunderbird, and I prayed fiercely that they would survive what was to come. They deserved it.

I returned to Gran's and took my first look at the papers in the box as Gran peered over my shoulder. Some of the first writings were notes in a childish handwriting, which matured as the dates advanced from 1954. This was going to take some time.

An impatient text from Mike asked when I'd be back to make my statement, and I reluctantly put the box into Gran's safe. One of my grandfather's "tinker around the house" projects, the fireproof box was bolted to the wall of her bedroom closet. It would be secure there. Plus, I didn't want it anywhere near Pineville.

Disappointed, Gran made me promise that I'd come back as soon as possible so we could go through it. I made her promise not to mention the box to anyone, even in passing.

I packed up the notes I'd made the night before and headed to Pineville and the police department. I found myself unexpectedly nervous and a little fidgety. For all of our flirting and randy banter, I'd never seen where Mike worked or lived. The city police department operated out of the first floor of the courthouse. Since the county seat had split, a larger, more modern courthouse had been built in another city, and many of the normal county functions had moved there. Other offices and functions had merely split. Thus the Pineville courthouse had a lot of empty offices. Courtrooms and judges' chambers occupied the third floor, along with two jury rooms and a lounge for the bailiffs. The second floor held one version of the county clerk's office, along with two ADAs, and a slew of conference rooms, many of which were never used. The elected DA and sheriff were located in the other courthouse.

The city management of Pineville had moved into the first floor. The police department was across an atrium lobby from the mayor's office, which was behind a wall of oversized glass, with small white bistro tables and chairs for anyone who had to wait. Ellis Patton's name was emblazoned in an arch across the wall of glass like the logo of a major retailer, including his tagline—"A man of the people for the people"—and office hours. One thing I could say about Mr. Ellis Patton—he certainly knew how to market and brand himself.

The police department, on the other hand, was a solid block wall with two openings: a small plexiglass window, probably bulletproof, where visitors signed in and a solid metal door with a numeric keypad and a buzzer lock.

I signed in, receiving a heavy-lidded and wary look from the sergeant behind the glass, a man who looked as if he'd been with the department since the 1600s. He sounded like he'd smoked since then as well. "Step to the door. Wait for the buzz." He coughed.

I did and found myself in a small anteroom. More block walls, another door with a keypad entry, two hard plastic chairs, and a silk ficus that was limp and covered in dust. I stood. Mike pushed open the inner door a few moments later and motioned for me to follow him.

As I passed by him, his hand closed gently on my elbow, and he tilted his head toward me. "How are you holding up? Did you sleep?"

I kept my reply soft as well. "Feeling safe at Gran's helped. And ibuprofen. I missed talking this over with you."

"Soon. I promise." His eyes gleamed as he led me through a cubicle farm of ten offices or so, most of them occupied by officers I'd spotted on the streets or at the crime scenes. On the far wall, the police chief's office was clearly marked, and I could see a relatively neat desk and computer behind the glass-windowed door. Along the wall next to it was a line of interrogation rooms. Mike opened the door to the one closest to his office and gave my arm a firm squeeze before letting go.

More block walls waited inside, although these were painted a pale gray. A square table and four chairs sat in the middle. Two video cameras were mounted up close to the ceiling in opposing corners. I sat facing the door and pulled my notes from my purse, spreading them flat on the table.

Mike sat opposite me and cleared his throat. He spoke in a clear, professional tone. "For the record, this interview will be recorded. Please state your full name, birthdate, and occupation."

"Star Renee Cavanaugh. January 23, 1981. Private investigator."

"Please describe, in as much detail as you remember, the events surrounding the murder of Roscoe Carver at Pine Grove Baptist Cemetery last Friday."

I glanced at the notes, then started with the items I had loaded into Belle for the trip to the grave. I gave the time of my arrival, what I'd done, and how Roscoe had scared the living daylights out of me by sneaking up behind me. I relayed what we'd talked about, as close to verbatim as I could. I described his behavior, including the profuse sweating and his coughing, my concern over his health.

Mike did his best to maintain a stoic expression, but when I expressed concern over Roscoe's health, he broke. His eyes widened, and his lips became a thin line.

I paused. "What is it, Mike?"

He hesitated. We both knew he shouldn't share anything with me, and he obviously wrestled with that. Finally, he rolled his shoulders back and sat straighter in the chair. "Do you remember how there wasn't a lot of blood at the scene? On Roscoe?"

I scowled, thinking back, going over the scene in my head. The windshield had been shattered. There was the neat, round hole in his chest

. . . *neat.* No ooze or spatter of any kind. In his sternum, but too high. A sudden dread settled in my chest. Not the relief I should feel at the news, but complete, nauseating dread. My head felt light, dizzy. I braced my hands on the table to steady them. "No . . ."

Mike nodded. "We got the preliminary coroner's report this morning. The bullet didn't kill him. Roscoe was already dead when he was shot. Heart failure."

"So even if we found out who shot him . . ."

"It's not murder. We might charge him with attempted murder, but a good lawyer would have a field day with this."

"I don't suppose you can keep this under wraps?"

He smirked and pointed at the cameras "We aren't exactly in this alone. Besides, in this state, coroners' findings and autopsy reports are public record. We can try for a while, but as soon as it's filed . . ."

". . . everyone will know."

"And I have two dead bodies and one big mystery."

I leaned forward and rested my arms on the table. "You may have more bodies than that. But there's no statute of limitation on murder in Alabama."

His eyes narrowed. "Talk to me."

CHAPTER TWENTY-SEVEN

Pineville, Alabama, 1983

ROSCOE LOOKED OVER both sets of his ledgers, annoyed by how much they made him feel like a criminal. Both represented his income from the shop, but one included the money that the organization was laundering through his accounts. The other tracked how much of that money had been exchanged with Alex and Bobby. He knew all too well that Alex was also keeping record of it, but at this point, Roscoe trusted no one, not even his own brother.

He'd caught William in one too many lies. Lies of omission as well as commission, as his preacher would say. *Scripture says a lie is a lie is a lie, no matter the intent behind it.* Roscoe hated lies . . . and liars. He hated that this whole operation had turned him into one as well, just as it had William. His little brother had always been a wild child, defiant, rebellious. But never a liar. Not until this.

William felt trapped. For a long time, Roscoe had not understood that sentiment. They had people in Birmingham, Nashville, Cleveland, Detroit. They would have helped William, Maybelle, and the kids get a fresh start. Just pick up and go. But no, William had refused.

Now Roscoe understood. It wasn't about William and his family. It was everyone he cared about.

The bell over the front door of the shop sounded, echoing off the metal surfaces of the washers, dryers, and refrigerators in the showroom.

"I'll be right with you!" Roscoe closed the ledgers and slid them into a bottom drawer of the desk. He locked it, then pocketed the key as he stood up. And froze.

The old man stood in the door of his office. Abner himself. "Hello, Roscoe."

Roscoe swallowed hard. "Good afternoon, sir." According to William, Abner was Buck Dickson's right-hand man and best friend. Of course, Buck Dickson reported only to the devil.

"We need to talk." He nodded at Roscoe's desk chair. "Have a seat." He glanced around, then pulled another chair close to the desk and sat.

Roscoe eased back down. The chair creaked as he shifted it toward his visitor. "Is something wrong?"

"I'm afraid so, my friend." The old man leaned back and crossed his arms. His spindly frame seemed to go on forever. Standing, he towered over almost all the men in town, but his lean look made him look frail, especially as he got older. Roscoe, however, knew better. He'd seen Abner lift his bulky older son, Chris, right off his feet.

"How can I help?"

The old man's eyebrows arched. "By following instructions, for starters. I've been having a few chats with my wife about you."

"Oh?" Such a sentence never boded well for a black man in the South. Roscoe's blood chilled, and his throat tightened.

He gave a dismissive sniff. "Oh, nothing like that. You know she's head teller over at the bank."

Roscoe found his voice. "I've heard as such."

"So she tells me you've never opened an account with us."

So much for bank privacy. "I just haven't had the opportunity. The store has been pretty busy lately. And the money is going through the Carterton bank just fine."

"That just means you've been lucky. Sooner or later one of those tellers will check the wrong bill and alert Isaiah. That would create a situation I don't want to have to clean up. You understand?"

"Yes sir."

"Good." He uncrossed his arms and braced his hands on his thighs. "So I can expect Janice to bring me good news soon."

"Does your wife know about all your businesses?"

The old man stiffened. "A husband and wife should not have secrets. But what business of that is yours?"

"So she knows about the girl with the daisy?"

Abner's eyes narrowed to mere slits. "You promised me you had forgotten all about that."

"Hard to forget something that almost got my daddy lynched."

"Ebenezer is a good man. I wouldn't have let that happened."

"Despite what that would have meant for Chris?"

"It wasn't—" The old man jerked to his feet and slung the chair away from him so hard it slammed into the wall behind Roscoe. He clenched his fists and leaned over Roscoe, their faces close enough that Roscoe could smell cabbage and ham on the old man's breath. Spit hit Roscoe's cheeks with the next sentence.

"Don't test me, boy." He straightened, but fury reddened his cheeks. "I'm the one who makes life pleasant and comfortable for everyone in this town. I'm the one who makes sure nothing gets burned and no one gets lynched. No one's little daughter gets taken. No one's wife gets hurt. You understand me? Everyone makes money, and no one gets hurt. We all work together, but I make it happen. Me. Without me, it all falls apart. Don't ever forget that. And you get that account open. Today."

He stalked from the office, but Roscoe didn't breathe until he heard the bell on the front door. When he did, one word came out on a slow exhale of air.

"Imajean."

CHAPTER TWENTY-EIGHT

Pineville, Alabama, Present Day

MIKE WANTED ME to stay in Birmingham for a few days, but he really couldn't stop me from talking to people in Pineville, as long as I didn't interfere with his investigation into Roscoe's shooting or his work to close the books on Dean's suicide. I knew people would still blame me for both, at least for now. It would take a bit for the autopsy reports to make their way into public knowledge. I especially needed to stay away from Miss Doris, at least temporarily. Mike had mentioned that Charlotte had moved back in with her parents and would probably stay there until Dean's funeral. Possibly longer. That alone would probably put Miss Doris in an exceptionally foul mood.

I needed to talk to Doc, but oddly, I didn't feel ready to discuss his role in this. My gut told me I needed to know more answers to the questions I had before I approached him. While my instinct on cases was not infallible—and in this case, it was certainly clouded—I still trusted it. If it said wait, I'd wait.

I did stop by the drugstore to officially turn in my resignation. He was alone when I went in. Late afternoon was always a quiet time, and he was in the back, making up a few prescriptions. He looked up when I entered, motioning me on back. "Afternoon, Star. How can I help you?"

"I'm sorry about the mess in your back yard."

He shrugged. "No worries, girl. Fuel for the feud."

I fought a smile. "Jake's upset."

He grinned at me over the top of his reading glasses. "When is he ever not?"

"Mike said it would be a couple more days. He also said he'd help me with hiring a cleanup crew."

Pills rattled as he poured them into a counting tray. "It's all good."

"Including me not coming back to work here at all?"

He looked over the glasses again, his eyes gleaming with amusement. "Star. I've already placed another advertisement."

"I could probably help in a pinch till you hire someone."

He shook his head, his mouth moving silently as he counted pills. I waited until he was finished. He capped the bottle. "That's a good offer. You were a great server. But seriously, I have it covered." He dropped the bottle into a bag and pulled the label off the printer, stapling it all together. He dropped it into one of the customer bins, then stepped from behind the counter. He took his glasses off and put them in his pocket. "So. This is not about you filling in, is it?"

"I think we need to talk. At length. Now is just not a good time."

"I figured as much. Sit." He gestured to one of the soda fountain tables near the back of the store. As usual he sat with his legs stretched out in front of him. "You have carried these three murders as a burden for a long time. Not only as a cop but as a daughter and granddaughter. I know you want to solve them. Just remember that not everyone was involved. Lots of innocent folks could get hurt. Please tread carefully."

"I will do my best."

The front door opened, and a woman with three children came in. Doc waved at them, then stood. "You're right. Not a good time. But let me know when you can, and we'll set a time."

"Sounds good."

"And tell Mike to watch his back."

My mouth dropped, but before I could say anything else, he turned and greeted the new arrivals by name. I got up and stumbled outside. I leaned hard against Belle. Was that a threat? Or a warning about a threat?

I watched Doc through the windows of the drugstore. As always, he was the grandfather helping out the younger generation, recommending an over-the-counter drug. I considered going back in and demanding an explanation, the way I would have as a cop. But unlike a cop, I had no authority, no backing of law enforcement peers. Not even Mike would stand with me if I stepped over the line. And in the back of my head, I knew that was what my father had done. He'd gone straight at it.

So what next? I walked around Belle and got in. I called Mike to tell him what Doc had said. He accepted it as a given. He was, after all, the top cop in town. But he didn't seem otherwise too concerned. So be it. I tried not to worry, and I tried to ignore the urge to talk to him at length, just to hear his voice. Instead, I ended the call and reached for the key, then paused as I glanced around the square. There might just be one other place in town where I'd still be welcome.

I got out, locked Belle, and strolled over to the Pineville Musuem and Historically Archives. I opened the door, the bell over it dinged, and by the time I'd closed it, Claudia Hall was at my side.

"Oh, Miss Star!" She threw her arms around me and hugged me as tightly as a long-lost grandmother might. "We hoped you would stop by. We are so sorry!"

I stared at her. "For what?"

Betsy joined us, wiping her hands on the ever-present bibbed apron. "We were out of town this weekend. We just heard about Roscoe and Dean. Miss Doris was in here telling us all about it."

Claudia bobbed her head. "We always go out of town on Decoration Sunday. We can't stand all that. Too much grief. Too much celebration of grief. Too much greasy food for our constitutions. All that horrid fried chicken and nasty potato salad. And our sisters are Episcopalian, so we go visit them."

I wasn't sure what being Episcopalian had to do with not celebrating Decoration Sunday, but I stored that for later. "But why are you apologizing?"

Betsy leaned in closer, her voice dropping conspiratorially. "Because we had no idea you were Bobby Spire's daughter."

Claudia grabbed my arm. "Come with us."

I let them take the lead because, to be honest, I was still stunned and sputtering. "Wait. You . . . the two of you . . . know . . . knew . . ."

Betsy patted my other arm as they turned me down the middle aisle. "Oh, darling, we know everything there is to know about Pineville. Including where a lot of the bodies are buried."

"Literally," Claudia proclaimed.

"We thrive on people thinking we're the ditsy biddies in the old house off the square," Betsy said. "They think we're crazy, so they say anything and everything in front of us."

We took a right, then another left.

"You know, like that movie, *What the Deaf-Mute Heard*."

"The movie was *What the Deaf Man Heard*, Claudia. *Deaf-Mute* was the book."

"Oh right, by Mr. Gearino." Claudia looked up at me as we entered a storage room at the back. "Probably out of print by now. It's old."

"Quite implausible as a plot."

"But it works pretty well when they think you're old and crazy."

In front of us was a large vault. The thick metal door stood partially ajar, and through the opening I could see a wall lined with safe-deposit boxes. On the front, a small bronze plaque announced that it had been built by the Diebold Safe and Lock Company of Canton, Ohio. One surprise after another.

"Wait. The dime store had a vault?"

Claudia let go of me and pushed the vault door farther open. "This wasn't always a dime store, dear. In the late eighteen hundreds it was a bank. It went bust in the Panic of 1893. Empty for a while, then . . ." She looked at Betsy.

"Our grandfather bought the building in 1915. Our family ran it as a general store for a bit, then Elmore's took it over in the late fifties. Was that for more than twenty years."

"Closed a few years ago."

"Now, Claudia, 1972 was not 'a few years ago.'"

"Right, I forget."

Betsy pushed her wire-rimmed glasses up on her nose and peered at me. "The city rented it for a while. Everything was growing like crazy, and the sheriff's department was running out of room in their old building. So the sheriff's department used it a while for their archives."

Claudia gestured toward the front of the building. "If you look closely, you can see the marks where they boarded up the front display window. The archive clerk said it made her feel too vulnerable to sit where everyone could see her."

Betsy snorted. "That woman had more problems than a little paranoia."

"Now, Sister. Play nice."

"Humph. Anyway, then the big split in the county came. They built a big new building for the sheriff on the other side of the county and a new building for the archives out on the Pell City Highway. The newly formed Pineville PD moved into the courthouse. So this place has been empty ever since. There was talk of turning it into an art gallery, like they did that Woolworth's up in Asheville, but this is not a town that would support something like that. So . . . empty."

"Sort of empty."

Betsy grinned at her sister.

I looked from one to the other. I could see the crazy-biddies act came naturally to them. "Meaning?" I asked.

Claudia pointed at the wall of safe-deposit boxes. "Like Betsy said, that clerk had issues. Lazy was one of them. She hated to file stuff, and it would just pile up all over the place. JoeLee would come in and yell about organization, and she'd start shoving stuff into the empty safe-deposit boxes. She decided they made great storage, and she wouldn't have to deal with filing anything. No one knew. Then JoeLee up and fired her one day, for reasons only known to JoeLee."

"Well, you know he had that little piece on the side, and he put her in here."

"Sister! Shame on you."

"Oh, Claudia, the man was a sleazeball."

"True, but we still don't have to gossip about it. I'm sure he took advantage of her."

I could also see why the entire town adored these two. I cleared my throat. "Um, the first clerk?"

Betsy pointed at me. "Right."

Claudia grinned. "When she left, she hid all the box keys. Told them they'd never existed, since the bank had been closed for almost a century and that the boxes were empty anyway."

"No one dared tell JoeLee any different—everyone was terrified of him—so when they moved, all that stuff stayed behind. With them splitting up everything between here and there and the archives out on Pell City Highway, no one noticed they didn't have all that they should have."

I felt a touch of excitement in my gut. "Have you found the keys?"

Their faces fell a bit. Betsy sniffed. "Not exactly."

Claudia picked up the tale. "We found her. The fired clerk. She's in upstate New York somewhere, living with a granddaughter, I think. We're waiting on a call back."

*

As a cop, I sometimes worked twenty-four to thirty-six hours straight to resolve a case. Every lead was urgent, not to be ignored. But with five people dead as a result of whatever it was I was investigating at this point, I had to pay closer attention to the people I was bringing into the case. And I had become convinced that I was no longer trying to solve only three murders. Whatever had led up to those deaths was starting to expand into something involving most of the town.

So when Betsy suggested it might raise too much suspicion for us to work throughout the night, I had to agree. They were as eager to dig in as I was, but they left the museum every day at five on the dot—because Miss Snopes, don't ya know—and people would notice if they burned the midnight oil. I had to trust that boxes that had been secure for more than a hundred years and unopened since the mid-seventies weren't going anywhere overnight, especially without the keys. Betsy promised to try the clerk again from their home.

Since they came and went through a back entrance, they let me out the front and locked the door. I walked slowly toward Belle, glancing back occasionally to make sure all the lights went out. I watched until their twenty-year-old Lincoln Marquis eased out the back lot and turned toward their home. Then I unlocked Belle and slid in. As I let some of the hot air inside dissipate, I punched a number on my speed dial.

I reached to close Belle's door, which shuddered to a halt as a hand blocked it and shoved the door back open. I yelped and twisted in my seat. Ellis Patton blocked the opening, with one arm on the door and the other on the frame.

"Star."

I caught my breath. "Mr. Mayor." I laid my phone on the dash.

"You've created quite an uproar in my town."

I tried to smile. "Not my intent—"

"Don't lie." His eyes were hard, his face impassive. He leaned closer, his body filling the space. His "man of the people" demeanor vanished. "It dishonors both of us."

I waited. This was obviously his conversation. After a moment, he leaned back and let go of the frame, but one hand remained on the door.

"You need to keep a few facts in mind, Star. Most of what you're investigating took place outside the city limits. Except for Sowers's suicide, Michael Luinetti has no authority to look into any of it. He's overstepping his bounds. The city council and I don't like it."

"Have you mentioned this to him?"

"I will be doing so tonight. And reminding him that we are the ones who hired him."

"That means the county sheriff would have to take over."

"Correct. If there's, in fact, anything to take over. Roscoe Carver died of a heart attack. Dean Sowers shot himself. But you can be sure the sheriff's office will have no interest in cooperating with an outside investigator."

"I would have thought you, of all people, would have wanted this to stay within the town's control."

He ground his teeth so hard the muscles in his jaw jerked and bounced. "You're an outsider. You have no idea what's important to this town. We value peace, quiet, and a certain contentment. Something you have no clues about. Just like—" He broke off.

"Just like my father?"

"And his mother."

We stared at each other in silence. Finally, I asked. "Anything else, Your Honor?"

"Yes. Get that monstrosity out of Taylor's yard. If you don't have it gone by this weekend, we'll pass an ordinance to outlaw it. Then we'll tow it to the junkyard and have it crushed to a block of solid metal."

"As soon as Mike releases it. Maybe you can talk to him about that as well."

"You can bet on it."

With that he stepped back and slammed the door. I watched him in the rearview as he marched away. Down the block, he got into his old pickup. I could see a second person in the truck, and if the shadow ballet that played out between them was an indication, they were not happy with each other. His grandson? Dandridge? Miss Doris had implied Dan was supposedly the Patton heir apparent. After a moment, Ellis started the truck and it roared out of the square.

I picked up the phone. "You get all that?"

"Nice to know I'm so valued in this town." Mike Luinetti's voice dripped with wry irony.

"He's probably headed your way now."

"No doubt. I'm glad I haven't had supper yet. So why did you really call?"

I filled him in on what I'd heard from Claudia and Betsy Hall. "They think they're invincible. But after my little chat with His Honor, I'm not convinced anyone is."

"Agreed. I'll keep an eye out. What time will you be back tomorrow?"

"They'll open at their usual time, around ten. I'll be there around then."

"Any chance you can drive something a little less obvious?"

I had to grin. "Possibly." In the background of the call, I could hear the muffler of Ellis Patton's old truck. "You have company."

"Right. Star?"

"I'll be careful. Promise." I hesitated. "You do the same. Please? I can't handle anyone else getting hurt because of me. Especially you."

After a moment of silence, he said quietly, "I've got your six. That's not going to change."

I heard a banging in the background, and he ended the call. I phoned Gran to let her know I was on the way home. When I got there, she had supper waiting. Fried chicken and potato salad.

I hugged her tighter than I had in a long time.

CHAPTER TWENTY-NINE

Pineville, Alabama, 1984

"HE THREATENED IMAJEAN, William. I won't stand for that."

"I know. He's threatened Maybelle and the kids. Even the baby. Usually every time Chris screws up or I want to quit."

William used his pitchfork to spear another load of hay and toss it into the stables below. Both stood in the loft of their father's barn, helping with the daily chores. The January chill eked through every crack of the old structure, chilling them to the bone. Roscoe's hands felt numb from the frigid air, even through his leather work gloves. His father had milked the cows that morning and set them out to pasture, but he'd had to retreat to the house after. Ebenezer's strength had failed steadily since Thanksgiving. Watching him totter up the narrow steps to the loft made them all nervous. For several weeks, Roscoe and William had been coming over in the morning to help.

"How can you stand that? Him threatening your family? I'm serious now—you need to take Maybelle and the kids and go up north."

"And leave y'all to bear the brunt of all that? I can't have that on me, Brother!"

"He wouldn't dare."

"He would. And Mama and Daddy. The man's beyond cruel. He'd kill all y'all if I left."

Roscoe grumbled. "Maybe we should all go."

William gave a harsh laugh. "Get a grip." He pointed to a pile of rough cloth sacks stacked in one corner of the loft. "And grab a sack of that corn while you're at it."

Roscoe leaned his pitchfork against the wall and headed for the sacks.

"Watch for snakes."

Roscoe froze, then twisted to glare at his brother. "What? It's too cold for snakes."

William shrugged. "The cats keep down the rats in the barn, so the rat snakes are usually around the crib. But Mama said she saw one in the barn last week. Spooked one of the cows."

"Thanks." Roscoe pulled a sack away from the pile slowly, his eyes peeled for anything slithery. He almost had it free when he felt pressure on his back. He screeched and whirled, trying to brush something, anything away.

William stood behind him, bent double with laughter. He pointed at Roscoe, his breath coming in gasps and gulps. "Man, you went four feet in the air! I ain't never seen you jump like that!" Then laughter took over again.

Roscoe glared at his brother. "I ought to toss you over the edge to the cows! That wasn't funny!"

"Oh yes it was!" William straightened and held his stomach. "Funniest thing I've seen in a long time."

"Humph!" Roscoe shouldered the sack of corn and headed down the worn steps at the end of the loft. His foot slipped at the bottom, and he almost lost control of the sack. He looked back at it, reaffirming that he didn't want his father going up and down them. Not all barns had a staircase to the loft, but his father had installed this one when his wife had been pregnant with Roscoe. Some of the hens had taken to nesting in the loft, and Ebenezer hadn't wanted his wife climbing a ladder to get the eggs.

Now you can't climb it either. Roscoe didn't like seeing his parents get older. *But I guess we all have to.* The alternative was too hard to think about.

"You think that's enough hay?"

Roscoe looked into each stall. "Yeah, that'll be fine. But we'll have to muck everything out this weekend. Getting kinda rank in here." He entered one stall and poured a measure of the corn into the trough.

William trotted down the steps. He lifted a basket from a nail on the wall. "I'm going to check the garden for the winter greens."

"I think there's still several rows of turnip greens. You know how Mama loves her turnips."

William's upper lip curled into a snarl. "Better her than me."

"She'll beg us both to stay for supper."

"I wish."

William left the barn, and Roscoe finished distributing most of the corn into the troughs. He scattered the rest of it out in the barnyard for the chickens, who descended on him with a flurry of feathers and clucks. *Everybody's gotta eat*, he thought.

Eating. Paying bills. A roof over the kids. That was what kept them both under the old man's thumb. Only after his last threat, Roscoe had called Bobby with as much information as he could get out of William on the big shipment.

Today. It was happening today. He'd already begged William to get out of it somehow. Convince Chris that it would be better if the other team took it. His brother had refused, even knowing Roscoe had passed the information along. Maybe he needed to make one more try. Roscoe draped the empty sack over a fence post and headed for the garden.

William already had a good mess of the greens tucked into the basket, along with several white-and-purple turnips. He used his pocketknife to snip another bunch free and added them to the basket. He straightened as he saw Roscoe and closed his knife, dropping it back into his pocket. He rubbed his lower back. "Man, I was *not* cut out to be a farmer. And I thought the trucks in the army were rough on my spine."

"Daddy would say we're both getting lazy. Sitting too much."

William looked over the rows of turnip greens. "How in the world do they survive this cold? I'm dying."

"Bred to it, I guess."

They stood in silence a few moments. Roscoe cleared his throat, but he didn't get a chance to speak.

"Don't."

"Don't what?"

"Don't even try. And don't pretend you weren't going to try to convince me not to go tonight. You know I have to."

"But you don't. This is major, William. You'll be arrested. And what if it all goes completely south?"

William picked up the basket and stepped closer to his brother. "Then you'll take care of Maybelle and the kids just like you promised."

"William."

"I need a Camel." William walked past him and headed for the house. Roscoe watched him go, a dark feeling of dread settling in his gut.

So he wasn't surprised when the knock on his door came at three the next morning. The banging woke them all up, and JoeLee's booming voice echoed through the house, but Maybelle never left her bedroom. She knew. Instead she gathered the kids around her in the bed. When Roscoe knocked once on the bedroom door, then opened it, Maybelle was already sobbing. She held the baby in her lap, and one arm had Jeshua clutched to her side. The boy leaned against her, a blank stare on his face.

The next day Roscoe opened his store as usual and ate breakfast in the drugstore. He wanted to hear it, wanted to know that everyone in town understood how badly it had gone. An accident like that—three cars and an eighteen-wheeler—hit the town grapevine before dawn. Three people killed, including the son of the town patriarch. Two hurt. But not many knew, however, that William and Chris had been killed transporting counterfeit and laundered money, along with a full load of stolen and bootlegged items. That it was all gone, burned to a pile of hot ash.

Dean Sowers, who had been running point for them in one of the patrol cars, had been caught up in it. He was still in the hospital, and the story now painted him as a hero, a first responder who couldn't quite prevent the accident and paid the price.

When Roscoe returned to his store from breakfast, the old man stood near the door. Inside the shop, Abner sat silently beside Roscoe's desk, staring at his fingernails. Roscoe waited. After almost fifteen minutes, the old man coughed. His hoarse voice matched the red in his eyes. "How did they know, Roscoe?"

"Sir?"

"The feds. How did the feds know about the run? Of all the times they could have shadowed those boys, why now? Why wait on the big run?"

"Maybe someone on the Tennessee side—"

"They picked them up on this side of the state line. Tailed them, then tried to close in." He finally looked up, every muscle tense, his face scarlet. "When I find out who got those boys killed, we'll have our revenge, Roscoe, you and me. I'll make sure they know they can never pull something like this. Not on us."

"No—"

"You know they won't even let me go in there and get my boy! Said it's all too hot. Too hot." He returned his stare to his hands. "Serves 'em right, if there's nothing left. No evidence. Nothing for them to hang on to. To hang us with." He sucked in a deep breath. "My boy!" Sobs rocked the old man's shoulders, and he buried his face in his hands.

Roscoe sat, numb, and waited. He had a feeling he'd be waiting a long time.

CHAPTER THIRTY

Birmingham, Alabama, Present Day

MY ROOM AT Gran's was now half guest room, half storage room. The closet had one narrow space for hanging clothes, and the dresser had one empty drawer. A stack of boxes in one corner carried various labels such as "baby clothes," "h.s. awards," "letters," and—my favorite—"school pictures." The collection inside reminded me that no matter how cool I thought my mom and uncles were, they had been just as dorky as the rest of us prior to age eighteen.

The letters box contained everything from Papa's love letters to Gran to the last letters she'd received from Uncle Jake. A few of my letters to her during my divorce era lay on top. I'd suggested she burn those, but she'd only whispered, "When I'm dead, they're all yours." I prayed that wouldn't happen anytime in the near future. I didn't hate Tony *that* much.

Roscoe's letter box, though, was a thing to behold. Impeccably organized, it held twenty-three envelopes, each dated on the front, with the earliest at the front of the box, the more recent at the back. After supper, I retreated to my room and began to read, absorbing the contents of each carefully.

The first envelope, dated simply "1954," held several newspaper clippings dealing with my grandmother's murder and the boy she left behind. One announcement about the abandoned "Bobby Doe" had been folded into a small square, the paper yellowed, the edges foxed, and the folds frayed.

The next envelope jumped a few years, "1969," but there was nothing between them. This one held an announcement from a Birmingham neighborhood paper about the graduation of a local boy, Robert C. Spire, from West Point and his deployment to the conflict in Vietnam. The photo on top of the announcement was obviously my father's graduation picture, although someone had scribbled "Bobby Doe" across the top of it. The envelope also held two folded pieces of paper, accounts of Roscoe's first two meetings with my father while they were both in Cam Rahn Bay. One passage stood out.

> *I told the LT I knew my father had either witnessed it or knew who did it. Daddy has made the last part of the field road, down next to the creek, off limits to me and W. No reason for that. Told us if we want to go fishing to get to the creek across the melon/bean patch.*

I stopped reading as a thought tickled the back of my brain. What was it Dean Sowers had said about the other deaths? *"Knows about the other graves at the end of the road. . . . Buried at the end of the road and forgotten, like nobody should be."*

A piece fell into place. A bare supposition of a piece, but still a piece. Doc had said Roscoe and his father had almost been lynched over the death of Daisy Doe. Why? Just because she'd been found at the edge of their field? What was it Dean said about my father's death? *"They would have disappeared too, if Roscoe's old man hadn't been such an early riser. Good old Ebenezer was already out, good farmer that he was, running the tractor in the fields behind their house before sunup. They didn't expect that. Had to improvise."*

Which didn't make a lot of sense. Two farmhands had found my father. Why wouldn't Roscoe's father have raised the alarm if he saw them dump the body? Supposedly they had duplicated the first murder because they couldn't get to the burial ground. But what if my grandmother's murder had been the same? They had to improvise because they couldn't get to the end of the road? Had they been lying? But why? And if the end of that road was considered a "dumping ground"—

I pressed my hand to my mouth. Exactly how many people were buried at the end of Ebenezer Carver's field road?

*

I called Mike on the way back to Pineville the next morning, to tell him about the boxes from Imajean as well as my suspicions about Ebenezer Carver's property. I used my earbuds because installing any kind of Bluetooth capabilities in Belle felt downright sacrilegious.

Mike, who had already been through a workout, a shower, and breakfast at the drugstore, was behind his desk, shuffling papers. "Actually, it wouldn't have been Carver's property."

"What?"

"The Carvers were tenant farmers. Ebenezer built the house and the other buildings, but he rented the land. He had no ownership of it at all. I didn't know about it all until I asked one day why Roscoe had not moved to his family's farm when he retired. Boy, Charles gave me an earful. What a raw deal they had."

"True dat." I knew about the tenant farmers, sharecroppers, in the rural South, but it had been a system mostly long gone. "So who owned the land?"

"I'm not sure, but . . ." Mike's voice trailed off.

Ah yes. Mayor Patton's visit. "It would be outside your jurisdiction. Did hizzonor give you a good talking-to last night?"

"More like a new orifice."

I didn't laugh. I almost choked on my coffee, but I didn't laugh. Heavens, I missed talking to this man. "So you have to stay out of this?"

"What he promised was if I didn't stick to my side of the street, I could lose my job. He didn't name specifics, but we both knew what he meant. He also insisted I release your trailer so you could haul it out of here."

"Any reason you can't clear it? You don't have to bring in the cleaning crew. I've cleaned up a few crime scenes before. As they go, this one isn't too bad."

"I took fingerprints off your door. Hoping I could find more than yours, mine, and Dean's."

"Any luck?"

"Not yet. But they aren't back yet. It's not like Pineville has a crime lab. Just the basics."

"Sometimes that's all good cops need."

He snorted. "Were you thinking about bringing those boxes here?"

"I'd thought about it, but now . . ."

"Now they could easily wind up in the sheriff's property room, if Patton takes a notion."

"Imajean wants to trade them out, one by one, so that I never have all of them at the same time. I'll keep what I have in Gran's safe."

"Good idea. Did you get anything more out of the first one? Because I know you stayed up until you went through all the envelopes."

"Of course I did! But there wasn't anything else there that I didn't already have in my files back home. Neither one of them signed the letters, but Daddy had kept a lot of the ones from Roscoe. I just didn't know it was Roscoe. I'm hoping that Roscoe kept other items as well, in addition to the letters. I'll call Imajean later today to see if I can set up a time to exchange the boxes."

"Good. I'll work on getting your trailer released. Although I hate doing anything that's going to make Jake Beason happy."

"Maybe he'll put a good word in for you with the good mayor."

Mike snorted. "That'd be the day. Between you and me, the gossip has already spread about Patton's visit to my house last night. The officers under my watch don't like it. They're starting to grumble, so I suspect they'll have my back."

"Excellent. I'd hate to have to follow you to wherever you land a new job."

There was a beat of silence. "A new town might not have any cold cases for you."

"Small towns always have cold cases. I'm sure I'd find plenty to keep me busy. Just don't think of going back up north."

"Never. I like living below the snow line. I like it where the weather is warm and the women sassy."

"Are you implying I'm sassy?"

"Nope. Not implying. I'm saying it outright."

I laughed. "Can we solve this thing so we do this in person again?"

"Sounds like a plan to me. Keep me updated."

"I'll definitely keep you posted."

"And you watch your back."

"Always."

I ended the call with a long sigh. Mike Luinetti had definitely wormed his way into my heart. It was a complication I didn't need, but at this moment, I cherished it. "Lord," I whispered, "please don't let me get him killed."

I pulled into a spot around the corner from the museum. As I crossed in front of the window, I stopped. At first I would have sworn that the Hall sisters had put a taxidermied bobcat on display. Then it turned its head and looked up at me. Large round eyes shone golden in the sunlight, and its mouth opened in a silent meow.

I hurried inside, not even greeting the sisters as I trotted to the window's display ledge. There, among the buckskin-covered mannequins, a rocking chair loaded with quilts, and an antique desk draped in maps, sat a particularly large Maine Coon cat. Its classic mackerel pattern of blue, red, cream, and brown blended perfectly with the sepias, blacks, and ivories of old furniture and papers.

I held my hand out to it, palm down, fingers relaxed but curled under. "Well, hello. Who are you? Where did you come from?"

It chirped in the way that Maine Coon cats did. It sniffed my hand, then head-butted it.

I felt Claudia and Betsy behind me. "I knew y'all would get along," Claudia said. "That's Ratliff."

"Ratliff. Between him and Miss Snopes, you've got a little Faulkner hamlet going on."

Claudia chuckled. "Mr. Billy is one of our favorites, don't you know."

"I can tell."

"It's a family love. Ratliff belonged to our sister, Dinah," Betsy replied. "We picked him up this weekend."

I couldn't take my eyes off Ratliff. I opened my hand, and he pressed the side of his face into it. I repaid him by scritching his jaw and throat, and his expression became blissful. "Let me guess. You found mice in among the antiques."

Claudia giggled. "Yep. First time in years I've heard Betsy scream."

"I did not scream. I yelped. I do not scream."

"You screamed."

"Well, this big boy will definitely be able to help. How big is he?" Ratliff stood up, stretched, and chirped at me. He put his paw on one arm, then leaned in toward my torso. I gave him a long, firm pet down his body. He was definitely one of the larger, more muscular cats I'd ever seen, even in his breed.

Claudia bounced up on her toes. "Almost twenty-five pounds."

"A little over three feet, nose to tail."

I spoke to Ratliff, quoting one of my favorite posters from my childhood. "'Love to eat them mousies,' don't you?"

Ratliff raised up and put his front paws on my shoulders. He pressed his face into my cheek and rubbed his jaw against mine. I wrapped my arms around him and lifted. It was like picking up a small child. I faced Betsy and Claudia. "He's a lovey."

They exchanged looks, then grinned.

"You may have to help us with him," Claudia said. "He's almost too big for us to pick up."

Betsy looked at me over her glasses. "I can still pick up twenty-five pounds, you understand. It's just a little harder when it's a squirmy feline."

I set Ratliff down on the counter. "I suspect you won't have to pick him up much."

"More like getting him down." Claudia pointed to one of the higher shelves. "He likes high places."

"Most cats do. And it's better for him to spot all the rodents."

"We just don't want him pushing stuff off. Miss Snopes clears off our dresser almost every morning."

I laughed. "I expect he'll adjust." I stroked Ratliff again. "So what are we doing this morning?"

Claudia pressed her palms together. "Oh, we have a surprise for you."

"Someone we want you to meet." Betsy motioned for me to follow them down the center aisle. This time we didn't detour toward the vault room but went straight back to the office. But as usual, the scent of old paper, leather, and dust made me sneeze.

Claudia chuckled. "You'll get used to it eventually.

Originally a storage area and break room, the sisters had converted it into a two-person office and a kitchenette with a microwave and fridge. The usual desks, filing cabinets, and computers were joined by a couch, wingback chair, and small appliances.

Essentially my first apartment. Except their sofa didn't turn into a bed.

On the sofa sat a diminutive man with steel-gray hair, rich brown eyes, a neat goatee, and dark-framed glasses. He forced himself to stand as we entered, leaning heavily on a dark cane topped by a silver wolf's head. His navy blazer, khaki slacks, and loafers were impeccable, and his height was between mine and Betsy's, probably five six or so. He extended his other hand to me as Betsy made the introductions.

"Mr. Prentiss, this is Star O'Con—um—Star Cavanaugh. Star, this is Harold Prentiss. We'd heard that you wanted to meet him."

"Yes, I did." I shook his hand. "My pleasure, Mr. Prentiss."

His grip was strong and sure. "All mine, Ms. Cavanaugh." He motioned at the wingback. "Please have a seat."

I did, fighting the urge to sit as formally as Mr. Prentiss's manner.

He lowered himself back onto the sofa, bracing firmly against the arm of it and his cane. "Please, feel free to call me Hal."

"And I'm Star."

Betsy and Claudia retreated behind their desks, as quiet as I'd ever known them to be.

Hal settled, then peered at me. "I understand, Star, that you are looking into the sordid underbelly of Pineville's past."

I cleared my throat. "Um. Yes sir."

He nodded. "It gets pretty gritty."

"They killed my grandmother. And my father."

"Yes, they did."

"Do you have any idea why?"

Another nod. "Star, many people who were alive at that time know what happened. A lot of them are dying to talk to you. But they are too terrified, still, to cross the people involved."

"You aren't?"

"I did two tours in Vietnam and saw the fall of Saigon. Also went to

Grenada and Panama. Was a mercenary for a while after that. I have cancer and cirrhosis, a fused spine, and a hip that has more screws than an erector set. I've wanted to talk about it for years. It's just that no one wanted to listen. My question is, are you ready to hear? It's not pretty. And it may not be what you want to hear."

I hesitated. This was exactly what I wanted—and it may be exactly what I was afraid of when I started this. The complete tarnishing of the golden figures who lived in my head. The harsh reality of the romanticized story.

I leaned forward, focusing on his face. "Tell me everything."

CHAPTER THIRTY-ONE

Pineville, Alabama, 1984

ROSCOE ROLLED OVER on his side and spit. A molar came out with the stream of saliva and blood. Another foot slammed into his back, and he felt like his kidneys would burst. He bellowed, the pain rocking through him.

The old man leaned over, his face only inches from Roscoe, his skin gray and sallow in the moonlight. "It was you, wasn't it, boy? You're the one who betrayed us."

The face vanished, and Roscoe squeezed his eyes shut, waiting for the next blow.

Like the Klan reborn.

Roscoe and his family had just finished dinner, a cool breeze through the open windows dissipating the heat of the stove. They'd heard the truck pull into the drive but didn't think too much about it. They'd had a lot of visitors since William's death.

Then the old man and two of his goons shoved through the back door and grabbed Roscoe, dragging him away from the dinner table and out into the yard. He could still hear the screams of Maybelle, Juanita, and the kids ringing in his ears. Roscoe had tried to resist, but he wasn't a fighter, not since 'Nam, and the two goons had pounded him immediately—face, back, groin, head—until Roscoe's body was nothing but fire and pain. He struggled for each gasping breath, his chest throbbing with an ever-tightening pain. His swollen tongue tasted like dirt and blood.

The old man's voice, however, found a new place of pain. "Get in the house. Shut those kids up."

"No!" Roscoe's was a harsh croak.

Abner leaned over him again. "This is your fault. You took my son. Whatever happens to them, this is on you. Chris told me before they left. Told me William wanted out of that run. Thought it was too much for him. Claimed he couldn't handle a big rig if things got tough. But that boy had driven everything from a pickup to a bulldozer. I knew it. Chris knew it. He just wanted out. Only one reason for that. He knew the feds had the info. Only one way he could know that. He knew who'd given it to them. You." The old man punched him, his bony fist landing hard on the side of Roscoe's neck.

"I didn't! I swear!"

Roscoe barely got the words out when the screams in the house escalated. He could hear Imajean's piercing wail, Maybelle's terrified shrieks, and Juanita's bellowing alto, bringing down the wrath of God on the men. His faithful bride. His love through all of it. Harsh male commands sounded through the windows followed by two gunshots.

The house went silent. The screen door slammed.

"This," the old man hissed. "This is on you. All of it on you. You took my son. Never forget that. Because I know I won't."

Roscoe's eyes had finally swollen shut. Every tiny movement sent reams of pain through him. But he could still hear.

The three men walked away. There was the sound of a pickup with a bad muffler starting up. Tires on gravel and an engine that needed a tune-up.

Inside the house, the screams had been replaced by racking sobs. Then Roscoe heard Maybelle on the phone calling the police.

Like the police would do anything. Like they *could* do anything. Except bring the coroner.

Roscoe curled into a fetal position, waiting to die. Hoping to die. Because the one voice he could not hear from inside the house was Juanita.

CHAPTER THIRTY-TWO

Pineville, Alabama, Present Day

HAL PRENTISS DID not mince words. "Pineville sent twenty-two boys to Vietnam. Seven came home. One ate his gun, one disappeared, presumed murdered. Two moved to huts on the 'Forgotten Coast' down off Highway 98, and one functions with less than a full deck on good days. That left Roscoe and me, and a sad lot we were."

Betsy Hall got up from her desk and sat down next to Hal on the couch. He patted her arm, then took her hand. My eyebrows went up, and she blushed as if she were fourteen. "We went out in high school."

Hal gazed at her fondly. "Betsy here tried to save my soul. She failed. I coped with the aftermath of war by involving myself in a whole lot of other wars." Hal turned back to me. "By the time I got back here permanently, the events you're investigating were over and done with. The syndicate shut down the primary criminal activity, and all that was left were the scars, the general corruption, and an ingrained political dynasty that may never be uprooted. Too many of the people still in power hold all the secrets. It could literally shut down almost every business in town. And people still disappear when they talk."

I stared at him. "That widespread?"

He nodded. "Passed down through the generations. You know Ed?"

"Owns the hardware store."

Another nod. "Ed is as upright and honest as they come. But his father got trapped in a scheme that would have sent him to prison. Blackmailed into being a part of it. Anyone who didn't cooperate found themselves burned out . . . or they just disappeared. That hardware store was built on that scheme. If it came to light today and the authorities could prove it's the result of a criminal enterprise . . ."

I understood. "Ed could still lose it."

"Or vanish."

Betsy's face lost color, and she looked at Claudia. "Sister?"

"We'll talk about it later," Claudia whispered.

Hal squeezed Betsy's hand, his gaze on her face. "Not everyone was involved. But a lot were." He focused on me again. "My father, Isaiah, ran the bank over in Carterton. When it all collapsed, he called me, asked me to come home for a while to watch out for my mother. They were both terrified they'd get caught up in it. They knew what was going on over here and had stayed alert and cautious about their business. That's why I know so much about it. After your father was killed, my father had Secret Service agents swarming all over the place."

"Looking for counterfeit money."

"Correct. But they found nothing. Not there. Not here. After the accident, after the murders, the syndicate cleaned everything out. All evidence of any racketeering, conspiracy, counterfeiting, smuggling, whatever they were into, all of it vanished within forty-eight hours. The town appeared spotless by the time the feds could react. And because of who all was involved, no one would dare speak up, even if they had proof. No one wanted to lose what they had. With the major part of the criminal activity—the smuggling and the counterfeiting—shut down, everyone thought it would all settle down and go away. They desperately wanted life to go back to some sense of normalcy. And in some ways, it did."

"Except there's no statute of limitation on those crimes."

He pointed at me. "Bingo. Even with no activity, if proof were discovered today, there would be a lot of consequences. So there is a lot of motive to keep you shut out and to keep the townsfolk who know silent."

"But was it truly shut down? Or just on hiatus?"

Hal had a crooked smile and a wicked twinkle in his eye. "Who knows for sure? If there is still activity, it is deep underground."

"So who was responsible? Who was the 'they' I keep hearing about? And what accident?"

Hal looked down for a moment. "Star, you ever read Carl Sagan?"

I knew where he was going. "Knowing something is not the same as being able to prove it. Sagan expressed it as 'Extraordinary claims require extraordinary evidence.'"

"And what I'm about to say is a pretty extraordinary claim."

"Without proof."

"None whatsoever. And the information I have came primarily from my father and a Secret Service agent who probably said more than he should, trying to pry information from my father. They were in a fine feather, determined to find the root of everything because they'd lost one of their own."

"Alex Trawler."

"Exactly. Who apparently was a good agent who underestimated the lethal nature of the rubes he was dealing with."

I understood that all too well. "Probably thinking that, like the Mafia of the time, they wouldn't kill a cop. Or a federal agent."

"Precisely. And miscalculating exactly how tightly the town could circle its wagons and turn the guns outward. Even to this day."

Betsy straightened and glanced at her sister. Claudia nodded, then Betsy spoke. "Star, when we heard why you were here, we prayed you could finally bring all this to a close. Even if some of the main players are already dead, a lot of us still live in fear, live with the idea that if we step out of bounds, we could be in for a world of hurt. It's going to take someone from outside, who doesn't have to live here, to break it open."

I watched Hal, whose face had been calm, almost impassive. Now he grimaced as he shifted on the couch, his eyes reflecting the obvious pain he was in. He rocked his hips side to side, searching for a more comfortable position. Finally he settled, draped his cane over the arm of the chair, and put both feet flat on the floor. He was ready to talk.

"Remember, everything I have is hearsay. No proof. I'm not even sure you could get anyone to confirm it."

"Understood." I leaned forward and rested an elbow on the arm of the wingback. "I've been gathering information from a lot of sources. Some of it is starting to dovetail together. For instance, I've been told that the Pattons pretty much ran the town during those days, with the sheriff's help."

"A fact most people know. The Pattons and the Taylors controlled, in one way or another, most of the major businesses in town."

I blinked. Twice. "The Taylors?"

He nodded, then used his hands to demonstrate the layout of the square. "Think about it. The Taylors had the drugstore on the corner—here—and the medical clinic just down the block. Those were the Taylor strongholds. Russell ran the drugstore, and his son, Andrew—our current Doc Taylor—ran the clinic until he took over the drugstore from his father. Across the side street was the bank—owned by the Pattons—and the street ended at the courthouse. So you had this square of buildings—bank, drugstore, courthouse—that all faced each other. Between the drugstore and the clinic was the hardware store—which belonged to the Walker family—and Roscoe Carver's appliance sales and repair shop."

"So how were the Pattons and Taylors connected?" I still had problems envisioning Doc Taylor as a crime syndicate boss.

"Like any good crime family. Marriage. Russell's sister Tess worked at the bank and married old Abner Patton, the patriarch. They had a girl, who died from polio in 1952, and two boys, Chris and our current mayor, Ellis. They lost two more boys in infancy, between Chris and Ellis. My mother said Abner wasn't a bad man until after his babies died, especially the little girl. After that, he turned sullen and mean. Really did a number on his surviving boys. Almost as if he blamed them for surviving.

"Then after your grandmother showed up, Tess put two and two together and packed her things and left. I guess around 1955. She's not been heard from since."

I scowled. "And she didn't take her boys?"

Hal hesitated, thoughtful. "No. I guess that's a little odd."

"Especially for 1955. Did he remarry?"

Betsy nodded. "Pretty quick, come to think of it. Young thing, worked at the bank. Didn't have the sense God gave a goose."

Something nagged at the back of my mind, but I shook my head to clear it. "I'll think about that later." I looked at Hal. "Please go on."

"Well, that made it all worse, and by the late sixties, you couldn't turn your back on Abner without getting bit. But way before that, he and Russell had teamed up with a guy named Buck Dickson out of Fort Payne to run moonshine into Pineville and all the surrounding counties. Buck had the connections with the bootleggers out of East Tennessee, and he'd been running 'shine into Birmingham and Montgomery. Abner and Russell had the rural connections, as well as enough law enforcement on the hook to spread into the small towns in a six-county area.

"As Alabama passed more open liquor laws, they started smuggling other items, eventually turning to counterfeit money. Money laundering had always been a part of it, and that expanded. Buck had avoided getting involved with the Dixie Mafia for decades, then gave in with the money laundering. Drug and theft money would come in, and Abner and Russell would funnel it through the local businesses, pass it through the bank, and send it on to Birmingham, scrubbed fresh and clean.

"It appeared to be the perfect setup. If the feds got wind of it, they'd planned to throw it back on the businesses. This would leave the bank, and the core of the group, in the clear. If a business wouldn't cooperate, Abner had no qualms about burning it down. Some folks just vanished in the middle of the night. Enough of your family goes missing, you start to toe the line."

"Why not leave?"

Hal shifted again, pain etched in his face. "Most families here are rooted deep. Would you leave if it meant death to your cousin second removed? Or your husband's elderly aunt?"

"People felt trapped."

"Unmistakably."

"It sounds like a sweet deal for the core group. So what happened?"

A slow smile crossed his face. "Roscoe Carver happened."

CHAPTER THIRTY-THREE

Birmingham, Alabama, 1984

ROSCOE HAD PRAYED all his life, but he hadn't prayed this hard since Vietnam. Prayed that Abner Patton and his goons would ignore Imajean, who he'd sent—along with his parents—to live with his aunt and her preacher husband. He knew that they'd protect her with their lives, and he prayed fervently they wouldn't have to.

Maybelle's sister in Mississippi had taken her and Jeshua in, and Roscoe prayed that she'd find a way to forgive him, forgive that his actions had taken her baby from her. One of the bullets that had killed Juanita had passed through her and hit the little one. But the last time he'd seen his sister-in-law, Maybelle hadn't even looked at him. She hadn't done much of anything actually. She'd just sat and stared. Shocked. Catatonic. Another thing he hadn't experienced since Vietnam.

Then again, he doubted he'd be able to forgive himself for all of this. His chest constantly felt tight, his heart crushed. His ache ran deep, and not just from the broken ribs, smashed left knee, and deep contusions. Also from the high cost of trying to stay on the right side of things. Was it worth it? Their lives would have certainly been more peaceful if he had just gone along and did what everyone else was doing.

But Roscoe had had enough of that. Enough of watching his father do it during the Jim Crow days. Of doing it himself in the military, jumping any time a slick-haired lieutenant right off the boat ordered men into terrifying danger. Enough.

Roscoe looked around the shed where he waited. He found a five-gallon bucket, upended it, and eased down on it, using his crutches to slow his descent. His uncle's sister-in-law's nephew by marriage ran a gas station on the north edge of Birmingham, a tidy place catering to the black community. Roscoe had shuttered his store and had been sleeping in the shed behind the gas station for a couple of days, to get out of the harsh light of Pineville. Quite a downfall from the pleasant and open house he and Juanita had bought. But infinitely safer. He'd take the smells of gas, oil, and kerosene over that of gunshots any day of the week and twice on Sunday.

Everyone, it seemed, knew what happened. The old man, Abner, had made sure, wanting the whole town to know what happened when he was crossed. The community was still reeling from the accident, the deaths of Chris and William, along with Dean's injuries. Most of the Secret Service agents who'd been trying to stop the big rig had been caught up in it as well. Four agent deaths and a lot of injuries. The accident site, two counties away, now swarmed with federal investigators. Everyone knew they'd be heading for Pineville next. And when he'd returned from the hospital, everyone had stared at him as if he'd personally driven that eighteen-wheeler off US Highway 11 into a ravine. Pineville despised him.

Roscoe heard a low, well-tuned motor pull behind the gas station. Tires passed from pavement to gravel, then the engine shut off. Roscoe used one of his crutches to push open the shed door. Bobby and Alex entered, their faces somber.

"Roscoe, I'm sorry." Bobby's voice was barely above a whisper.

"Thank you." He gestured around the shed. "Pull up a bucket and have a seat." The request had the desired effect—they relaxed and found their own makeshift seats.

"Is the rest of your family safe?" Alex asked.

Roscoe sat straighter, pressing one hand against his broken ribs. His torso was wrapped, but the dull pain remained, making it hard to breathe. "They are, at least for now. Besides, the old man has more on his mind right now."

"Such as?" Bobby leaned forward, bracing his hands on his knees.

"They think that the devils of hell are going to descend on Pineville." He gestured at Alex. "Aka the Secret Service."

"That's pretty much what's about to happen," Alex responded. "The accident investigation has the focus right now, and a second team is busily tearing up a couple of locations in eastern Tennessee. They'd hoped to find the printing plates, but they didn't turn up. They do have a line on the printer who was running them, so they may be there."

"Somebody who Buck Dickson had under his thumb from his moonshining days?" Roscoe had heard enough from William to know that the methods the old man used to control Pineville weren't isolated—and that Abner Patton had learned a lot from Buck Dickson.

"Pretty much. They'll be raided tonight. Do you have any other information?"

"I do. But not about that." Roscoe shifted his left leg to ease the pull on the cast and put all his focus on Bobby.

Bobby caught the move and straightened. "What? You found out about my mother?"

Roscoe inhaled deeply and released it slowly. "My father came to see me in the hospital. This attack destroyed him, almost as much as William's death. He begged me to tell him how it all started."

"And did you?"

Roscoe nodded. "I told him it all came down to the time the girl with the daisy came to town. He broke down, then he told me what he knew. Confirmed what I had seen in the woods that day when I was hunting."

Bobby stiffened. "Who?"

Roscoe looked from Alex to Bobby. "Tess Patton killed your mother."

Bobby stared at Roscoe, his mouth opening slowly. His voice cracked. "Tess? Abner's *wife*?"

Roscoe gave a slow nod. "I didn't believe it either, especially after what I heard in the woods that day. But I got it wrong. Turns out that your mother went to the Patton home that night to confront Abner. He wasn't home. Tess listened to her, then lost it, probably fed up and more furious at Abner's cheating than at your mother. Chris was in his bedroom and heard the fight. But he didn't get there in time. By the time he got downstairs, your mother was dead."

Bobby whispered, "I can't believe it."

"Chris is the one who dumped the body, trying to cover it up. To protect Tess. Dr. Taylor, Andrew Taylor, helped. They were going to dump her in the creek at the end of my father's field road, set him up as the killer, but Daddy was up too early, before dawn, working in the barn with the livestock. They were afraid he'd see their truck coming and going. So they left her for us to find, hoping the Klan would do the rest. It was the doc's idea to pose her like that gal in California. Realized too late that was their mistake."

Alex frowned. "Why was that a mistake?"

"My father's illiterate. Everyone in town knows it. No way he'd ever have heard of the Black Dahlia, much less read enough about it to copy it. Once the Pine Grove Baptist preacher got that detail in his craw, my father wouldn't be blamed by anyone in town. JoeLee had to step in, make it all go away."

Bobby swallowed hard, then scrubbed his face with his hands. "What else? I want all of it."

Roscoe hesitated, but they had come this far. "Chris and William became friends toward the end. Chris trusted him, especially as his old man started pushing Chris out of the operation. One night when Chris was nine sheets to the wind on his own moonshine, he told William about the murder, that he'd intercepted letters between Daisy Doe and his father. Chris and Andrew had been best friends in 1954. They'd been in the drugstore that day she showed up, and Chris knew immediately who she was. Daddy watched them follow her out of the drugstore. Apparently they followed her to the motel, thought she'd stay there."

"And he didn't say anything to anyone?" Outrage touched the edge of Bobby's voice.

Roscoe glared at Bobby. "In 1954? The Jim Crow South? They hadn't lynched anyone in Alabama for eleven years at that point, but my daddy wasn't about to test that. He wasn't a brave man—he was a survivor! A family man. Besides, who would he tell? JoeLee Wilkes? The man whose very existence and fortune depended on the Pattons and Taylors?"

Bobby looked away, a bright wetness reflecting in his eyes as his head turned. Roscoe relented. "Bobby, these men slaughter anyone who crosses them. Your mother didn't stand a chance—even if Tess hadn't killed her, they would have. I don't doubt that for a second. And if they had known my father had watched them follow her, he would have been just as dead."

Bobby cleared his throat. "I know that."

"Did you know that Tess disappeared a year or so later?"

Alex made guttural sound deep in his throat. Bobby glanced at him. "Disappeared?"

"The old man told everyone she'd run off with a lover. No one would have doubted him. Six months later, he divorced her and married a bank teller, the same one who helped him with the money laundering."

Silence settled in the shed for a few moments, then Roscoe looked at Alex. "What now?"

Alex rolled his shoulders. "You said they're expecting us."

"To the point that you'll probably find nothing left."

"They're destroying evidence?"

"As fast and furious as they can. Did you expect any less?"

"Not really. We may have miscalculated how much we needed the Tennessee-based information. We knew the cash originated there. We expected to find as much as we needed for the Alabama operation in the truck. We saw Pineville as a stop-off, a place the money came and went, not the base of the operation. That lay with Buck Dickson."

"Probably not too far off, to be honest," Roscoe muttered. "As far as the core of things lay. You had no idea how mean these men are or how willing to kill they are."

"You saw Patton's men shoot your wife?"

"No. But Maybelle did."

"Would she testify?"

Roscoe shrugged. "Right now she's in shock."

Alex stood. "We'll start there. We can pick him up tonight."

"I thought you were just counterfeiting."

"We can make arrests for other crimes if we need to, especially if in connection with a crime under our normal purview. Juanita was killed as part of an ongoing conspiracy involving counterfeiting and smuggling."

Roscoe used the crutches to stand. "And if you find any of their books, probably tax evasion."

A slow smile spread over Alex's face. "You know this for sure?"

"The Pattons and Taylors both squirrelled money away. I can promise you that."

Alex glanced at Bobby. "Let's go. I want to call in backup before we head down there."

Roscoe watched the two men leave, listened to their car back out and pull away. The night felt soft and muggy as he settled back on the cot. This part of Birmingham fell almost as silent as the farm at night, since it was primarily residential. The nightspots were a few miles away, and only the echoes from Interstate 65 disturbed the quiet. A dog barked, and Roscoe could hear a child squealing with glee. He should rest, but he couldn't shake the feeling that Alex was acting too quickly, without regard to what could actually happen.

"Wait for your backup, Alex. Please."

Lying back on his pillow, Roscoe stared up at the shed's ceiling and went back to praying. Hard.

CHAPTER THIRTY-FOUR

Pineville, Alabama, Present Day

THE BELL OVER the front entrance chimed. All four of us froze as Mike Luinetti's baritone echoed off the high ceiling.

"Ahoy, the museum! Anyone home?"

Betsy twisted on the sofa to face Hal, her eyes wide. "No! He couldn't have known!"

Claudia hopped up from her desk. "I'll take care of this." She left the office, pulling the door closed behind her.

Betsy's alarm escalated. "Your car is not here. We brought you in through the back at the crack of dawn!"

Hal looked down at his hands, slowly shaking his head. "I should have known. Ellis Patton has eyes all over this town."

I stood up. "Anybody want to tell me what's going on?"

Hal looked up at me, and his shoulders drooped. "I wanted to talk to you. I insisted Betsy make it happen. This is not your fault."

"What is not my fault?"

The office door opened, and Mike Luinetti filled the door. Claudia bounced up on her toes, trying to peer around him, mouthing, *I'm sorry*. Mike looked from me to Betsy to Hal, and he seemed to sag against the frame. "Hello, Hal. I hoped it wasn't true."

"Would someone *please* tell me what's going on?"

Mike glanced at me, but his focus was on Hal as he stepped into the room. "Please stand up. Harold Raymond Prentiss, you're under arrest for tax evasion, illegal sale of a firearm, and evading arrest. And I ought to cite you for putting these ladies at risk for harboring a fugitive."

Hal pushed to his feet, and I resisted the urge to help him. Instead, I backed away as Mike turned Hal around and placed cuffs on his wrists.

"Grab my cane, would you, Michael?"

"Sure." Mike picked up the cane and tucked it under one arm as he escorted Hal from the room, matching his pace to the older man's.

Betsy and Claudia followed them, rocking up on their toes with each step. Betsy seemed the most frantic, occasionally tugging on Mike's arm. "Michael, please don't do this!"

They paused at the door, and Mike looked from one sister to the other. "You two need to realize what kind of trouble you could be in if anyone could prove you knew where he was before this. Now, let this go, and let it play out through the system." His gaze shifted to me. "I've released the trailer. You can take it anytime. And please take care of them." He nodded at the sisters.

"I will."

He led Hal out, reading him his rights as they went. I stopped Betsy and Claudia at the door, although Betsy tried to push by me. I blocked her with a hand on the doorframe. "Listen to him. Let this go for now. Do you know if Hal has an attorney?"

Betsy still stretched, leaning over my arm, in an effort to watch the two men, but Claudia nodded. "I think so. One handled his daddy's estate."

"No, he needs a criminal lawyer who knows tax law."

Betsy finally settled down as Mike's cruiser backed out of a parking space and drove away. "Yes. We know someone."

"Go call him. Her. Whoever. Explain what's happening."

With a slow nod, Betsy headed back to the office. Claudia started to follow her, but I snagged her arm. "Wait. Let her make the call. And would you please tell *me* what's going on?"

Claudia rocked up on her toes, watching her sister enter the office and close the door. Then she motioned for me to follow her away from the window. She lowered her voice to barely above a whisper, even though there was no one to hear.

"After his father died, Hal went off the grid. He'd survived so many battles and wars and coups and all the cruel things people can do to each other. After everything went south with the Secret Service raids and his father was under suspicion, he just barely hung on. Once Isaiah was gone, Hal just walked away. Real survivalist stuff. Cabin in the woods, no electricity or sewer. Grows his own food. No address. Hunts for his meat. No one knows where he lives, where that cabin is."

"Not even Betsy?"

"Absolutely not. No one."

I got it. "Including the IRS."

"Right. He had no income, had made plenty of money as a mercenary, inherited even more. He didn't have to earn."

"But estates come with taxes."

"And he had investments that paid dividends."

"I bet the first year or two didn't get their attention."

"No. It was year four and five when they started taking note."

"How did they find him?"

Claudia looked around, as if checking for eavesdroppers. As far as I could tell, the only listening ears were Ratliff's, from where he sat on a high shelf about five feet over our heads. He meowed, and Claudia jumped.

I put a hand on her arm. "It's OK. There's no one else here."

She let out a frustrated sigh. "I know that. But just . . . how did they know he was here? Michael only did this because someone else insisted. But we brought Hal in the back way early this morning, before even the drugstore or Ed's was open. In our car. How did they know?"

Good question.

"Let's back up. How did the IRS find Hal?"

"There's a flea market, a permanent one, not too far from here. It's open every weekend, and a lot of long guns get traded there. Pistols too. Usually it's just farmers trading shotguns, rifles for pests and game, that sort of thing. Utility stuff, not for sport. Private sales like that aren't regulated in Alabama, with a few exceptions. Unfortunately, Hal sold a pistol to a man who turned out to be a felon."

"Which *is* illegal."

Claudia sighed. "Eventually he broke the law again, and when they checked out the serial number, it tracked back to Hal. The ATF got involved, and the guy who'd done the trade told them Hal had a cabin somewhere around Pineville. So they issued a warrant and logged it with every law enforcement officer in the county. But how did Michael know he was here?"

"I'll ask him. But it's clear you're being watched."

"At six in the morning?"

"Whoever's watching probably has someone reporting 24-7."

"But why us?"

I put an arm around her. "Because you're helping me, and there's still enough people in this town who don't want me tracking all of this down. Y'all think there's no proof. Hal thinks there's no evidence, just information to be had. Apparently the folks on the other side think the evidence exists and that we're close to finding it."

Claudia walked with me back to the office. Over our heads, Ratliff followed, leaping agilely from shelf to shelf, landing lightly.

Claudia stopped at the door. "Wait a minute. If they think that there's evidence to be had . . ."

"Then there probably is. They don't want us to find it. Our job is to track it down."

Ratliff chirped once, then landed with a thump behind us. We both jumped, and Claudia grabbed her throat. "Oh, that cat!" She let out the breath she'd been holding. "I swear he's going to be the death of me!"

Ratliff looked up at her, then did a circle eight around her ankles.

I couldn't help but grin. "Apparently, it's treat time."

"He's a cat," Claudia said sharply. "It's *always* treat time."

She knocked once and opened the office door, stepping around Ratliff. Betsy stood behind her desk, just hanging up the phone, and she motioned with a pen for us to come on in. She made one last note, then said, "It's taken care of. The lawyer will meet Hal at the police department and stick with him through any arraignment. I still can't believe they've done this!" She threw the pen down on her desk.

"I'm sorry."

She put her hands on her hips. "This is not on you. This is on all of us who've never stood up to these people. Who let them think that we're too bullied to ever ferret anything out. I think it's time to start making some phone calls."

"Sister?" Claudia walked behind the desk and put her arm on Betsy's shoulder. "What are you thinking?"

Betsy let her sister's arm fall away. "I've had it. We've lived under this tyranny all our lives. It drove our other sisters out of town, out of our lives. It put our father in an early grave and left our mother to grieve herself to death."

Claudia's eyes rounded in concern. "Betsy . . ."

Betsy's hand slashed through the air. "No. I'm done." She focused on me. "Our father was in on it. Trapped by it." She thrust a pointed finger toward the floor. "We *own* this freakin' building! Free and clear. He could have stood up to the Pattons."

"He tried!" Claudia had gone stark pale. "You know what they did!"

Betsy's breath came in deep, rapid gasps. "I know all too well what they did." She glanced at me again. "When Daddy tried to resist, threatened to turn them in, they kidnapped Abby, our oldest sister. They tied her to a tree at the end of Ebenezer Carver's field road and left her there. She managed to get her gag off, and Ebenezer eventually heard her screams. He rescued her and called Daddy."

My knees felt weak. "How old was she?"

Claudia dropped onto the couch. "Sixteen. We were stairsteps. I'd just turned thirteen."

"And I was nine. Even then I knew Abby would never be the same."

Claudia clutched her hands together, twisting the fingers back and forth. "She wound up at Bryce."

I sat next to her. "The psychiatric hospital."

Betsy nodded. "She attempted suicide when she was in college." She began to pace. "Two days after Ebenezer found her, Abner Patton paid Daddy a visit here in the store. He had no idea that I was playing in the back room. I heard the whole thing. He reminded Daddy that he had four more daughters."

"So your father gave in."

"Yep, but what Patton didn't know is that Elmore's had been courting Daddy. He took revenge by leasing the whole kit and caboodle to a national chain, which Patton wouldn't dare mess with. Daddy rented the house here, and all of us took an extended vacation to Fairhope. Our sisters stayed there."

Claudia still stared at her hands. "When Elmore's closed, we thought we could come back. The tenants had moved out of the house. We hadn't been here three days when Patton showed up and informed my father that the town was suffering without a general store."

I looked from one sister to the other. "He reopened?"

Betsy paused in her pacing. "No. He died. Heart attack. Shortly after, the sheriff's department took over. Rent free."

"Of course."

Betsy resumed pacing. "But when everyone came to offer Mother their condolences, they talked. About all of it. And you heard Hal. He wanted to talk. I think other folks do as well. They just need persuading."

A thought niggled at the back of my brain. Something that Miss Doris had said. It began to swirl around the threat from Patton about Mike's job, and it formed and popped out my mouth before I could stop it. "What does Ellis Patton have on Mike?"

Claudia's head snapped up, her mouth in a small O. Betsy froze in her tracks.

"I mean, more than just his job. Ellis has threatened to fire him if he doesn't toe the line, which is why he came to get Hal this morning. But it has to be more than that. Mike's a good cop, with the best training possible. He could get a job anywhere in the country. Unless Ellis has something that would ruin his career."

Claudia closed her mouth with a soft "Ummm." Then she looked at Ratliff, who had found a new perch on top of the refrigerator.

Betsy crossed her arms. "Are you sure you want to know? You don't really need to know *what*, just that there is something."

"I'm sure. Please tell me."

And she did.

CHAPTER THIRTY-FIVE

Pineville, Alabama, 1984

THE NEXT FORTY-EIGHT hours were excruciating. No calls, no word at all from Pineville. Roscoe spent it on the cot, praying—and hoping he'd heal faster than the doctors anticipated. He took his pain pills, washed in the gas station bathroom, and ate takeout the manager brought him. He hated waiting. Even more, he despised hiding. He'd resented it as a kid, seethed when he had to do it in Vietnam.

The pills helped, but he felt himself growing as numb as Maybelle had seemed to be. He stared at the rough beams over his head, slowly losing any sense of anger or resentment. If this was his new normal, he was in serious trouble.

The night of the third day, Roscoe drifted in and out of sleep until a soft knock on the door just after midnight roused him. "Yeah?"

The door opened, and the young manager appeared, his face twisted with anguish. "I just gotta phone call, man. You need to get to Pineville."

Roscoe struggled to sit. "Now?"

"Yeah. It's bad."

Roscoe slipped on a sweatshirt. He'd been wearing the same pair of jeans with one leg cut off for a couple of days. It'd have to do. Suddenly, he was grateful for the rest. He felt stronger for it. He stuck the pain pills in his pocket but was glad he'd been a few hours without them. His ribs ached, but he breathed and moved easier. He grabbed his crutches and headed for his car.

The hour drive to Pineville seemed to last all night. The stretch of Interstate 59 northeast of Birmingham held few cars, but a forest of pine trees on either side of the road went on forever, a mesmerizing blur of green and black. Roscoe used Motown soul on the radio to stay awake, letting his mind drift to a different time, a more pleasant existence. A true fantasy.

A fantasy that dissipated even before he pulled into the Pineville square. He smelled smoke and slowed, expecting to see an array of emergency vehicles. But the empty, silent square felt ghostly, deserted. A normal 2:00 a.m. on the square, except for the smoke hovering in and around the buildings, a gray fog filling his nostrils. As he turned the corner that took him by the bank and drugstore, he saw the source of the smoke.

His store. His cherished and carefully cultivated appliance and repair store was a smoldering hulk. The fire had taken it to the ground, along with half of the two buildings on either side: the hardware store and a sewing notions shop. Tendrils of smoke spiraled up from hot spots, drifting slowly toward the heavens.

Roscoe pulled up and stopped, pushing himself out of the car. He stood, leaning heavily on the crutches, numb as he watched the last of his life drop into ash.

He felt rather than saw the old man ease up behind him. He'd obviously been waiting, responsible for the stark emptiness of the square.

"Abner."

"Roscoe." After a moment, Abner leaned closer, his voice low and hard in Roscoe's ear. "You wouldn't listen. You never did. Not even as a kid when your daddy tried to tell you what you should and shouldn't do. You step out of bounds, you pay the price."

Roscoe shifted his weight to his good leg and let his right crutch lean lightly against his side. "Is that what happened to Chris and William?"

The old man's teeth ground so hard Roscoe could hear his jaw crack. "No, that's on you. Like I said. If you had just listened." Abner stepped to Roscoe's left, and he motioned to the smoky ruins. "Just like this. And just like those two federal boys you've been meeting with."

Roscoe straightened his shoulders, and his left crutch fell to the ground.

Abner laughed, a low, mean chuckle. "Oh yes. They're gone too. Has no one told you? Found out at your daddy's field just like that woman. Two of your daddy's hired men found them. Or didn't he tell you?"

Roscoe glanced sideways at the old man. "Why would he? My daddy's gone. In hiding from you and your goons."

The old man's eyes narrowed, and his brows came together. "What? No. That can't be right. They told me—"

"What? Don't tell me someone lied to you." Roscoe shifted his grip on his right crutch, moving his hand down to the main support.

"They wouldn't—" Abner stepped a few inches away.

Roscoe twisted, swinging the crutch fiercely across his body, his left hand clutching it mid-swing to add more force. It hit with the force of a baseball bat, the twin beams of the upper section catching Abner Patton across the face with a blow that crushed his nose and cheekbones. A harsh shout of pain burst from him, but he stumbled into the gutter and fell backward, his head slamming into the fender of Roscoe's car. His skull splintered, caving inward, and Abner slid to the ground, smearing blood and gray matter down the side of the sedan.

Thrown off balance, Roscoe tumbled down over Abner's body. His casted leg skidded out from under him, and he rolled over on his back, down the old man's legs. Pain roared through him, making him bellow as he tried to thrust himself away from the body. He lay on the sidewalk, gasping for air, trying to completely grip what he'd just done. He'd been so numb as to not believe his eyes when he'd spotted the store. But Abner had managed in mere seconds to stir a lifelong fury from dormant to full bloom.

The square returned to silence, except for Roscoe's harsh gasps. No calls for help, no sirens of warning. He looked at the old man, whose eyes stared blankly. Abner's face had been so damaged as to be barely recognizable. The back of his head seemed concave. Roscoe struggled to sit up, leaning back on his arms, still sucking in air. He sat there, letting the blood rage leach away. As it did, he took a few deep breaths, even though his ribs ached anew. Finally he reached into his pocket and then swallowed three of his pain pills dry.

This night was about to get a lot longer.

Roscoe scrambled for his crutches, scooted to the curb, and used his car and his crutches to shove himself upright. Then he opened the back car door, tossed the crutches into the floorboard, and reached for Abner Patton. Placing all his weight on his right leg, he tugged and shoved the old man into the back seat. He slammed the door, glanced once more at his demolished store, and shoved himself into the driver's seat.

The trip to his daddy's farm seemed as long as the drive from Birmingham. Adrenaline coursed through him, and Roscoe felt as if every nerve, every sense was on edge. He couldn't shake the image of Abner waking up and bashing him in the back of the head.

Crime scene tape still littered the area, bits of it tied to trees, the edge of the porch, a few stalks of corn. All other signs had already been cleared. Roscoe stopped the car at the house only long enough to grab a shovel from the equipment shed, then he headed down the field road. With the windows down, the pungent scents of ripening corn and soybeans threw Roscoe back into his childhood, including the night he'd hidden in the cornfield from the Klan.

No more hiding. Not after tonight.

He slowed the car, dodging mud puddles and depressions where the sandy soil had sunk under the recent rains. Edging in under the trees at the edge of the creek, he looked for the bare ground he knew had to be the syndicate burial ground—the reason his father hadn't let his boys take this route to the creek for fishing. He found it near a boat ramp reclaimed by kudzu and moss. Several mounds looked recent, and Roscoe pushed who they might be out of his mind. He needed to get through this.

The ground was soft, but digging still took every ounce of his strength. His ribs felt as if they were breaking all over again, and by the time he got a shallow trench opened, he'd swallowed two more of the pain pills. He'd fallen twice, and his jeans and sweatshirt were caked with thick, wet mud as well as blood.

Finally, he dragged Abner to the trench and rolled him in. Roscoe stopped, leaned over the hood of the car, and gasped for air. He had to finish; he had to rest.

So it went, until a new mound had been neatly padded down.

Roscoe drove back to the farmhouse and stopped, knowing he'd not be able to drive much farther with the number of pain pills in his system. He parked behind the equipment shed, which he hoped would be out of sight from the two boys his father had hired to take care of the livestock while he was gone.

Roscoe stripped in the back yard, balled up his clothes, and shoved them into one of the grocery bags his mother kept stored on the back porch. He went into the house and fell across the bed of his childhood. He slept off and on for the next two days, expecting the cops to show up at the front door at any moment. Or the Klan to appear and drag him away.

But no one came. The phone didn't even ring. On the third day, Roscoe wrapped his cast in plastic and took a shower so long and scalding that the hot water ran out. He burned his jeans and sweatshirt in the kitchen's wood-burning heater, ate some bread and butter his mother had stashed away, took more pills, and went back to sleep.

Roscoe awoke slowly the fourth day, a soft breeze pushing the curtains on his bedroom window. The morning light had a bluish tint, a sure sign of a coming storm, and he could smell rain in the wind. A rooster crowed, and for just a moment, Roscoe felt warm and safe and at home. Then he heard the hired boys' rattling truck pull into the drive, circle, and park behind the house. Morning sounds of a farm. Lowing cows, fussy chickens, barn cats eager for spilled milk. The squeak of wood on wood, the thud of doors. The boys chattered as they shelled corn for the chickens, exchanging gossip and tales about yesterday's raids on the banks and courthouse. And the disappearance of Abner Patton. They called him a coward for running away, for going into hiding when the Secret Service was turning everyone else's lives upside down.

Sadness rolled over Roscoe again, the ache of deep loss. Juanita was gone. William too. But the rest of his family was safe, and maybe, just maybe, with Abner Patton gone, they would stay safe. His store was gone too, but the raids would clear out most of the dregs. Roscoe prayed that Pineville could find a sane center.

CHAPTER THIRTY-SIX

Pineville, Alabama, Present Day

NOON HAD COME and gone by the time I left the museum, so I drove to a fast-food place, snagged some lunch, and went back to the Taylors to get the pink beastie ready to roll. On the way, I called Gran to let her know I'd be pulling into her back yard later that evening, and I left Imajean a voicemail asking about a time we could exchange box one for box two. Back at the trailer, I began locking down everything, making sure dishes were secure and that nothing would shift as I was driving. I ignored the remnants of Dean's suicide. Cleaning up blood required some special care, and I didn't have the time or energy at that moment. I knew Gran and I could do a better job once I got the beastie back to Birmingham.

But even though I stayed busy, every moment of that morning swirled in my head, fermenting. I had learned a lot from a variety of sources over the past few days, and a lot of it made sense. A lot of it didn't. At least not right now. And even if I could put it together, I would still only have a lot of information—and no proof, no evidence. Nothing to show that any kind of crime had actually been committed. I still hoped I would learn not only all the answers but where the proof was as well.

That was the nature of cold cases, and I had known that when I took this sudden left turn with my career. After all, I got into this not only because of my own personal cold case but because I liked the nature of the game. Police work of any kind was never as flashy and dramatic as it appeared on television, and DNA was seldom the perfect solution. Even when it was, as with the solving of Marcia Trimble's murder in

Nashville forty years after she was killed, the answer lay in the tedious and meticulous work the Metro Nashville PD did in gathering evidence at the time of the crime. Without their careful work, there would have been no DNA to test.

Solving cold cases was far more about gathering lots of information, talking to endless numbers of people, and slowly putting the puzzle together. Once the puzzle was complete, it would either direct you to the evidence or provide enough irrefutable information that no doubt remained.

For now, I knew without a doubt that the murders—and far more than three of them—had been committed to protect and encourage an ongoing enterprise of theft, counterfeiting, money laundering, and political corruption. Many of the players, especially those from the last generation, were dead. The ones remaining were still culpable, but a lot of answers remained out there: What was Doc's role in all this? How did Roscoe, as Hal had implied, bring everything to a screeching halt? Had he been more involved with my father and Alex Trawler than as a witness?

As if by appointment, my phone rang. I stepped outside and sat in one of the lawn chairs. "Hey, Darius. Whatcha got?"

"Hey, darlin'. What I've got is a hankering to come down there and protect you."

"Oh?"

"Have you run into a guy down there named Roscoe Carver?"

I sat a little straighter. "Yeah. He was one of the people I was looking for down here. I think he was my dad's main contact. A witness to Esther's murder."

"More than that. Alex had him down as a confidential informant in a counterfeiting scheme that was about to blow wide open. They had information from him, including some of the counterfeit money, leads on all the players—just about everything they'd need to make the case. Then it all went south."

"What happened?"

"The bad guys decided to make one last big run. Everything in a big rig, coming south out of Tennessee on US 11. They had two escort cars.

Just after they crossed into Alabama, the agents closed in. No one was sure what happened, but they all got tangled up. The truck went into a ravine and exploded. Everything was destroyed. Four agents were killed, along with two people in the truck, and two in one of the escort cars."

"Unbelievable."

"The second escort crashed, but the driver survived."

Nausea swept over me. I leaned forward, bracing my elbow on one knee and resting my forehead in my palm. "Dean Sowers."

"Yep." Darius paused. "You OK?"

"No. But go on."

Darius cleared his throat. "Alex Trawler had not been in charge of the operation. He was working the Pineville side of it."

"With my father."

"Not officially."

I heard Darius clicking keys. "What is it?"

"Did you know your father and Alex were college friends?"

"Not a clue."

"Alex left a note in his files that he had been helping out an attorney friend, a guy he knew from college, with a private matter, when they had run across this operation. They thought it might be connected, but they weren't sure how. They met with Roscoe one more time after the accident. There was a delay in getting a team into Pineville, but Alex tried to light a fire under it. He requested backup and headed back to the town.

"Apparently with my father in tow. And they didn't wait for the backup."

Darius went silent. "I'm sorry."

"Anything else in the file?"

I heard a few keyboard clicks, then pain shot through my head, turning my vision white-hot. My phone shot from my hand and slammed into the side of the trailer. I plunged forward, and my face hit the grass, shoving the pain to the back of my skull. I screamed, a far distant sound in my roaring ears.

Then . . . silence. For a brief moment, I heard Darius calling my name. Then more silence. And darkness.

*

The pain came back first, shooting sparks down my spine and into my hips, jerking me awake. My head felt like a throbbing raw sore. The pinching ache across my shoulders moved up into my biceps.

Up?

My eyes were caked shut, but as consciousness returned with intense agony, tears filled them, breaking through the gooey seal. I blinked a dozen times, finally forcing the lids to stay up. The dim light, a late-afternoon gold, filtered through a thick canopy of leaves overhead. Slowly the totality of my situation sank in. I was tied to a tree trunk, my arms pulled over my head and affixed to the trunk in some way I couldn't see. I was sitting, my rear wet from the damp mud. My legs stretched out in front of me, my knees were strapped together by a belt. My ankles were bound with duct tape. The same kind of tape covered my mouth, its adhesive pulling taut and hard against my skin.

I blinked again and again, trying to focus. An odd, undulating pressure crossed my leg, and I stared down to see a water moccasin slithering across my thighs. I froze, holding my breath, fighting the adrenaline-driven panic that surged through me. I waited, and finally it wandered away. I heard a wet rustle in the leaves, then a soft splash. As I listened, I could hear other soft splashes and bubbles. I was near water, which explained the mud under my rear. A stream? A creek?

I let out my breath, then took six more deep ones, trying to leach the adrenaline away. In four counts, hold four counts, out four counts. It helped. But not much. The desperate itch to struggle, to fight, to try to claw my way out of this ran deep, even though I knew it would do no good.

I looked around. In front of me, a barely graveled road came to an end, dissolving into a loop of sand. Beyond the sand lay a broad arc of mud and scraggly patches of grass and wildflowers. Trees and undergrowth covered the rest of the area—a lot of pines, but also a scattering of maples, pecans, and cottonwoods—as far as I could see. Even the road seemed to emerge from a tree tunnel.

Over my head, squirrels fussed and chewed, their teeth making a familiar scraping sound on the nuts they'd found. I could hear crows, mockingbirds, and the occasional cardinal. As a light breeze cooled my face, the scents of decay common to creek banks stung my nostrils: dead leaves, earthworms, fish, and feces. The wildflowers growing from the mud did nothing to ease the fecund smell.

This had to be the burial ground, the end of Ebenezer Carver's field road. In the arc of mud and grass, the ground undulated, with the higher mounds the perfect size for graves. The perfect hiding place.

A place I'd been left to die.

The tears that had brought relief to my eyes now stung as more flowed. The panic ripped through me, destroying my resolve, and I yanked my hands, trying to pull them down. My body bucked hard, and I kicked with both legs, a mermaid thrust, determined to remove myself from the tree.

Nothing worked. My torso was strapped to the tree with a thick rope, and my thrusts only resulted in aching ribs. Whatever held my hands to the tree refused to budge, and my wrists felt stretched and raw. My heels dug blunt-ended trenches in the mud, which gave me something to brace against but offered no help in escaping.

My rapid, desperate breaths burned my nostrils, and I forced myself to make my breathing long, deep, and slow, finally calming again. I knew I could wait to be rescued—eventually someone would miss me. But it seemed unlikely that they'd put the pieces together before dehydration—or some of the woodland creatures less friendly than the snake—put in an appearance.

Lord, is this it? Is this the way I'm meant to die? I thought about Gran being alone, the times I'd hope to still spend with her. I glanced upward, as if God really were hiding above the trees. *Send help? Please?*

As the air shifted from gold to blue to purple, frogs and crickets filled the air with the noise of a night forest. A rabbit emerged from the woods to munch on the wildflowers, and it froze for a moment when it spotted me, the new denizen of the small glade. When it realized I wasn't about to pounce on it, it ate a bit more and hopped into the undergrowth.

I shivered, the moisture in my wet jeans causing a chill to spread through by body. My hands had no sensation left, and my mouth felt cottony and swollen. Cold and the dull ache of my joints kept me agitated and exhausted.

Then as the dusk deepened, a tuxedo cat eased from the woods, its black-and-white paws padding carefully through the grass and strewn leaves, its white chest almost a beacon in the waning light. It paused and looked at me, eyes dark and solemn. Its tail twitched, then it continued on its way into the brush. A few minutes later, it emerged again, this time only a few feet away. Curiosity perked its ears, and it stepped closer and paused. It sniffed, and a few more steps brought it close to my legs. It began a serious snuffling investigation of my calves.

Ratliff! It smelled Ratliff on my jeans. This supposition was confirmed by a series of headbutts and a slow rubbing of its jawline along my calves and knees. Finally, it stepped up on my lap and investigated my torso and face. Much smaller than Ratliff, but larger than Miss Snopes, it must have weighed about ten or twelve pounds, so I *oof*ed when it put front paws on my belly and stretched up to sniff my face.

Satisfied, it began to knead one thigh, its claws piercing the denim while I tried not to jerk or wince. Finished with its prep, it curled and lay down on my lap, front paws and head braced on my stomach. Its body was wide and long enough that it covered my entire lap, and its long, fluffy tail draped down over my calves. A moment later, the purring commenced.

The effect was immediate. The cat's body emitted a deep warmth that seeped through my body like a salve. The purring seemed to echo in my chest, as calming as ocean waves lapping on a beach. I braced my head against my bicep and slept.

CHAPTER THIRTY-SEVEN

Pineville, Alabama, 1984

FIVE DAYS AFTER Abner Patton died, Roscoe Carver finally returned to the land of the living. He called his father in Birmingham and told him to come on home and bring the family. He called his insurance agent about the store fire and filed the initial claim. Then he dialed an emergency number that Alex had given him. The agent on the other end of the phone was curt but seemed genuinely grateful Roscoe had survived. The man promised to send Roscoe some paperwork to fill out regarding his part in the investigation and all it had cost him.

Finally, Roscoe called a real estate agent about the house that he and Juanita had bought. He and Imajean would stay with his parents for now. No way could he ever return to that house.

Covering his cast in plastic again, Roscoe drove his car up close to the house and used a hose pipe to scour his back seat and floorboard. Then he took another shower and fixed a proper lunch. As he cleaned up the dishes, his parents returned with his daughter in tow, and they all sat at the kitchen table, the misery of the past few days weighing down on them. Roscoe pulled Imajean onto his lap.

She squirmed at first. "I don't want to hurt you, Daddy."

He gave her a quick squeeze. "You won't, baby, if you'll sit still."

"Oh." She froze, gazing at his face.

"Listen, we're going to stay here for a little while. Is that all right with you?"

She nodded vigorously. "I love Nana and Poppy. I like it here."

"You're OK with not going back to the other house?"

She scowled, her brows coming together. "I don't want to. That's where everyone got hurt. It gives me bad dreams."

Roscoe glanced in alarm at his mother, who nodded sadly. He pulled Imajean close to his chest. "Well, we'll see what we can do about that, OK?"

She nodded.

"All right, I need you to go play in the front room. I need to talk to Nana and Poppy."

She kissed him, then scooted off his lap, grabbed a bag of toys she'd been carting around, and skipped out of the kitchen.

He straightened and faced his parents. His father nodded solemnly, then whispered, "Go through it again. Your mother needs to hear it too."

So he told them everything, his father nodding along with the details Roscoe had told him in the hospital, his eyes widening at parts he hadn't known. From Bobby Doe to Vietnam to the counterfeiting to Alex to the fire. What William's involvement meant and why it had led to the accident. Explained exactly what happened to Juanita and Maybelle's baby and why. Told them why they had crime scene tape in the front yard.

As he talked, his mother slowly reached for her Bible, which never left her side for long, and hugged it to her chest. Her lips began moving in silent prayer long before he finished. His father just listened, with the occasional nod. When Roscoe finished, his father muttered, "Evil people. I always knew those men were evil."

Roscoe, however, did not explain the last five days. He'd have to work up to that. But the knock he'd been expecting came that afternoon. He opened the door to find the oversized, mythic figure of JoeLee Wilkes standing on the porch. He did not invite the man inside. Instead Roscoe suggested that he and JoeLee sit on the front porch to chat. The old sheriff agreed readily and wedged his girth into a sturdy cane-bottom rocker. He accepted Mrs. Carver's offer of ice tea with a grateful smile. JoeLee rocked. Roscoe listened.

"Old man Patton has been missing almost a week now. You sure you didn't see him when you came back to town?" JoeLee took a sip from the moisture-laden glass, but his eyes narrowed over the top of it.

"I did see him. That night." Roscoe continued as JoeLee set the glass aside. "I got a call about the fire, and I drove up. Got here about 2:00 a.m. Course, most everybody was gone by that time. 'Cept Mr. Abner."

JoeLee stopped rocking. "What happened?"

"We talked. He said he was real sorry about the fire."

"Yeah, I bet he was." JoeLee apparently had no illusions about how it had all gone down.

"Said the fire marshal wasn't sure what caused it."

"Right."

"Asked if I had insurance. Promised he'd make sure the bank gave me a good deal on a loan to rebuild."

JoeLee leaned back in the rocker but held it still. "Right generous of him."

"I thought so."

"Then what?"

"Then nothing. I got in the car and came here. I couldn't stand to look at my burned-out store anymore. Staring at it wasn't going to change anything. I was too beat up to do much about it. Leg in a cast and all. Could barely move."

"Right. So you left him there."

"Standing next to that beat-up old truck of his. I figured he was waiting for someone else when I showed up."

"Who called you?"

"No idea. Thought it must have been one of your deputies."

"Not one of my men. I checked."

Roscoe shrugged. "Maybe Ellis. Or Andrew. It was a message left with a friend."

"You ever hear of a guy named Alex Trawler? Or Robert Spire?"

Roscoe's throat tightened. "Nah. Not from around here. Who are they?"

JoeLee pointed at the crime scene tape.

Roscoe tried to act surprised. He wasn't sure he succeeded. "You mean the boys that were found dead out here?"

JoeLee nodded, his eyes unblinking as he watched every muscle of Roscoe's face.

Roscoe took a deep breath. "Man, I wish you white people would stop dumping bodies on Daddy's land. Makes the Klan jumpy and all jittery." Roscoe watched JoeLee just as closely.

"Well, whoever killed these boys won't have to worry about the Klan. They'll have federal trouble."

Roscoe widened his eyes. "Seriously?" JoeLee nodded, and Roscoe let out a long sigh of relief. "Then I guess it's a good thing none of us were home when it happened. Mama and Daddy have been out of town since Juanita."

JoeLee slowly picked up the glass of tea and downed the last half of it. As he set it down again, he cleared his throat. "Are you telling me that your father was not here last week when those two farmhands found the bodies? Wasn't up at the crack of dawn like normal, out working?"

"Nope. In Birmingham. Staying with Mama's sister. The one married to the big preacherman. The one who's got the ear of the TV folks these days. Those two who found the bodies were men we had looking after the animals. Probably a good thing they were still coming around or those boys might not ever have been discovered."

JoeLee stared at Roscoe a few moments, then smiled slowly. "Good thing, that, huh?" He wormed his way out of the rocker and stood up. He walked to the steps, then looked back, all cynicism gone from his voice. "Roscoe, be careful. Ellis is fit to be tied about his daddy and the way everything has fallen apart. He's going to be looking for someone to blame."

"And *you* know they ain't got nobody to blame but themselves."

"Just be careful. And you might want to put some distance between you and him." He glanced at the screen door. "Tell your mama that was some mighty good sweet tea."

"She makes the best."

JoeLee strolled beyond his car and snagged the tattered remains of the yellow tape. He rolled up the pieces and tossed them in his passenger seat as he squeezed behind the wheel. He drove out, and Roscoe leaned back in his chair, energy draining from him. He considered for a moment the wisdom of getting out of town for a while, then rejected it. His parents needed him here.

But another thought nagged him, something that Abner had said, as well as JoeLee. The questions about his father being out working when those men's bodies had been dumped. Someone was using his father as an excuse, but there was way too much proof his father had been in Birmingham when that happened. He dearly hoped this would come back to haunt them—and soon.

CHAPTER THIRTY-EIGHT

Pineville, Alabama, Present Day

"Higher, Daddy!"

He pushed the swing harder, making me arc so high that the swing chains bowed and went a little slack. I giggled, but he caught me on the return arc and stopped the swing. I pouted, but he grabbed me up and spun and held me tightly against his chest. I snuggled into his shoulder as he sat down at the picnic table.

He smelled so good. Like Daddy. Sweat and peppermint and Old Spice. Mama would tease him any time those sailor commercials came on TV. Unshaven, he tickled me by nuzzling his face into my neck, and I squealed.

"See, peanut, some things don't have to change."

"But we're leaving our friends!"

"And going to a lot of other friends."

I sulked. "I don't know them yet."

"You will. And God will take care of you, just like he does me and your mama." He put his face close to mine and whispered, "You are special. You are strong and smart. You love adventures and going higher. You are going to have a lot of change in your life, and every single change will be for the better. It'll all be just like going higher."

"What if I fall?"

"We all fall sometimes. And we all get up and start again. It's not about the falling. It's all about getting up and doing it again."

I jerked, and the cat looked up at me, annoyed. I'd had a dozen dreams overnight that caused me to disturb the cat's slumber, but it never left my lap. Some of the dreams seemed more like visions or hallucinations while I was half awake, making me wonder how long before I really lost it. And I'd developed complete sympathy for Abigail Hall, whose abandonment here had altered her reality forever.

Please, Lord, not three days.

Dawn passed from blue to pale yellow, and the first golden rays poked through the leaves, bouncing over both of us as a light breeze stirred the trees. The cat yawned, extended all four legs in different directions, and rolled over onto its back. When no belly rub was forthcoming, it got up, stretched its front legs again, and trotted off. Time for breakfast. I tried to stretch my legs as well and only succeeded in launching a charley horse in my right calf, which left me squirming and screeching behind the tape. Which had an abrupt, and interesting, effect.

Duct tape sticks to skin like nothing else. Forget what's seen on television. Well-applied duct tape can remove the epidermis if yanked off. What it doesn't like, however, is oil. And makeup. Or in my case, oily skin covered in makeup. I produce enough oil on my face every night to top off my Carryall in hard times. When I screeched in pain, the tape closest to the edge of my mouth popped free.

I sat still for a moment, not quite believing what I felt. My mouth had collected a little saliva in the night, and I let myself drool, pushing the liquid out with my tongue and exploring the area that had pulled loose.

Strange what odd little things could produce a jolt of hope.

I turned my head and rubbed the tape as hard as I could against my left bicep. Slowly, as oil from my skin worked in under the tape, it began to slip. Just a little at first, with a pull and tug that made my skin burn and itch. Then a little more. Finally, the still-sticky edge caught on the cloth of my sleeve, and I gradually worked the tape off my left cheek. It dropped away, hanging from the right side of my face.

I caught my breath, trying to calm my excitement. Noise meant nothing if it went unheard. Still . . . hope bloomed in my chest. I took a deep breath and I screamed, a bellow as long and loud as I could make it. Then I listened. Nothing.

I waited, counting off ten minutes. I knew my voice wouldn't hold out long, not as dry as my throat was. But I had to try. Birds scattered out of the trees with the first and second screams, and a squirrel scolded me fiercely with number three. Then came number four. And in the silence that followed, I heard a faint voice. Then another.

"Did you hear something?"

Young, male. *What were they doing out this early?* I didn't care.

"No. Hush. You're scaring the fish."

Also male. Older. Fishing. *On the creek?* I screamed again, this time with a word: *Help.*

At first there was just silence, then came the first voice again, still closer. "Hello? Is someone there?"

I smothered a nervous giggle. "Hello! Can you hear me?"

A pause. Then, "Yes! Where are you?" It was louder this time.

I called back, speaking slowly. "I need help! Please call 911! Tell them I'm at the end of the Carver's field road. Please!"

The voices were closer now, and I heard the distinctive bump of wood on metal. Then a splash. A boat. They were on the creek. I prayed furiously that they had their cell phones with them.

"Who are you?" The second voice, closer. We no longer had to shout.

"My name is Star! Please call them."

Silence, and I found myself praying they weren't some of the people responsible for me being here in the first place. Then finally I heard the first voice, firmer this time.

"Yes, we're fishing on Canoe Creek, and we hear someone calling for help. She says her name is Star and that she's at the end of the Carver field road. Does that make sense to you? Oh! OK." Another moment of silence passed, then he said, "Star?"

"Yes!"

"They're on the way."

Hallelujah.

"Thank you, God," I whispered. For a cat. And a boat. Miracles.

*

Dehydration. Contusions. Mild concussion. Ultrasounds on hands, arms, legs, and feet to check for blood clots. IV fluids. Broth. Eventually, toast.

I felt like a balloon leaking air. An extremely sore, grouchy balloon.

Mike hovered. He'd been on duty when the call came in and had led the ambulance down the rutted field road. He'd cut my bonds and helped lift me onto the gurney. I couldn't stand; I couldn't even feel my feet or hands. Then as the blood flow resumed and the nerves woke up, the electric shocks shot through me, and I screamed, twisting under the belts of the gurney. Massages helped, but I was an absolute mess. I hadn't really cried since I'd regained consciousness from the attack. In the ambulance, I sobbed like a child.

In the coolness of the hospital room, normalcy returned slowly. I would be sore for several days, complete with headaches and dizziness. But nothing was broken. No permanent damage. At least to my body. With a second meal of broth and toast warming my tummy, I sat up in the bed, leaning heavily against the pillows on the upraised head of it. I told Mike everything I could remember, but I'd been blindsided. I'd neither seen nor heard anyone come up behind me. That was when the really bad news hit.

"Star, your truck and trailer are gone."

I stared at him. "Gone? What do you mean gone?"

Mike paced again, from the door to the window and back. "Meaning the Carryall pulling the trailer left Doc's yard about the time of your attack. We thought you'd left to take it back to Birmingham because of Ellis's order."

"What about my cell phone? It went flying when I was hit."

"They probably grabbed it, threw it in the truck. It's not in Doc's back yard. No one thought you were missing until your friend Darius tracked me down."

Darius? Right. "I was on the phone with him."

Mike paused at the window, glanced out, then back at me. "He heard the attack."

"What?" I grabbed the rails of the bed and pulled myself a little higher. "What did he hear?"

"Your scream, for one. Lots of thumps and bumps, scrambling, then the call went dead. He knew something was up. Started trying to get in touch with law enforcement in Pineville, but it took a while for him to get through to me. Then when you didn't show up at your grandmother's last night, she called every half hour. We've been looking for you all night. I had a BOLO out on the Carryall. And you." Another glance out the window, then he started to pace again. "But no one had seen anything, until the 911 call came through."

"I'm surprised it didn't go into the sheriff's office instead of your office."

"Luck of the draw. The creek is the jurisdictional border."

I watched him fidget and pace, back and forth, looking at the window. Whatever had his nerves turned inside out had nothing to do with jurisdiction. In fact, the hospital in Gadsden was even in a different county.

"Did Ellis order you off this case too?"

He paused, his eyes narrowing. "Said Darius didn't know what he was talking about. That you'd obviously just up and left. And even if you hadn't, it wouldn't be a case for at least forty-eight hours. Even then, kidnapping would be a federal case."

"Doesn't know much about the law, does he?"

"His legal knowledge all comes from reruns of *Car 54*." He hesitated, then muttered, "But he knows about other things." He walked back to the window and stared out through the blinds.

I had to ask it. "Mike, does this have anything to do with Jessica Carter?"

Mike continued to stare out at the parking lot in absolute silence. Nothing moved. I wasn't even sure he breathed. I waited.

After several minutes passed, he looked at me. "What?"

"You're prancing around like a bug in hot ashes, and you keep looking out the window as if aliens had landed in the parking lot. This is more than about my attack."

"How do you even know about Jessica Carter?"

"Miss Doris mentioned that something in your past tied you to this place. I got curious."

"Doris Rankin doesn't know the details. Betsy?"

I nodded. "What happened?"

He hesitated, then his shoulders sagged. He sat on the end of the bed, and I drew my legs up to make room as his words cascaded out. "Jess and I dated twice. Seemed like a sweet girl. I'd seen her around town for a few weeks, and there aren't many women in town that I don't already know. Then I made the mistake of mentioning to Ellis I thought it was time to move on, expand my skills in a larger market. The next night, I find Jess in my bed, unconscious and bloody. I call 911, get her to the hospital, where they tell me her blood alcohol level was twice the legal limit and her body appears to have been put through some rough sex games, if not rape. She'd been choked and had two broken ribs. She woke up, became hysterical, couldn't remember any of it but knew it had to have been me because she'd never sleep with anyone else." He paused to catch a breath.

"Let me guess. You'd never slept with her either."

"No! We'd only gone out twice. We hadn't even gotten around to discussing a future relationship."

"But since she had been unconscious . . ."

He nodded, staring at the floor. "The sheriff started talking about assault and rape charges. Not his fault. He'd have no choice."

"Which would have ruined your career."

"Without a doubt."

"And Ellis said he'd make it all go away."

His head snapped up. "How—"

"I was married to an Ellis type. I know how they work. Pictures? Video? Some guy in a police uniform?"

No response. He simply stared at me.

"Everyone here knows you're innocent. Not so much a potential employer."

A single nod.

"What happened to Jessica?"

Mike glanced away from me, his gaze turning into a thousand-yard stare. "They told me she tried to kill herself. That she's been in Bryce ever since."

"Psychiatric commitment." A twinge of a thought plucked at the back of my mind, but I couldn't pull it forward. Maybe later . . .

"Because of me."

I coughed, jerked back to the conversation. "Uh, no. Because Ellis Patton is a demon who can't bear to lose control of the slightest element in his world. But no one here can do anything about it."

"He keeps them terrified."

"Whereas I am a private investigator specializing in cold cases, and I consider him a mad dog who needs to be put down."

He looked at me again, and a smile played around the corner of his mouth. "You would help me?"

"I do believe I owe you my life."

"I suspect you owe that to God."

"Him too." I told him about the cat. "It was weird, it coming out of nowhere like that. But it really did save me. And part of me thinks it was one of God's little miracles that Gran keeps telling me about."

"I can believe it. I depend on those almost every day." Mike reached for my hand. "Although I am wondering why they didn't kill you when they had the chance."

"Been wondering that myself. But I think I might know. Do you know what happened to Abigail Hall?"

His brows furrowed. "The oldest Hall sister." When I nodded, he scooted a bit closer. "All I know is that she had some mental issues."

I went through what Claudia and Betsy had told me. "I think that I was meant to be a reminder. They wanted me to suffer before I died, a reminder that no one crosses these people, even to this day. A message to the Hall sisters to keep their mouths shut."

He didn't look convinced. "Maybe." He slid a finger under my hospital bracelet, caressing my wrist. "When will you get out of here?"

"We're waiting on one more scan of my brain. If it's positive and shows I still have one, maybe later today. Tomorrow for sure."

"What do you want to do next? Find Belle?"

I shook my head. "No. Do you by any chance ever work with cadaver dogs?"

CHAPTER THIRTY-NINE

Gadsden, Alabama, 1985

ROSCOE SNAGGED HIS suit coat off the back of his desk chair and slipped it on. "I'll be back in an hour."

His coworker acknowledged the statement with a faint wave, but didn't even look up. "Have a good lunch."

Roscoe chuckled as the front door of the shop closed behind him. He'd been working for the appliance sales and repair store in Gadsden for almost six months, and he barely knew the man who sat at the second desk in the showroom. The store had more traffic than his own shop had on its best days, and having a colleague to help out with breaks, lunches, and inventory had been a relief. But the man kept to himself so much Roscoe didn't even know his last name.

All of it fuel for thought on making a decision about opening up his own place again. If he did, it would be here in Gadsden, not back in Pineville. He'd never go back into that again, even though the main source of the corruption was gone. Dead and buried, so to speak. But the Pattons and the Taylors still held sway over the town. Probably always would. It was like kudzu. You could cut all the tendrils, but if you didn't get the deep roots, it just came back.

With Old Man Abner missing and Chris dead, Ellis had slipped easily into control. At thirty-five, he was too young to be mayor, but whoever took the post would be his puppet. And his own sons were not far behind. The oldest, Thomas, had just turned sixteen, got his license, and had started making deliveries for almost every business in town. Roscoe knew the pattern. It was a job that would ingratiate him to almost every citizen in Pineville. Thomas would become the beloved son, groomed to take over for Ellis in the family business.

Russell Taylor had made noises about retiring, and the scuttlebutt was that Andrew was about to close his clinic and go back to pharmacy school. Another dynasty at the heart of everything. Andrew and Maude had not had any children, so maybe he'd be the last Taylor medicine man controlling that part of the community. But for now it all meant Pineville was out of the question for Roscoe.

Roscoe strode down the sidewalk, grateful for the late-August sunshine, a good summer breeze, and his new tan suit. He knew he looked good. His knee was almost back to normal, and helping his father on the farm had trimmed off a few pounds—which would be easy to put back on eating his mother's cooking and sitting behind a desk. The suit cost a little more than he usually paid, but he could afford it.

The insurance had paid off on the store, and the government had come through with a victim's fund check for Roscoe as well as Maybelle. They'd even sent one to Imajean, which he'd immediately set aside for college. At first Maybelle had been reluctant to accept the money—she didn't consider William or herself as "victims." But Roscoe reminded her that the money would put Jeshua through college if he wanted to go.

Sweet Maybelle. He hoped she could find another husband someday. She was gorgeous, kind, and a delight to be around. But for now, she still grieved, even more than he did. However good life might be at this moment, they had gone through hell to get there.

He pulled open a restaurant door and stepped into the cool, looking around. He spotted Maybelle, Imajean, and Jeshua in a booth near the rear, looking over the menus. Imajean had been staying with Maybelle and her family for the summer, and they were back. Man, he'd missed his little girl!

Imajean saw him, and her face lit up. She scooted out of the booth before Maybelle could stop her and ran toward him. Roscoe scooped her up, smothering her cheeks and neck with loud smacky kisses. She squirmed but hugged him tight. Roscoe set her down and did a fake pant and grab at his back. "My, you have grown this summer. Getting heavy."

"Stop it, Daddy!" She shoved at him, then slid into the booth.

He joined them. "I'm glad to see y'all too."

Maybelle actually smiled. "She really missed you this summer."

"Maybe!" Imajean tried her best to look grown up. At twelve, she did a pretty good imitation of it, which made Roscoe's heart ache a little more than he expected.

"Thank you for bringing her back. I could have come got her."

Maybelle shrugged. "I wanted to see your folks. I don't want to lose touch, especially for Jeshua's sake."

Roscoe peered at his nephew. The boy who'd once pulled Imajean's hair and chased her with lizards had turned sullen and withdrawn since his father's death. Maybelle acknowledged the silent observation with a nod. "It's a journey. For all of us."

The server appeared at their table, and they ordered. The conversation moved to summer fun, movies, and school plans. Imajean started the seventh grade in two weeks; Jeshua the eighth. They avoided the topics of William, Juanita, and the events of 1984. Roscoe and Maybelle both seemed to recognize the need to move forward.

Roscoe paid the bill, and as they walked out, Maybelle touched him on the arm. "Can you walk us to the car? I have something for you."

At her late-model sedan, Maybelle told the kids to get in the back, and she pulled a wooden box from the front seat and set it on the trunk of the car with a thunk. The size of a large boot box, it was made from unfinished pine and had a hinged lid. From the way Maybelle hefted it, the box had a lot of weight to it.

She glanced around before explaining. "I found this in some of William's things. It took me a long time to start sorting through them."

"Believe me, Maybelle. I understand."

She touched his arm. "I know you do. It had a letter taped to the top addressed to me, containing instructions to give it to you without opening it. He said that it was his insurance and that you'd know what to do with it." She paused, chewing briefly on her lower lip. "I opened it."

"Natural curiosity."

"Maybe. But before you look at it, please know that I did not touch anything inside it. Nothing, not even the inside of the box. To tell you the truth, this terrified me."

Before Roscoe could gather his thoughts about that last statement, Maybelle lifted the lid. There, nestled deep within bunched rolls of velvet, lay four metal blocks, each neatly engraved with the images of US currency. The two on the left were the front and back of the ten-dollar bill. On the right were the front and back of the twenty-dollar bill.

Roscoe placed his hand on hers and slowly closed the lid.

Maybelle licked her lower lip. "So they are what I think they are?"

He nodded.

Her voice trembled. "Then can you get them as far away from us as you can? Not just you and me, but the kids too. And your folks."

Roscoe latched the box and clutched it to his body. "I will. I'll take care of this."

"Thank you," she whispered.

Roscoe stepped back to the sidewalk and watched her drive away. He headed back to the shop, walking slowly, as if he were carrying lighted sticks of dynamite. Because, in essence, he was.

CHAPTER FORTY

Gadsden, Alabama, Present Day

ALTHOUGH WE KNEW the Pineville grapevine would have spread the news of my kidnapping and salvation by now, Mike and I decided to play everything close to the chest. He left the hospital, with his first stop at the sheriff's office in Carterton. He'd heard good things about the man in charge, and we had to trust that Ellis Patton's reach had not encompassed that side of the county.

The hospital wanted to keep me overnight for observation, and I used the time to make some calls. I started by updating Darius, as well as warning him that we might be about to open up the counterfeiting case again. I also thanked him for being persistent when our previous call went crazy.

"I'm just glad I was the one on the phone."

"Me too. So you think you can stir some interest up in the case?"

His voice shifted from friend to agent, and most of the Texas accent vanished. "The unsolved murder of an agent? A counterfeiting cold case? I had people standing at my desk before I finished the first search on Alex Trawler. They're chomping at the bit. Are you sure there are other bodies where they found you?"

"Darius, at least three people have told me that I didn't understand how many people had died over this. How many people had vanished. If those aren't graves, they have a serious mole problem down here. You ever see an abandoned graveyard? Or an archaeological burial site?"

He hesitated a moment. "I've seen killing fields."

"Like undulating waves on a lake, frozen in time."

"No more dropping your guard, Star."

"Not even here in the hospital."

"I'll see what I can stir up. How long before Mike can get the dogs down there?"

"A couple of days. There aren't many around here, and the ones who are stay pretty busy. He thinks the county sheriff is on the up and up. He's going to ask him to go after the warrants. And he'll be the one to call you or the FBI for help."

"The more the merrier?"

"I was thinking more like there's safety in numbers. If all goes according to plan, he should call you later today."

"Keep me posted if he doesn't."

I then called Gran to let her know that everything was OK. Mike had called her as soon as they'd found me, but he'd not given her any of the details. I hesitated to tell her about the trailer, at least until we knew for sure what had become of it. I fully expected it to be in some ravine halfway between here and Chattanooga, but no need to deliver the bad news until it was finalized. So I just assured her I would be out the next day and all was well.

"Hmm. I don't believe you."

"Gran . . ."

"Don't you 'Gran' me, young lady. Your police person was a mess when I talked to him."

"He's not my police—"

"Just hush. I'll be there in an hour or so."

"Gran . . ."

"And I'm bringing chicken and dumplings."

My stomach growled. "Well, if you insist."

She laughed, a sound that was good for my soul. "See you soon, sugar."

"Don't speed." My eighty-year-old grandmother had a lead foot.

"Will do my best."

My stomach rumbled again. After twenty-four hours with nothing but broth and toast, her chicken and dumplings sounded like the world's greatest panacea. I laid my head back on the pillows and closed my eyes, more exhausted than I wanted to admit. Even with the IV fluids and a bit of nutrition, my brain still felt a little scrambled, my muscles weak and prone to cramps. I hurt all over, and I had avoided mirrors since I'd been admitted. The concussion had left me with a dull headache and nausea if I moved too quickly.

All of it a hard reminder that I wasn't the young rookie anymore. I couldn't "take a lickin' and keep on tickin'," as the old slogan went. "Lord," I whispered, "aren't cold cases supposed to be mostly research and conversations? Uncovering old secrets?"

Then again, some people would kill to keep their old secrets buried.

"Star?"

The soft voice from the door was gentle and familiar. I opened my eyes to see Imajean in the doorway. I straightened and pushed myself up against the pillows. "Imajean. Please come in."

She did, bringing with her a large canvas tote bag. She wore a trim navy-blue pantsuit with a pink blouse. A navy-and-pink scarf delicately circled her neck, accenting the matching earrings. "I don't want to disturb you. Were you sleeping?"

"No. Praying, I think."

She smiled. "Definitely not something I want to interrupt."

I motioned for her to sit in the chair closest to my bed. "No worries. God and I aren't on particularly good terms anyway. I'm definitely one of his errant children."

"Aren't we all?" She sat, placing the bag on the floor next to her, although she didn't turn loose of the handles.

"Probably. How did you find me?"

"After I got your voicemail, I kept trying to call back. It went straight to voicemail, so by this morning, I knew something was wrong. I called the police department first. When they wouldn't tell me anything, I called the museum."

"Ah. Betsy and Claudia know all."

"Always have." Imajean paused, her mouth tightening into a slight frown. "They also said to give you a message. Something about finding the keys?"

That sparked a fire in my brain. "They found the keys?"

"Something like that. Betsy said she'd call you later."

"Excellent." I tried to tamp down my excitement, but it wasn't easy.

Imajean obviously saw it. "This is good news?"

"Probably the best we've had in a while."

"I doubt that."

I stared at her. "Why would you say that?"

She gestured at the tote bag. "Because my guess is that I'm carrying the best news you've had in a while."

I looked from her face to the bag and back, feeling oddly wary. "How so?"

She leaned back in the chair, finally letting the handles drop. She loosened the scarf around her neck, then rested her hands in her lap, one on top of the other. "Star, my father changed after he saw you the first time in the drugstore. It's almost as if he'd been dormant, waiting to die. All of a sudden, he came alive again. He'd been living with us since he had his first stroke two years ago, and most of the things he'd kept from his house were in a walk-in closet. He started going through some of it, organizing it. He got Charles to show him how to use our computer. He asked me about you, some of the oddest questions, like if anyone at church had any run-ins with you. That kind of thing."

Ah. "Like he was investigating me."

"Exactly. That's when we talked about the letter boxes, and I insisted he put them in a safe-deposit box. He did, along with some other things he thought were valuable." She glanced down a moment, her lips pursed. When she looked back up at me, her eyes glistened. "After he died—" She stopped, swallowing hard. "After he died, I wanted to know why he had . . . what had spurred him on so. I went to the bank and got those letters—"

"I still think that they are vital—"

"And I found something else. He had also put this in the safe-deposit box. At first I thought it was old coins he'd colleced, but these were taped to the top of it." She reached down in the bag and pulled out two envelopes. "He obviously wrote these once he decided to talk to you."

"Why is it obvious?"

"They're both typed, printed from our computer. One is for me. And one is for you." She looked out the window, silent, and this time I just waited. She brushed tears from the corners of her eyes and focused on me again. "Star, Daddy knew that if he talked to you, there was a great chance he'd be killed. He knew that. What happened is not on you. I know that now. He chose this path, and he walked it decidedly and with courage."

"From what I've seen and heard, your father was one of the bravest men I've ever known."

She nodded. "More than you can imagine." She stood up and handed me one of the envelopes.

I opened it and pulled out a single sheet of paper.

Star,

I had hoped to hand these to you in person. Since that was not possible, I'm asking Imajean to do it for me. Please get these to the proper folks. I don't want Imajean to do that, because I don't want her more involved than she already is. She was a child when all this went down, and I guess we always see our kids as kids, not adults able to handle our affairs.

Don't touch them. I'm sure they've been handled, and I'm hoping they will bear the appropriate fingerprints. If so, they will be all the evidence you need to blow this all wide open.

I'm sorry about what happened to your grandmother and father. If my father and I could have stopped it, we would have. But we didn't act quickly enough in light of the poison that has soiled this entire town. I hope you will forgive us. And I hope you will finally bring the healing to Pineville that it's needed for more than three generations.

God bless you.

Roscoe Carver

I folded the paper slowly and returned it to the envelope. I looked at Imajean and nodded. "What's in the bag?"

She picked up the bag and stood, setting it on the end of my bed with the opening toward her. The weight of it pressed down on the mattress, and I shifted my feet away from it. She reached in and slid out a wooden box about fifteen inches square and six inches deep. She brought it up and rested it on my lap, my eyes widening as it pressed hard on my thighs. It had to weigh close to twenty pounds. She nodded at me, and I slipped the latch open and lifted the top.

Time stopped. So did my heart. I stared, captured by the exquisite craftsmanship . . . and the overpowering impact of what we had. Fear speared through me in a way that almost froze me to the bed. Finally, I blinked and closed the lid slowly. I latched it and looked at Imajean's face. My first words were hoarse, choked, and I had to stop to clear my throat.

"Have you . . . have you looked in this box?"

She nodded.

I pushed it toward her. "Please take this, now, without stopping, to the sheriff's office in Carterton. Don't stop. Just get there as fast as you can. I will text Mike and tell him it's coming."

She lifted the box and slid it back in the bag. "Are you sure?"

"Yes. You cannot keep it now that you know what it is. We certainly cannot leave it here. Don't say anything about it except that you found it in your father's stuff after he died. Don't let them press you for more information."

She scowled. "I don't have any other information."

"I know. They don't."

Understanding cleared her eyes. "Ah." She picked up the tote bag. "Now?"

"Now. We'll talk about the other boxes later."

She left, and I sent Mike a frantic text, then a second one to Darius. The replies snapped back almost immediately. *On it*, from Mike. *Will call sheriff back*, from Darius.

"Back?" I whispered, then smiled. Darius, always skilled at sending two messages in one. I put my phone on the tray table, and my door opened again.

"Halloo? I come bearing good food and good company!" Gran stuck her head around the edge of the door.

"Come in! I could use some of both."

She pushed the door, then faced me, skidding to a halt as she saw my face. Her mouth dropped open.

"I know I must not look very pretty . . ." Neither Mike nor Imajean had such a reaction to my appearance.

"Pretty?" she whispered. "Half your face is purple. Both your eyes are black."

"That probably explains the headache."

"Oh, Star . . ."

I held up a hand. "Gran, please don't. You've seen me looking worse."

"Not since Tony."

"No. Don't go there."

Gran sniffed, then set an oversized Laura Ashley bag on the chair. "So what else hurts?"

"Mostly my head. They hit me on the back of it, and I landed on my face. That's why I'm half purple."

"Mostly. Right." Gran pulled a small slow cooker from the bag, placed it in the center of the bedside table, and plugged it in. "It's only been unplugged an hour, so it should heat up quickly." She returned to the bag and pulled a small leather case out and held it toward me.

This time it was my mouth that dropped. I snatched the bag from her grip. "Gran! What are you doing? How did you even get in here with this?"

She waved away my concern. "This isn't some big urban medical center. The only metal detector is in the ER."

"I'm in the hospital just for tonight. I don't need my gun."

"If you'd had your gun, you might not be in the hospital."

"Or I might be dead."

"This is why you need someone to take care of you."

"Not anytime soon. I'm too stubborn and independent."

"Which is why you need the gun."

This was definitely going nowhere. I tucked the case under my thigh. I'd find someplace to hide it later. "I thought you said God would take care of me."

She lowered her head, her eyes narrow. "Don't make light of God's protection. He doesn't keep you from making foolish choices. But he does help you get through them." Gran pulled bowls and spoons from the bag, put them next to the slow cooker, then shoved the bag under the bed.

I suddenly pictured a tuxedo cat picking its way through dead leaves. *Thank you, Lord, for your help.* "Sometimes he even sends a cat."

Gran stilled. "A cat?" As I told her about the odd appearance of the tuxedo cat in the woods, she pulled the chair close to the bed, sat, and reached for my hand. "I knew there was a reason for that weird gift you have with cats."

I wondered if I looked as disbelieving as I felt. "You think God gave me a gift with cats as a kid to save my life in my thirties?"

She squeezed my hand. "In a word, yes. But it goes deeper than that, Star. First, a lot of people have an affinity for animals, but your gift with cats is almost bizarre. You don't see it because it's just part of your life. Johnny and I were convinced you'd become a vet. But with all that happened with your parents, your daddy being a lawyer, we could see how becoming a police officer was in the works as well."

"You believe God weaves all the elements of our lives into one story."

"I do. I've seen it often enough. God is not some convenience-store guy in the sky who showers us with gifts whenever we ask in prayer. It's a relationship, up close and personal. We make choices, take steps, and he weaves them into the tapestry of our lives. As hard, as awful as some of these events have been, you are meant to be here, right now, in this way. If there's a resolution to be had to all of it, you're the catalyst. It simply would not happen without you."

I tried to absorb what she was saying, but I couldn't quite accept it. "Gran—"

"Look, when you didn't show up, I was scared half to death. I just knew you'd jackknifed that trailer and was lying dead in a ditch somewhere. So I prayed. Hard. Then in the midst of it, this sense of peace came over me. An unbelievable calmness. And I knew that whatever was happening, God was with you." She gestured at my face. "I believe this will have an outcome that will help a lot of people. I'm just sorry you have to go through all this."

I put my hand over hers. "I know. And I'm sorry too. I've been so obsessed about this for so long. And we're close. Closer than we've ever been. I just want it done."

"And then what?"

I blinked, confused at her shift in tone. "What do you mean?"

"I mean that your whole life has been centered on this one case. Even more than your father ever was. You became a cop because of it. You left that and became a private investigator because of it. You pursued cold case expertise because of it. If it's done, are you going to keep going in that direction?"

My mouth twitched. "It's not like I'm trained to do anything else. You even said you think God brought me here."

"Yes. For this case. But will it make you happy if this case is no longer the heart of what you do? Are you going to be open to other directions?"

Good question. "I honestly have no idea."

"Something to think about. Something to pray about."

And think about it I did. Maybe even prayed some about it. Through chicken and dumplings and into the evening. Gran left, and I hid the gun in the drawer of the bedside table until after the shift change at 11:00 p.m. I dragged my IV pole to the bathroom and back, fluffed all pillows, then made my nest for the night. Lying flat was still uncomfortable, so I kept the head of the bed raised. It also helped me feel a little less vulnerable to be able to see most of the room. A little less. Lying in a dark room with no lock on the door when someone had tried to kill you was more than a little unnerving. And not a good case for sleep.

So I pulled the Glock from its case and tucked it under my thigh. I felt silly, but I knew I'd sleep better if it were handy. An old cop habit, perhaps. It was a good justification anyhow.

But I felt a lot less silly three hours later, when I awoke with the uncomfortable feeling that someone was in my room. I blinked, not moving, expecting to see a nurse working around the room, checking my vitals. Instead, I saw a silhouette against the window, a man. I turned my head to look directly at him, and I slid my hand under the covers. He spoke, the hoarse voice sending a chill straight through me.

"Hello, Star."

CHAPTER FORTY-ONE

Pine Grove Baptist Church Cemetery, 1986

ROSCOE BRUSHED LOOSE sand away from the gravestone, then stood back and admired the craftsmanship.

"They did a good job for you, Daisy. Esther. Esther Renee Spire. It looks really good. I wish we could put your real name on there, but that would put Daddy and our whole family on the hot seat. And from what I know of you, you wouldn't want that. You fought the crooks from one war. You know what it takes. The sacrifices it takes.

"By the way, I hear you have a granddaughter. Bobby showed me pictures. She's a cute little thing. Looks just like you, with those dark curls and big eyes. Said they even named her after you. We couldn't keep you or Bobby safe, but we'll do what we can to keep Little One safe."

He squatted again and smoothed over a rough patch of ground next to the headstone. "See. They won't even let me plant a rosebush for you. This is two somebody's ripped up." Roscoe's mouth twisted into an amused grin. "Let see how they like daisies. And just maybe they'll leave the stone alone, since everybody saw it last week on Decoration Sunday. Now Miss Doris, she's a smart one. Marched right in my store on Monday and asked if Daddy had done this for you. I fessed up. I thought she'd be mad, but she seemed right pleased. Said it would serve them right for it to be tossed in their faces. She's got some spunk, that one."

He stood again. "We fixed something else for you too. All the paperwork Bobby had. It's gone missing. Old JoeLee is fit to be tied. He smacked one of his deputies right upside the head, and he up and fired the clerk. What he didn't know is that the clerk is the one who made it go missing. But we'll make sure it turns up again when the time is right."

Roscoe saluted her and turned to walk away, then stopped. He looked back. "Oh, and that man who did you so dirty, left you with Bobby, then hung you out high and dry to get killed? Well, Abner's gone too. And he'll never have a headstone or a rosebush or anyone to pay respects to him on Decoration Sunday. He's down yonder in the mud, right where he belongs. So you rest, my friend. We'll take care of this."

CHAPTER FORTY-TWO

Gadsden, Alabama, Present Day

I CLEARED MY throat. "Ellis."

"Surprised?"

"More surprised that I'm still alive. Y'all are getting sloppy."

He made a guttural sound of derision. "My . . . grandson . . . can't seem to focus on the proper outcomes. He has a weird mindset."

"Dandridge."

He stepped closer. "It should have been Thomas. My eldest. The brightest. But no, he had to get killed and leave me with a boy who can't even point a gun straight. My so-called heir apparent is weak, incapable of taking over the family business. And then you come along."

"The sins of the father, is it? 'And by no means clearing the guilty, visiting the iniquity of the fathers upon the children unto the third and fourth generation.'" I pulled my knees up at the same time my hand closed around the butt of the Glock.

Ellis snorted. "You're one to quote Scripture. Sinner that you are. Dandridge was supposed to kill you, but he wanted to prove himself to me, that he could be just as cruel. He wanted you to suffer before you died, leave a message for those two deranged sisters. But he couldn't even do that right. He underestimated your resilience."

"Maybe he just doesn't have the right teacher. Why are you here?"

"To kill you."

We stared at each other in silence, the cool darkness oddly oppressive. After a few moments, he chuckled, which made me cringe. He held up both hands.

"I am unarmed. This may be a minuscule hospital, but it still has cameras. And nurses everywhere. Too many eyes to see me come and go. Even Luinetti wouldn't miss a gunshot in the dark. Are you still sweet on him? Has he told you about his little perversions? The kind that can make a girl absolutely lose her mind?"

Every muscle tensed, creating sparks of pain in my legs and back, but my brain fought back. *Don't fall for this!*

"So since you hold everyone's secrets, what's yours? I promise I won't tell. I'll even take them to my grave."

He chuckled, a sound more of cruelty than mirth. "This is why I like you, Star. You don't give up."

"Who killed my grandmother?"

He paused, his head tilting in curiosity. "You really don't know, do you?"

I waited, and he let out a sigh. "My mother. My dear sainted mother."

My eyes widened. "Your mother? Not Abner?"

He shook his head slowly. "Nope. My father was out of town. Business. He'd already put my mother through hell and back, and when your grandmother showed up on the doorstep, my mother lost all good sense. My brother tried to cover it up, protect my father. You know about Buck Dickson?"

I nodded.

"Yeah, Buck had a weird sense of morality. It's OK to lie, steal, launder money, but don't cheat on your woman. And we were all terrified of Buck."

"Is that why my father was killed?"

He took a deep breath. "No, that was business. He and Roscoe Carver were trying to turn the business inside out. He came down here to find out who murdered his mother. But just like you, he had no idea what he was stepping in.

"You killed them."

A nod. "Doc actually shot them. I wanted to make them tell me what they knew, but he wanted it over. To protect the business. In a way I guess Buck was right. If my father hadn't slept with your grandmother, none of this would have happened."

Sins of the fathers.

"But you're the one who shot Roscoe."

Another nod. "Then Dandridge was supposed to shoot you. But he couldn't handle that either."

"Maybe he didn't like the idea of shooting his cousin."

"You are not–" He stopped, then cleared his throat. "Then that would make him even weaker, don't you think?"

"Or maybe you're just not as important to him as you think you are. Ellis, if you're *not* really here to kill me, then why show up in the middle of the night?"

He lowered his head, examining me. "I just said I was unarmed, not that I wasn't going to kill you. It's all about to come tumbling down, thanks to you. You turned over too many rocks, from poor Sowers all the way through Imajean Thompson. Oh yes, I know about her. My people tell me she took a huge tote bag into the sheriff's office, and about fifteen minutes later the place looked like someone had thrown gasoline on a fire ant hill. Now I wonder what could have been in that bag."

"Something you misplaced about forty years ago perhaps?"

Ellis Patton stood silent, staring. Then he walked toward my bed. "It's time, Star."

I shifted, sliding the gun closer to my side as I pushed up in the bed. My other hand reached for the controls on the rails. "Stop. Don't come any closer."

He did. He looked quickly at my hand on the controls, then back at my face. "You could call the nurse. But what would you tell her? And in the middle of the night, she'll take a while to get here."

With that, he closed the distance, his hands thrusting toward my neck. I brought the gun up under his chin, and his momentum shoved the barrel back toward his throat. It pressed hard into his Adam's apple. He gagged, and his hands dropped, catching the railing to brace himself.

"Back. Up."

He did, again putting his hands in the air. "I'm unarmed, remember."

"Right."

"You shouldn't have a gun in a hospital."

"I shouldn't be attacked in my bed in a hospital either. But it happens." I switched on the light, and we both jerked, blinking, but I held the gun steady. "Sit!" He sat down, and I reached to call the nurse, when the door opened.

Mike and Darius stepped into the room, guns drawn but held down at their sides. They stopped, assessing the situation immediately. Darius spoke first, snapping his gun up into firing position. "Don't move."

Not a chance.

Mike stepped closer to me and holstered his gun. "Is he armed?"

I stayed focused on Ellis. "Not that I can tell. He says not."

"I am not. I give you my word."

"Your word is worthless. You tried to kill me."

"I tried to hit you. There's a difference."

"Couldn't tell it by me." But I pointed my gun at the ceiling and took my finger off the trigger.

Darius crossed to Ellis, pulled him up, and pushed him against the wall. Mike stepped forward and eased my gun from my hand.

"See? I told you that you didn't have to worry about me in the hospital."

"Uh-huh."

"What are y'all doing here?"

"I asked the nurse to call me if any unusual visitors showed up. She called as soon as dimwit over there came around the corner."

"Didn't think I could take care of it?"

"I was kinda hoping they would give you something to knock you out." Mike looked at Darius, who had frisked Ellis and was putting handcuffs on him. "Was she always like this?"

Darius shot both of us a sharp grin. "All the time."

Mike focused his smile on me. "I'll consider myself forewarned."

Ellis had been right about what happened after Imajean delivered the plates. Everything had kicked into high gear, and by the time Gran had left with her slow cooker and the nurses made their 7:00 p.m.

rounds, the Secret Service had landed in Pine County with both feet. Only by the time they got there, Ellis and Dandridge Patton had vanished. But Ellis had apparently decided running was not worth it after all, not at his age. With the family business about to go up in smoke and no one left to run it, he had decided revenge—killing me—then flipping on his business partners was his best option. After his arrest in my room, he clammed up and stood fast behind his lawyer, waiting on an offer from the DA. Cruel, self-serving, and calculating—that was our mayor, our "man of the people."

A BOLO had been issued for Dandridge and his car, but he was still in the wind when I walked out of the hospital the next day.

I'd arranged for a rental car, and while I waited on the pickup, I knew it was time to let go of Daisy Doe. I needed to drive back to Birmingham and settle things with Gran, then get back to Nashville. I had most of the story, and what was left to complete it would fall into place over time. I'd finish getting the letters from Imajean, and Dandridge would eventually turn up. No one disappeared forever, not in this day and internet era.

The sheriff's office had already started working with the cadaver dogs at the end of the Carver's field road, and a text from Mike that morning told me they had already pinpointed multiple bodies. That was an excavation that could take months, and if the sheriff was smart, he'd ask the FBI for help. But just maybe there were dozens of families in Pineville that could finally have closure on the fate of their loved ones.

I did want to say goodbye to Betsy and Claudia and to ask if their search of the safe-deposit boxes had turned up anything intriguing. Any relevant evidence would have to be given to Mike or the Secret Service, but I knew they'd be excited over almost anything historic.

Besides, I really liked them.

I pulled up and parked in front of the museum, but I didn't get out right away. I wanted to savor this visit, since I most likely wouldn't be back. When I'd first arrived in Pineville, my only connection to this town was murder, three of them, now solved. I had developed a number of strong friendships, including Mike, but I had a lot of unfinished business elsewhere. I needed to get back to the rest of my career, and the chances that I'd ever visit Pineville again seemed pretty remote, even though it had wormed its way into my heart on quite a few levels.

And I had to give myself space to heal, somewhere other than the town that had covered up the murders of my father and grandmother. I needed time and space away from the lies and deceptions, even on the part of a man I'd grown so fond of that I had become wary of my own emotions. Ellis Patton's cruel manipulations had affected everyone I knew in this town. I needed clarity.

I would miss them all. Especially Mike. But I had to go.

I smiled at the misspelled sign, left up because the art teacher couldn't yet get to the window painting and the wording on the poster board had been done by a helpful elementary school class. The collection of items in what used to be a dime store display window represented more about what the town—and the museum owners—loved as opposed to true historical remnants. A leather chair from their father's store, a trunk shipped from Sears, Roebuck & Co. in 1910, a stack of ledgers from one of the first grocery stores, and five quilts draped artfully across and over most of the items. And resting casually on the chair, Ratliff, who still looked more like a bobcat than the Maine Coon that he was.

I sighed. Time to go pet the cat and say goodbye. I went in. As the bell over the door chimed, I called out a hello. Ratliff looked at me, then stood up and stretched. He posed, waiting, and I almost laughed. I stroked his head and scratched under his jaw. "Where are your mamas?" He chirped, but that wasn't helpful.

I looked around but could neither see nor hear any activity. "Claudia! Betsy! Are y'all here?"

Nothing.

I scowled. Definitely unlike them, and I moved quietly and cautiously forward, the hair on the back of my neck standing at attention. Ratliff leaped down and followed me as I walked around the checkout area and wandered down the center aisle. About halfway down, Ratliff paused and jumped up on one of the lower shelves, scrambling a bit, then I heard a metallic thud one aisle over. Claudia had told me that he often climbed to the top shelf by leaping across the aisles to the next higher perch.

I left the cat behind as I checked the office. Empty. "Betsy?"

I heard a scuffling sound, but I couldn't tell if it was cat created or just the sounds of the old building. Definitely odd that the sisters would leave the museum unlocked if they had left. I pushed open the back door. Nope, the Lincoln Marquis remained in the back lot. I closed the door and leaned against it, listening. Where could they be that they couldn't hear me? Did this place have an attic? As I paused there, I sent Mike a quick text, telling him I was at the museum but couldn't find the sisters. Had he heard anything?

As I waited for a response, I heard scuffling again. This time it sounded as if it was coming from the vault, which had been dark, with the door almost closed, when I had passed the center cross aisle on the way to the office. All of my street instincts snapped on alert. Something was definitely wrong. I pocketed my phone and stepped quietly down the outside aisle toward the vault. As I moved closer, I heard Betsy's hushed voice.

"That was the back door. She's gone."

Claudia's voice sounded choked as well. "Michael said she was leaving. Going home. She probably just stopped to say goodbye."

Who were they talking to?

"Please turn the light back on. Claudia gets claustrophobic."

The response came from a male voice as cold and dispassionate as I'd ever heard. "Who cares? I should kill you both and be done with it. Now which box is it?"

But I had heard that voice before. Where . . .

"Well, I can't exactly see it in the dark, now can I?"

Practical Betsy. I sent Mike a frantic text, then silenced my phone.

"Not till I know she's gone. I keep hearing noises."

"The cat. Looking for mice." Claudia still sounded on the edge of hysteria.

As if on cue, from a high shelf near my head, Ratliff complied with a chirp, then a low, threatening snarl. He too knew something was up.

"See? Cat! Please, light!" Claudia's clipped voice had slipped into panic. Any minute now she'd do something crazy, I was sure of it.

"And we need to open the door, let the air circulate." Again, Betsy, the practical one.

The light snapped on, and I pressed hard against the wall behind the door as it opened wider.

"Thank you," Claudia said. I could hear her panicked breathing.

"Where is it?"

"Box one hundred twelve. Please put down the gun." Betsy sounded resigned but calm.

My chest tightened. Mike still had mine. I had no way of confronting the man.

I heard another snarl from Ratliff, and I looked up. He was glaring intensely at the action beyond the door, his bottlebrush tail conducting fierce, sharp circles through the air. His neck arched and his chin tucked, Ratliff leaned forward, his chest over his front feet. His ruff flared, and Ratliff's eyes followed every move in the vault. His people were being threatened.

"Where's the keys?" The man's voice—the absolute absence of emotion, even of desperation—chilled me to the bone.

It was the voice from outside my trailer, the day Dean Sowers shot himself. And it could only be Dandridge Patton.

I knew he planned to kill them.

"In that box."

I heard a metallic scrape and a rattle of multiple items.

"These aren't numbered."

"You have to look closely at them. They're etched on the end, just the last two digits."

"How do you know it's one hundred twelve? Could be any of these boxes."

"The clerk told us when she told us where the keys were. Said what we'd be mainly interested in was box one hundred twelve."

For the first time, a touch of anger edged his voice. "So she knows too? How many people know about this?"

"Apparently more than we realized," Betsy said. "So it would do you no good to kill us."

I stepped to the edge of the entrance but was mostly hidden by the door. As I had imagined, Claudia sat on the floor, her head between her knees. Betsy stood between her sister and the man brandishing the gun. Even in profile I knew who it was. I used my cop voice, as commanding as I could make it. "None at all."

Claudia gasped, and her head snapped up. Betsy whispered, "Star!"

The man whirled. Dandridge Patton. He'd been the most handsome of the Patton men, with dark hair and a slightly more muscular frame than his grandfather. Now the flat expression in his eyes and exhausted look to his entire body made him appear haggard and old. His arm snapped up, pointing the gun at me, but he snorted a half laugh.

"I knew you were still here. You can't stay away, can you? My grandfather said you were persistent. Couldn't keep your nose out of our business. Everything was fine and dandy until you showed up. Your whole family is like a curse on this town." He stepped closer to me.

"You're wrong about that, Dandridge." I dropped the cop voice, making my tone more congenial, motherly. "I was just the catalyst. The real people who stood up to your empire were already here. They had the tools and the guts to use them. All they needed was a little support, a little push. A catalyst."

"They never would have acted without you."

I nodded. "Oh yes, they would have. Just a matter of time." In the distance, I could hear sirens.

Betsy moved behind him, and he swung back around, thrusting the gun at her. "Back up, or I'll shoot you just for the fun of it."

I stepped a bit more from behind the door and shook my head at her and Claudia, then I called his name. "Dandridge, do you know where your grandfather is?"

He nodded, then faced me again. "He gave up on me. He had plane tickets. We were going to get out of the country. But he gave up on me."

I dropped my tone a little more, and as I spoke, he closed in on me. "Dandridge, your grandfather realized that he was too old to spend life on the run. That his best bet is to turn state's evidence. To betray those who loved and protected him. Including you. Can you hear the sirens? The police are on the way here. So let's end this."

His smile was as cold and flat as his voice. "Really? So I guess there's no reason not to kill you, huh? Think of it as an honor killing, for what you did to my family."

"If you want to. Just remember that Alabama has the death penalty. Do you really want to die for a man who has betrayed you?" I pushed the door all the way open and stepped backward into the center cross aisle. Dandridge closed the distance, raising his gun. He aimed it directly at my face, and his finger moved over the trigger.

An unearthly yowl resounded over us. Dandridge's head yanked up as twenty-five pounds of angry cat landed on his chest and face, all claws extended. He screamed, and I threw up my arm and shoved his gun hand to one side. The weapon went flying as Dandridge stumbled back against the vault door. I jumped, pushing Ratliff aside. I landed hard on Dandridge, carrying both of us to the ground. His head hit the marble floor with a sickening thunk, and he stopped screaming. He moaned, then lay still. Still breathing but out for the count.

I looked up at Betsy, who stood pale and wide eyed, staring at me. "Twine? Belt? Zip ties?"

She blinked, then jumped into action, pulling her own belt out of the loops of her jeans. I rolled Dandridge over and bound his hands with the belt. It wouldn't hold long once he was awake, but the sirens fast approached.

So maybe, just maybe, all of this was truly and finally over.

CHAPTER FORTY-THREE

AND IT WAS. Dandridge and Ellis Patton were arraigned at the end of the week. Box 112 contained all the evidence and paperwork my father had gathered on the bootlegging, counterfeiting, and money laundering the Patton "empire" had been engaged in for more than seventy years. The letters that Imajean still had included Roscoe's and William's own observations of the operation, as well as notes about who had been killed and buried at the end of the field road. That information helped match names to some of the corpses, bringing much-needed closure to some hurting families.

Other safe-deposit boxes also held key evidence, including two more of the printing plates for the counterfeiting operation, and ledgers listing the local businesses that had been trapped into laundering the money, some of which were still doing it. As expected, there would be consequences, but Darius assured me that the blackmail used to get them involved would be taken into account.

And much to my dismay, Doc Taylor had been involved, in some form or fashion, since his father's day, including shooting my father and Alex Trawler. There was no statute of limitations on murder, but he stepped forward, helping with information on the bodies and handing over private records he'd kept for more than forty years. He would still go to prison, but his age and his help in unraveling everything would be taken into account. He admitted to the part he'd played in the crimes in the seventies and eighties and said he'd wanted to break free of the syndicate for years. He'd just been embedded too deep and had been terrified they'd take any betrayal out on Maude.

As I looked back over our long conversation, he'd tried to tell me as much, but I'd been too blind to see it, too enamored of his grandfatherly interest in me. I had to absorb and process that, examine why it had happened, and make sure it never happened again. Obviously, as Gran had often pointed out, I had issues with men of all ages.

Maude stood by him, even confessing to me that she'd known much of what was going on—that they'd even chosen not to have children because of it.

Between Doc and Ellis agreeing to testify, more arrests came, but when the dust and arraignments settled, I returned to Gran's for a few days, then retreated to Nashville. I might be called to testify at some point, but what I'd said to Dandridge had been the truth. The people of Pineville had been the ones to bring down the criminal conspiracy that had held the town hostage for so many years. I had been merely a catalyst, spurred on by a love of family and an obsession about what we leave behind.

My grandfather, for instance, had left behind a renovated 1969 Overlander with a six-foot pink flamingo painted on one side. Now gone, along with Belle, more victims of Ellis Patton and his crew. Belle, even more than the Overlander, had served our family since 1973.

Because the Overlander wasn't the only thing I'd inherited. Belle had belonged to a young JAG officer named Robert Caleb Spire. Purchased with pride for his growing family just after he returned from Vietnam. Other than boxes of papers about an unsolved murder, she had been the only thing I had of his. Now she was gone, and the feds had all the paperwork.

I had to let go.

Nashville helped. I slowly healed. As I regained my health, my friends began dragging me out in the evenings, trying to get me to reengage. But it was hard, and I talked to Gran often. She sent me a Bible that had belonged to Uncle Jake before he left, and I actually read it. I did some research at my father's old law firm, talked to one of the lawyers there about a case, but I declined two cold case jobs. I just didn't have the focus to work.

I knew I grieved for all that was lost. And grieved hard. But knowing what's happening to you and being able to take steps to change don't always coincide.

But sometimes the greatest steps in healing come from unexpected sources. Such as a phone call from someone you miss and are trying exceptionally hard not to think about.

I was lying on my couch, staring out at my back yard, still in my pajamas at three in the afternoon, when my cell phone vibrated. I stared at the number for a long time, almost letting it flip to voicemail. Just before it did, I answered. "Hello?"

"I know I promised not to call, but I have news you have to hear." Mike's rich baritone sent an unexpected ache through my chest. I missed him.

I forced my voice to remain even. "OK."

His voice, however, almost trembled with excitement. "We found Belle and the beastie."

My brain went numb. "I'm sorry. What did you say?"

"We found Belle and the Overlander. They were in an abandoned barn on one of the Patton tenant farms. It came out when he was giving information to the feds. Just took them a while to share the news. You said he kept wanting to buy the Carryall. Turns out he couldn't bring himself to destroy it."

"And this is not a joke?"

"Would I joke about a six-foot flamingo guaranteed to upset Jake Beason when it's anywhere in the vicinity of Pineville?"

I sat up. "And they're OK?"

"The Overlander took a couple of scrapes when they pulled it into the barn, but everything looks good. They just parked them and left."

"Where are they now?"

"The sheriff's impound lot. Ready for pick up."

Which meant that if I wanted them, I would have to return to Pineville. I hesitated, a dozen thoughts running through my head.

Mike mistook my silence. "We don't have to see each other when you come." His soft words held a slightly wounded lilt to them. And they forced me to focus.

"I want to see you. I've . . . I've been researching something. We need to talk. And not on the phone."

His tone became curious. "Anytime you want."

"Baker's? Saturday night?" Today was Thursday. "Around six."

"I'll be there."

CHAPTER FORTY-FOUR

BAKER'S ON A Saturday night was busiest between four and six, when the older people in the area ate supper at their favorite meat-and-three. Mike had always referred to it as the senior happy hour. After six, their business was mostly takeout from families heading home from ball practice and too tired to cook. And a few couples looking for privacy.

Mike's cruiser was already in the parking lot when I arrived in my nondescript rental. I hadn't yet retrieved Belle, but I had made arrangements to pick her and the beastie up on Monday. I hesitated, watching people come and go from the restaurant, my nerves more rattled than they should be. I wanted to see him.

And I didn't. Mike Luinetti had gotten under my skin in a way no man had since my divorce more than a decade ago. The lightest touch of his hand on mine made my heart leap. He was the first man who didn't make me think immediately of Tony O'Connell. The first man to make me think that not all men had a dark, evil side lying in wait to trap and hurt everyone around them.

And yet even Mike had his secrets.

I guess we all do.

I wanted to sink into his arms and never emerge. And I never wanted to see him again, never be vulnerable again.

I slid out of the car.

He sat near the back of the restaurant, in a corner so that he could see all the exits. When I entered, he stood immediately. No smile, but his eyes gleamed. He pulled out a chair as I approached, his hand gently grasping my elbow as I sat. And yes, my heart leaped in my chest, and I swallowed hard, nodding my thanks. He took his seat.

"I went ahead and ordered you a half-and-half sweet tea. The specials are salmon patties or pork chops. Anything you want. I'm buying."

"Thank you." The man did not chatter. Obviously, he was as nervous as I was.

"I mean, I don't mean to patronize. But I know you've not been working . . ." His voice trailed off as he realized he'd revealed too much.

My eyebrows went up. "You've been talking to my grandmother?"

He crossed his arms. "I knew she'd want to know about the Overlander."

"You didn't think I'd tell her?"

He uncrossed his arms, and his shoulders slumped. "OK. She called me. She's worried about you."

I sighed. "Mike, I'm not mad. She keeps trying to bring you up in our conversations as well. It doesn't matter how many times I tell her I don't want to talk about you."

His eyes creased. "You don't?"

"No. I do. So I don't. She knows I want . . . I can't talk—" This was not going well. "You terrify me!" I blurted.

He leaned back, stunned. "How? Why do I terrify you?"

It was out now. *Get it over with, Star.* "Because I've not wanted to be with anyone *ever* as much as I want to be with you. No one. But I can't handle being with you. I can't even handle *wanting* to be with you. Not right now. I just can't."

"And your solution to this is to completely sever contact?"

"It's the only one I can think of. Try to get you out of my head. My heart."

He leaned forward, bracing his arms on the table. "How about something more reasonable, like just taking things slow? Staying in touch? Seeing what happens?"

"When have you ever known me to be reasonable?"

"There's always a first time for everything."

Lord, I have missed this man. "You're willing to take this slow?"

"You are living in another city. Do we have a choice?"

He reached and took my hand. His fingers were warm, and his thumb gently caressed my palm. And it felt as if every nerve in my body fired. My voice cracked as I whispered, "You keep that up and we won't be able to take anything slow."

His grin shifted to a mischievous one as his eyes brightened. "I'll consider myself forewarned . . . and forearmed."

A server appeared at our table, delivering my tea and breaking the mood. Mike released my hand, we ordered, and she left. I sipped from the glass, grateful that Mike had remembered to ask for half sweet and half unsweet. Baker's sweet tea was so syrupy, a spoon could stand upright in the glass.

"So what else did you want to talk about?"

I straightened my shoulders and took a deep breath.

"Is it that bad?"

I grimaced. "You'll have to decide. I may have overstepped here, but I couldn't get something out of my head. So I've been talking to one of my lawyer friends about Jessica Carter."

His stunned look returned. "What?"

"I promised I'd help you, remember? I didn't forget that."

"But you didn't need to—"

"Yes, I did. Intrusive or not, I did need to. It was the only way I could think of to repay you."

He leaned forward, his eyes intense. "You didn't need—"

"Jessica Carter is a pro."

He stopped, his mouth open for a second. Then he closed it and swallowed. He shook his head.

I plunged on. "Look, I know all this is moot now that Ellis Patton is under indictment. But I thought you should know. When you told me about it, something felt familiar. It's a blackmail setup as old as time. So I had my friend look for similar cases. Just to see what we could find out. Who told you she attempted suicide? That she had been committed?"

I barely heard his hoarse response. "Ellis."

"Right. There's no Jessica Carter at Bryce." I pulled a mug shot out of my purse. "Is this her?"

Mike took the picture as if it might be poisonous. He stared at it, then nodded once.

"That's Jessica Carson. She's been arrested a half dozen times for this same scam, although it's usually for blackmail for money, not blackmail for leverage."

He put his hands flat on the table, fingers spread. "I saw her. She was bruised. Bloody. Brutalized."

"And she wouldn't let you near her. She was terrified of you."

The facts began to sink in. "But the blood test . . ."

"Oh, I'm fairly sure she was drunk. And some of the injuries were probably real. They had to make it look good for you and the doctors, and makeup only goes so far. But it was a setup between her and Ellis Patton. Some women will do anything for money. Shortly after the incident, Jessica Carson deposited fifteen thousand dollars into her savings account. My friend got a warrant for a trace on the cash, as a part of the ongoing investigation into Ellis Patton. They traced the money to an account in Dandridge's name."

Mike leaned back against his chair, and one hand scrubbed across his mouth. "So I don't have to—"

"You don't have to feel guilty that you ruined a young girl's life just by being here, by being caught in Ellis Patton's web. The story won't follow you anywhere. The feds don't need any additional charges against Ellis or they'd tack on this fraud. You can leave Pineville anytime you want to."

"If I want to." He glanced over my shoulder. I took a quick look, and a woman approached us with a slow saunter that could have come directly from a New York catwalk. Her tailored suit and designer bag had probably once been there as well. Her dark hair was secured in a French braid, and her makeup looked professionally applied.

"New girlfriend?" I asked.

He chuckled. "Hardly. Someone I want you to meet." He stood up and greeted the woman with a handshake. I did the same as he introduced her. "Star, this is Jill Turney."

Ms. Turney may have earned her looks in the big city, but her voice was straight out of north Alabama—and all business. "Ms. Cavanaugh. I understand you handle cold cases. Well, I've got a doozy for you."

I shot a sour look at Mike. "Interesting. And this cold case would be located . . ."

"Right here in Pine County. Been tormenting my family for more than twenty years. Time for it to stop. Can we talk?"

From the corner of my eye, I could see that the grin on Mike Luinetti's face was positively wicked.

Slow indeed.

CHAPTER FORTY-FIVE

Pine Grove Baptist Church, Alabama, Present Day

THE NEXT DAY, Mike and I returned to the Pine Grove Baptist Church in his Jaguar, garnering almost as much attention as we had the first time. Miss Doris and her girls smothered me in hugs, and it was as if I'd been gone for years instead of a few weeks. Betsy and Claudia Hall filled me in on Ratliff's latest exploits, and everyone wanted to know the latest on Belle and the beastie. Of course, everyone had already heard about their recovery.

There was definitely an ego boost to being a big fish in a small pond.

As we left, Imajean Carver Thompson waited by the Jaguar, and she and Mike exchanged a look that told me he'd been expecting her.

She reached and took my hand. "Star, can we take a walk? I need to talk to you."

"Sure."

She slipped her hand inside my elbow, and I went where she guided me. But as we headed into the graveyard, I had a feeling I knew where we were going. We stepped slowly across the uneven ground and around graves, Imajean speaking as we went.

"I wish you'd known my daddy better. He was a remarkable man. He didn't leave much behind. The store was sold after his first stroke, and his medical bills ate all of his savings. I have his Bible. All those letters."

"That's an incredible legacy in itself."

She nodded. "Charles calls it 'a legacy of honesty, bravery, and faith.'"

"He's right."

"In the letter he left for me with those plates, he laid out how it had all happened. Who killed who and when. Told me I could give the letter to the police, but after all you had dug up, I didn't see the need. Those are his last words to me, and I didn't want to give them up."

"I don't blame you."

"But he also asked me to do something for you. Told me where I could find the money to make it happen."

I stopped and looked at her. "Imajean, you don't owe me anything."

She released my arm. "Star, it's not just for you. It's for him. For us. For Pineville. We need this to happen." She pointed at the Daisy Doe gravesite.

Even from a distance I could see that the headstone had been replaced. My breath caught in my throat, and Imajean nudged me gently toward it. In the place of the small granite stone stood a black obelisk with a Star of David carved prominently near the top. As I closed in on it, the letters became readable, and my steps grew shaky. Next to the grave, my knees gave out, and my trembling fingers traced the inscription.

ESTHER RENEE SPIRE
JUNE 21, 1922–MAY 8, 1954
BELOVED MOTHER
"OUR SHINING STAR"

A row of daisies circled the base of the obelisk. I lightly touched the blossoms, then my eyes stung as the tears filled them and flowed down my face. I covered my face with my hands and sobbed, leaning against the stone.

Imajean put a hand on my shoulder. "They buried an unknown Daisy Doe. It was time we gave Esther Spire the burial and respect she deserved. Unknown no longer." She paused, then began to pray.

"Our Father God, you are filled with mercy. Please bring proper rest to our sister and mother Esther. May you who are the source of all mercy shelter her beneath your wings eternally, and bind her soul and sweet memory among the living, that she may rest in peace. Amen."

The tears slowed, and Imajean's prayer settled a soft solace in my soul. "Thank you," I whispered.

After a few moments, she stepped away, and I pushed myself up, using the obelisk for balance. I turned to find Mike standing close behind me. Beyond him, Miss Doris and her girls. Then the Hall sisters . . . and about half the congregation of the Pine Grove Baptist Church stood between me and the church, watching.

I hugged Imajean, then stepped toward Mike, still a little uncertain on my feet.

He took my arm. "Ready to go?"

"Maybe." I glanced back at the obelisk. "Yes."

He put his arm around my waist to steady me. We walked in silence, and everyone drifted back toward their cars. Mike opened the passenger door of the Jaguar for me, then slipped in behind the wheel. "Where to?"

My stomach chose that moment to snarl rather audibly.

"So . . . lunch?" Mike asked.

I cleared my throat, still somewhat clogged with tears. "Did you know that it's a pretty universal fact that grief can make you really hungry?"

"At least according to Mrs. Patmore on *Downton Abbey*."

I stared at him. "You watch *Downton Abbey*?"

"I had a girlfriend who did. Before I came to Pineville."

"Really? What happened to said girlfriend?"

"She didn't want to move to a small town."

"Man, you can really pick 'em. You may never get married if you keep this up."

"Ya never know when the tide will change. Top O' the River? I hear they have good fried dill pickles."

"I heard Yankees don't eat fried pickles."

"They are an acquired taste. But I've learned to like a lot of other things about the South." He brushed my arm with the back of his hand.

"Michael."

"What?"

"Drive."

"Yes ma'am. Wherever you want to go."

ACKNOWLEDGMENTS

WHEN I FIRST conceived of Daisy Doe and Star Cavanaugh in 2006, I had no idea how long and how many people it would take to bring this story to completion and put it in the hands of readers. From the contest judges, who praised the concept and compared me to famous authors, to my beta readers, who gave me tips and advice, an entire legion of people lifted me up and encouraged me to continue. They are precious because it is far too easy to give up on a story when it doesn't sell and the trends don't match up. I told my agent more than once to abandon it. I could have moved on; she didn't.

I have been blessed by these people. Here are a few of the standouts:

- Bonnie S. Calhoun, author, friend, and veteran, who helped me with Roscoe's history and point of view;
- Julie Gwinn, my agent and friend, who would not give up on this story;
- The Moody (Alabama) Police Department, who introduced me to small-town and county policing;
- The entire team—and I do mean *team*—at Kregel, especially the editors who pushed me to the next level, caught numerous gaffs, and made me laugh more than once at my mistakes. I thank God for each and every one of them;
- And Jack, who reminded me that you're never too old for sparks to fly.

Any mistakes or missteps left behind are my own.